Destiny

This Large Print Book carries the
Seal of Approval of N.A.V.H.

Destiny

Carly Phillips

WHEELER PUBLISHING
A part of Gale, Cengage Learning

Detroit • New York • San Francisco • New Haven, Conn • Waterville, Maine • London

Wheeler Publishing Large Print Hardcover.
The text of this Large Print edition is unabridged.
Other aspects of the book may vary from the original edition.
Set in 16 pt. Plantin.

LIBRARY OF CONGRESS CATALOGING-IN-PUBLICATION DATA

Phillips, Carly.
Destiny / by Carly Phillips. — Large print ed.
p. cm. — (Wheeler Publishing large print hardcover)
ISBN 978-1-4104-5073-9 (hardcover) — ISBN 1-4104-5073-2 (hardcover)
1. Large type books. I. Title.
PS3616.H454D47 2012
813'.6—dc23 2012018602

Published in 2012 by arrangement with The Berkley Publishing Group, a member of Penguin Group (USA) Inc.

Printed in the United States of America
1 2 3 4 5 6 7 16 15 14 13 12

This book is dedicated to my readers — those I've met in person, online, and those I've never met but hope to someday. Thank you for investing your valuable time and hard-earned money on my books. I'm so grateful, and I hope you love the Serendipity series because there's more to come.

A special note —

As hard as this is for me to believe, Destiny *is on bookshelves exactly one year from the day we lost our beloved Wheaten Terrier, Buddy. Rest in peace, my best boy. I think of you every day. A special shoutout to the current dogs in my life: Bailey (a Wheaten) and Brady (a Havanese puppy) — thanks for making me smile and for being by my side while I work! And to my family for humoring my obsession with the dogs: You do know I'd save you first! To Phil, Jackie, and Jen — I LOVE YOU!*

One

Nash Barron might be cynical about life and more recently about love, but even he normally enjoyed a good wedding. Today's affair had been an exception. The invitation had requested the presence of "close friends and family." Nash wondered if he was the only one in the group to notice the irony.

The groom's two brothers, Nash included, were a step short of estranged, and they'd only known the flower girl, their newly discovered half sister, Tess, for six weeks. The bride's father was in jail, which left her flamboyant decorator friend to give her away, while her mother spent the afternoon downing wine and bemoaning the loss of her beloved home, which just so happened to be the site of the wedding. The landmark house on the hill in their hometown of Serendipity, New York, was now owned by the groom, Nash's brother Ethan.

Come to think of it, the irony of the situation might be the only thing Nash had enjoyed about this day.

That and Kelly Moss, the woman sipping champagne across the lush green grass of the backyard.

Tess was Nash's half sister, a product of his father and Tess's mother's affair. Kelly, Tess's half sister on her mother's side, was a sexy woman who by turns frustrated him, intrigued him, and turned him on. Complicated yet simple enough to be summed up in one sentence: Kelly Moss was a beautiful woman and they were in no way blood related.

Which didn't make his desire for her any more acceptable. A simple acquaintance-like relationship seemed the safest route, yet Nash had been unable to find comfortable ground with either Kelly or Tess in the time since they'd been in Serendipity. Nash had no idea why he couldn't connect with his fourteen-year-old sister, who seemed determined to freeze him out.

As for Kelly, at first Nash blamed his frustration with her on the fact that she'd unceremoniously dumped Tess, a sister the Barron brothers knew nothing about, on Ethan's doorstep back in August. She'd demanded he parent the out-of-control teen. Nash hated to give Ethan credit for anything, but he had to admit his older brother had turned the wildly rebellious kid around in a short time. But Nash still had issues with Kelly's methods. So when she'd resurfaced and moved to town, he'd been both understandably wary and shockingly attracted. And she'd been getting under his skin ever since.

Nash turned away and his gaze fell on Ethan, his brother whose luck seemed to have done a one eighty since he'd abandoned his siblings ten years ago. He had chosen the perfect day for a wedding. Though early October, the temperature had hiked into the low seventies, enabling him to have the wedding outdoors. Ethan stood with his arm around his wife, Faith, talking to their youngest sibling, Dare. Even he had forgiven Ethan for the past.

Nash couldn't bring himself to be so lenient.

He glanced at his watch and decided his time here was over. The bride and groom were married, cake served, bouquet thrown. He finished what remained of his Ketel One, placed the glass on a passing waitress's tray, and headed toward the house.

"Leaving so soon?" a familiar female voice asked.

"The festivities are over." He turned to

face the woman who'd hijacked his thoughts just moments before.

Kelly, her hair pulled loosely behind her head, soft waves escaping and grazing her shoulders, stood close beside him. Her warm, inviting lemony scent enveloped him in heat.

Nash was a man who valued his personal space. Kelly was a woman who pushed past boundaries. Yet for a reason he couldn't fathom, he lacked his usual desire to find safer ground.

"The band is still playing," she pointed out.

"No one will realize I'm gone."

Or care. His leaving would probably ease any tension his presence created.

"I would." She gazed at him with perceptive brown eyes.

Intelligent chocolate-colored eyes that seemed to see beyond the indifferent facade he presented to the world. One he thought he'd perfected in his late teens, when his life had been turned upside down by his parents' deaths followed quickly by Ethan's abandonment of both Nash and their younger brother, Dare.

"Why do you care?" he asked, even though he knew he'd be smarter to walk away.

She shrugged, a sexy lift of one shoulder

that drew his attention to her soft-looking skin.

"Because you seem as out of place here as I am." She paused. "Except you're not a stranger to town or to this family."

Out of place. That one comment summed up his entire existence lately. How had she figured him out when no one else ever could?

"I need to leave," he said, immediately uncomfortable.

"What you need is to relax," she countered, and stopped him with one hand on his shoulder. "Let's dance." She playfully tugged on his tie.

He glanced over to where the rest of the family gathered next to the dance floor. "I'm not really interested in making a spectacle."

"Then we won't." She slipped her hand in his and led him to the far side of the house beneath an old weeping willow tree.

He could still hear the slow music, but he could no longer see the dance floor, and whoever was out there couldn't see them. She tightened her hold on his hand, and he realized he'd better take control or she'd be leading him through this dance. He wrapped an arm around her waist, slid his other hand into hers, and swayed to the sultry sound of the music coming from the band.

A slight breeze blew through the long dripping branches of the tree. She shivered and eased her body closer to his, obviously in need of warmth.

He inched his hand up her bare back. "Cold?" he asked in a gruff voice as her body heat and scent wrapped around him him.

"Not anymore."

He looked into her eyes to discover an awareness that matched his own, glanced down and caught sight of her lush lips. As they moved together to the music, warning bells rang in his head, but nothing could have stopped him from settling his mouth on hers. The first touch was electric, a heady combination of sparkling champagne and sensual, willing woman. Her lips were soft and giving, and he wasn't sure how long their mouths lingered in a chaste kiss they both knew was anything but.

His entire body came alive, reminding him of what he'd been missing in the two years since his divorce. That this woman could awaken him both surprised and unnerved him. It made him want to *feel* more. He trailed his hand up the soft skin of her back and cupped her head in one hand. With a sweet sigh, she opened for him, letting him really taste her for the first time. Warmth, heat, and desire flooded through him.

"Oh, gross! Just shoot me now!" Tess exclaimed in a disgusted voice.

Nash jerked back at the unwanted interruption. "What the hell are you doing?" he asked, the annoyed words escaping before he could think it through.

"Looking for Kelly. What are *you* doing?" She perched her hands on her hips, demanding an answer.

Wasn't it obvious? Nash shook his head and swallowed a groan. The kid was the biggest wiseass he'd ever come across.

"You found me," Kelly said, sounding calmer than he did.

Like that kiss hadn't affected her at all. A look at her told him that unless she was one hell of an actress, it hadn't. She appeared completely unflustered, while he was snapping at Tess because the hunger Kelly inspired continued to gnaw at him.

"Ethan and Faith want to talk to you," Tess muttered in a sulking tone.

Obviously she didn't like what she'd seen between him and her sister. Unlike Nash, who'd liked it a lot.

Too much, in fact.

From the pissed-off look on Tess's face, kissing Kelly and biting Tess's head off had resulted in a huge setback in trying to create any kind of relationship with his new sister. And to think, if asked, he'd have said things between them couldn't get any worse.

"Why don't you go tell them I'll be right there?" Kelly said patiently to Tess.

The teenager now folded her arms across her chest. "How about not?"

Kelly raised an eyebrow. "How about I'm the one in charge while Ethan's on his honeymoon and if you don't want to find yourself grounded and in your room for the next two weeks, you'll start listening now."

With a roll of her eyes and a deliberate stomp of her foot, which wasn't impressive considering she was wearing a deep purple dress and mini-heels from her walk down the aisle, Tess stormed away.

"Well done," he said to Kelly, admiring how she'd gotten Tess to listen without yelling or sniping back.

"Yeah, I did a better job than you." She shot him an amused glance. "But I can't take any credit. You saw what she was like before Ethan took over. This change is due to his influence, not mine." Her expression saddened at the fact that she'd been unable to accomplish helping Tess on her own.

He knew the feeling. "Don't remind me about Saint Ethan."

She raised her eyebrow. "There's always

tension between you and Ethan. Why is that?" she asked.

He definitely didn't want to talk about his brother or his past. "Is asking about my life your way of avoiding discussing the kiss?" He deliberately threw a question back at her as a distraction.

An unexpected smile caught hold of her lips. "Why would I want to avoid discussing it when it was so much fun?" she asked, and grabbed hold of his tie once more.

Her moist lips shimmered, beckoning to him as did her renewed interest, and he shoved his hands into his pants pockets. Easier to keep them to himself that way.

"Kelly! We're waiting!" Tess called impatiently, interrupting them again and reminding him of why he had to keep his distance from Kelly from now on.

"Coming!" Kelly called over her shoulder, before meeting Nash's gaze. "Looks like you got a reprieve." A mischievous twinkle lit her gaze.

A sparkle he found infectious. She had spunk, confidence, and an independent spirit he admired. His ex-wife had been as opposite of Kelly as he could imagine, more sweet and in need of being taken care of. Kelly could obviously hold her own.

And Nash didn't plan on giving her the

upper hand. "I don't know what you're talking about," he lied.

She patted his cheek. "Keep telling yourself that."

He would. For as long as it took to convince himself this woman would only cause him and his need to have a relationship with Tess boatloads of trouble.

Kelly Moss stood at the bottom of the circular stairs in the house that was nothing short of a mansion and yelled up at her sister. "Tess, let's go! If you want to have time for breakfast before school, get yourself downstairs now!" It was the third time she'd called up in the last five minutes.

"I said I'm coming!" came Tess's grumpy reply.

Ethan and Faith had left yesterday morning for their honeymoon, one week on the beautiful, secluded island of Turks and Caicos, where they had their own villa complete with private butler. *Talk about living the life,* Kelly thought. Hers wasn't so bad either, since she got to stay in this huge house with her own housekeeper while they were gone.

Tess's door slammed loudly, startling Kelly back to reality as her sister came storming out of her room, then stomping down the stairs.

The old days, when Kelly had been raising Tess alone and doing a god-awful job at it, came rushing back, and Kelly clenched her fists. "What's wrong?" Kelly only hoped it was something easily fixable, not a problem that would lead Tess to turn back to running wild.

"This!" Tess gestured to the school uniform she wore, a navy pleated skirt, white-collared shirt, and kneesocks. "I hate it."

Kelly knew better than to say it was better than the all-black outfits the teenager used to wear, including the old army surplus jacket and combat boots. "You'll get used to it."

Tess passed by Kelly and headed for the kitchen. "It's been a month and I still hate it."

The clothes or the school? Kelly wondered as she followed behind her sister. "Is it the skirt? Because you didn't mind the dress you wore at the wedding." In fact, she'd looked like a beautiful young lady.

"It's the fact that I *have* to wear it. I hate being told what to do."

"Tell me something I don't know," Kelly muttered, having been Tess's primary caregiver for longer than she could remember.

"I heard that."

Kelly grinned. Tess really had come a long way, thanks to Ethan Barron. Kelly shuddered to think of what might have happened if she hadn't taken drastic steps.

Both Tess and Kelly's mother, Leah Moss, had been a weak woman, too dependent on men and incapable of raising Tess. She'd been different when Kelly was young, or maybe that's how she wanted to remember her. Or maybe it had been Kelly's father's influence that had made Leah different.

Kelly would never know because her father had died of a heart attack when she was twelve. And Leah had immediately gone in search of another man to take his place. Her choice was a poor one. Leah struck up an affair with her married boss, Mark Barron. Yet despite how wrong it was, for Kelly, her mother's years as his mistress had been stable ones, including the period after Tess was born. But with Mark Barron's passing ten years ago, Leah had spiraled downward, and both Kelly and Tess suffered as a result.

She'd immediately packed up and moved them to a seedy part of New York City, far from their home in Tomlin's Cove, the neighboring town to Serendipity. Leah said she wanted them to start over. In reality, their mother had wanted an easy place to search for another lover to take care of her.

But Leah never found her next white knight, turning to alcohol and a never-ending rotation of disgusting men instead.

Since Tess had only been four years old at the time, a sixteen-year-old Kelly had become the adult, juggling high school, then part-time college with jobs and raising Tess. Fortunately, her mother had moved them into a boarding house with a kindly older woman who'd helped Kelly too.

But last year, their mother had run off with some guy, abandoning her youngest daughter, and something in Tess had broken. Angry and hurt, she'd turned into a belligerent, rebellious teenager, hanging out with the wrong crowd, smoking, drinking, and ultimately getting arrested. Desperate, Kelly had turned to the only person she remembered from their years in Tomlin's Cove, Richard Kane, a lawyer in Serendipity who'd put her in touch with Ethan Barron.

Kelly's heart shattered as she basically deposited her baby sister on a stranger's doorstep and ordered him to step up as her brother. But it was that, Kelly sensed, or heaven knew where Tess would end up. So here she was months later, starting her life over but still rushing Tess out for school, she thought, grateful things were finally looking up.

She and Tess ate a quick breakfast, after which Kelly dropped off Tess and headed to work. Another thing for which she owed Richard Kane, her job, working for him as a paralegal, in downtown Serendipity.

She stopped, as she did daily, at Cuppa Café, the town's version of Starbucks. Kelly had worked hard all her life and she'd learned early on to save, but her entire day hinged on that first cup of caffeine. It had to be strong and good.

Kelly stepped into the coffee shop and the delicious aroma surrounded her, instantly perking her up as if she were inhaling caffeine by osmosis.

She was pouring a touch of milk into her large cup of regular coffee when a familiar woman with long, curly blond hair joined her at the far counter.

"You're as regular as my grandma Emma wanted to be," Annie Kane joked.

Kelly glanced at her and grinned. "I could say the same for you."

"Good point." Annie laughed and raised her cup in a mock toast.

Small-town living offered both perks and drawbacks. Running into a familiar face could fall into either category. Kelly and Annie frequented Cuppa Café at the same time each morning and they'd often linger and chat. If pressed, Kelly would say Annie was the closest she had to a real friend here, if she didn't count Faith Harrington, Ethan's wife.

Annie was Richard Kane's daughter, though from the pictures on Richard's desk, Kelly noticed Annie looked more like her mother than her dad. From the first day they'd met at her father's office, Kelly had liked this woman.

Kelly took a long, desperately needed sip of her drink.

"So what's your excuse for being up so early every day?"

"Routine keeps me young," Annie said.

Kelly rolled her eyes. "You *are* young." She looked Annie over, from her slip-on sneakers to her jeans and light cotton sweater. "I bet we're probably close to the same age."

"I'll be twenty-seven next month," Annie said.

"And I'll be twenty-seven in December."

Annie raised her cup to her lips, and Kelly couldn't help but notice her hand shook as she took a sip.

Kelly narrowed her gaze but didn't comment on the tremor. Instead, she dove into cementing her life here in Serendipity.

"Listen, instead of quick hellos standing over coffee, how about we meet for lunch one day?" She was ready for a real friend here, someone she could trust and confide in. Kelly adored Tess, but a fourteen-year-old hardly constituted adult company.

"I'd like that!" Annie said immediately. "Let me give you my phone number." As she reached into her purse, her cell phone rang and she glanced at the number.

"Excuse me a second," she said to Kelly. "Hello?" she spoke into the receiver.

Kelly glanced away to give Annie privacy, but she couldn't help but overhear her end of the conversation.

"I'm feeling better, thanks. Yeah. No you don't need to stop by. I called the plumber and he said he'd make it to the house by the end of the day." Annie grew quiet, then spoke once more. "I can afford it and you don't need to come by. You weren't good with the pipes when we were married," she said, amusement in her tone.

Some more silence, then Annie said, "If you insist, I'll see you later," she said, now sounding more annoyed than indulgent.

She hung up and put the phone back in her bag. "My ex-husband," she explained to Kelly. "He thinks because I have MS I need his constant hovering."

The admission caught Kelly off guard and she felt for Annie, being diagnosed so young. Richard liked to talk about everything and anything when he was in the office, but he'd never mentioned his daughter's disease. Kelly didn't blame him for omitting something so personal. In fact, she was surprised Annie had mentioned it at all.

"I'm sure you noticed my hand shaking earlier, and if we're going to be friends, you might as well know," Annie said as if reading Kelly's mind.

Kelly met Annie's somewhat serene gaze. Obviously she'd come to terms with her situation. "Thanks for telling me."

"Hey, if I go MIA one day, at least you'll know why." She shrugged, as if the notion were no big deal.

Kelly didn't take the other woman's confidence or situation as lightly. "Well, if you ever need anything, just let me know."

Annie smiled. "Thanks. But I think my ex will always be around to handle things," she said through lightly clenched jaw.

"That could be a good thing," Kelly mused, "having someone at your beck and call when you need something."

"Not when you've told them you want to be independent," Annie muttered. The frustration in the other woman's voice was something Kelly understood.

Like Annie, Kelly didn't need or want a man who felt the need to take care of her. She was determined to be smart and self-sufficient, the opposite of her mother in every way. No matter how many obstacles life threw in her way. And unfortunately, there were more to come. Utter humiliation loomed in the not-so-distant future courtesy of a man she'd once loved. The affair was long over. The fallout was not. Kelly could handle the mess. Her younger sister could not. And Kelly did not want Tess exposed to gossip and innuendo just as the teenager was doing well and making better choices. Kelly only hoped the distance between Manhattan and Serendipity would spare Tess when trouble hit.

"Men just don't get us women, do they?" Annie asked, a welcome interruption from Kelly's troubling thoughts.

Kelly shook her head and sighed. "No, they do not."

"Firsthand experience?" Annie asked.

"Unfortunately, yes." Kelly frowned, the memory of spending the last year getting over having her heart and trust betrayed still fresh.

"I'm sorry." Annie blew out a long breath.

"I don't know about yours but my ex means well. He just takes the word 'responsibility' to the extreme."

Kelly swallowed hard. "And my ex-boyfriend took the word 'commitment' way too lightly."

"Excuse me," an older man said, indicating he needed to get to the counter so he could pour milk into his coffee.

"Sorry." Kelly stepped out of the way and walked toward the exit with Annie.

"So how about I call you at my father's office later today and we'll exchange phone numbers and make lunch plans?" Annie asked.

Kelly nodded. "Sure. That's fine."

They parted ways and Kelly headed toward Richard's office in the center of town. The buildings stretched along the road, stores on the main level, small apartments above, like hers over Joe's Bar. The small town appealed to her, coming from the overcrowded city with tall buildings and too many people.

Using her key, Kelly walked into the office of the man she credited for helping to save her sister and her family. "Richard?" she called out.

No answer.

The small office was empty. Obviously

she'd beaten him here, which was unusual. Richard was an early-to-the-office, late-getting-home kind of man, though his wife had been trying to get him to work fewer hours, maybe take in a partner to lighten his load.

Kelly settled in to her desk in a small room with a window that she appreciated. She already knew which case she had to work on and what she needed to do today, but she pulled out her calendar anyway. As part of her work routine and a way to make sure she never forgot an assignment, Kelly glanced at today's date and the list she'd made on Friday before leaving work for the weekend.

Seven P.M. — parent-teacher conference for Tess.

Which she was attending with Dare, since Ethan was away. Better Dare than the other Barron brother. The one she'd deliberately put out of her mind since the kiss on Saturday.

And what a kiss it had been.

Kelly prided herself on her poker face but she still wasn't sure she'd pulled off being nonchalant after Tess interrupted them. Her sister had sulked all the way home but hadn't mentioned what she'd seen, nor had she brought it up the next day. If Tess wasn't going to discuss it, neither was Kelly.

And considering she hadn't heard a word from Nash, neither was he. Which bothered her. A lot.

Sure, she'd been a little tipsy and a lot aggressive, but she'd felt his body heat and obvious reaction firsthand. He'd obviously liked the kiss, but he'd been hard to read afterward.

She told herself she shouldn't care what Nash thought or felt. She'd learned from her mother's choices and her own past not to rely on anyone but herself. So though she might be attracted to Nash, his feelings on the subject didn't matter. Even if he was equally interested, a brief affair would be disastrous because it would hurt Tess. And short term was all Kelly would let herself believe in from now on.

Two

Nash walked into the Family Restaurant where Dare had asked him to meet for lunch. The request wasn't unusual. Dare and Nash had been close forever. Not even going to separate foster homes had been able to break the bond between them. And nothing ever would.

The diner-like establishment was located on a plot of land on the edge of town, a staple of Serendipity for the last two decades. The owners remained the same, generations of the Donovan family members taking over for each other as circumstance dictated.

Nash waved to Macy Donovan, the hostess whom he'd gone to school with before the Rossmans took him in, adopted him, and sent him to private school. She waved back, gesturing to where Dare sat at a booth in the back.

Nash would have found him in a heartbeat, his blue police uniform making him stand out. He joined his brother, easing into the worn, cracked vinyl seat.

"Hope you don't mind, but I ordered for you. I don't have much time today," Dare said. "I'm on a quick lunch break."

As an attorney, Nash could pretty much make his own hours. "Good by me, thanks." He gestured to the waitress, a Donovan cousin by marriage.

"What can I get for you?" Gina, a middle-aged woman with red hair and a bright smile, asked.

"Coke for me," Nash said.

Gina eyed Dare's empty glass. "Want a refill, Officer?"

Dare nodded.

"Be right back with your drinks and your food," Gina promised.

"Thanks," Nash and Dare said in unison.

Nash leaned back in his seat. "So, have you recovered from the wedding?" He'd watched his brother enjoy his day off.

Nash wasn't sure if Dare's drink had been water or vodka, but he could tell his brother had had a good time.

Dare laughed. "Yeah. I'm just glad I was off duty on Sunday. It could've been ugly if I didn't get a day to rest."

"Who says it wasn't ugly?" Nash asked,

having not had nearly the fun his brother had.

Until the end, when he'd been blindsided by a sexy woman and a mind-blowing kiss.

"All things considered, I'd say the day was okay," Dare said.

"How do you figure?" Nash asked, always shocked that somehow, despite the fact that Dare had gone to a foster home with too many kids and too little money except what the state provided, he'd ended up with a better attitude than Nash.

"Tess behaved, you and Ethan didn't come to blows, and Faith's mother didn't insult us Barron boys too much." He slung his arm over the back of his booth and grinned.

"That's only because the great Lanie Harrington couldn't take her focus off the wineglass in her hand." Everyone in Serendipity knew Faith's mother thought she was better than the rest of the world, even after her husband had disgraced their family name.

Dare shrugged, his expression showing compassion not disgust. "Well, if I'd lost my house and all my money because my husband turned into a self-styled Bernie Madoff, I might spend most of my days drunk and not save it for special occasions. Just saying."

When the Harrington fraud scandal had broken, few were spared. Even Nash's adoptive/foster parents had taken a hit, and Nash currently represented many Harrington clients in a civil class action suit, but the likelihood of ever seeing any money grew dimmer by the day. Only Ethan prospered from the scandal, returning to town wealthy, thanks to his software abilities and army training. Apparently he'd sold some aircraft development system to the military, resulting in his ability to buy the Harrington mansion at auction after Faith's father's fall from grace.

Nash leaned back in his seat while Gina placed their food on the table. "Thanks, Gina."

"I love serving you boys. My husband, Tony, speaks very highly of you both. A lawyer and a policeman. He says your parents would be proud," she said quietly.

Nash met his brother's gaze, a silent knowing look in his eyes that spoke of the past and shared pain. "Thank him for us," he said.

"Will do. Can I get you anything else?" she asked, changing the subject.

"I'm good for now," Nash said.

"Same," Dare added. He waited until Gina walked away before leaning forward. "Now, where were we?"

"Talking about the Harringtons." Nobody in Serendipity ever tired of the subject.

"Right." Nash loaded his burger with ketchup before passing the bottle to Dare, who did the same.

"I might feel sorry for Lanie Harrington if I thought she didn't know anything about her husband's business. But how the hell could she live with the man and not know he was defrauding every one of his clients?" Friends, family, and strangers alike?

Dare's gaze darkened. "You can live with someone, be close to someone, and not know nearly as much as you think you do," Dare said with utter certainty and a note in his voice Nash rarely heard from his sibling.

Not knowing how to reply, Nash took a bite of his juicy hamburger. They ate in silence, Dare's sudden and unusual mood change reminding him of why the brothers tried so hard not to revisit the past.

Nash preferred to live in the present and had done well at it until Ethan returned to town, dragging all the ugly stuff with him.

"So what's the favor you needed?" Nash asked as he finished his meal.

Dare wiped his hands on his napkin and

tossed the paper onto the table. "A bunch of guys came down with the flu. We're short-handed so I said I'd work another shift tonight."

"Sucks," Nash said.

Dare nodded. "So I need you to go to Tess's parent-teacher conference at Birchwood."

"I think our sister might have a thing or two to say about the change of plans," Nash said.

When Dare had offered to go in Ethan's place, Nash hadn't argued. Considering how the kid felt about him, he figured she'd appreciate Dare attending and not him.

"No doubt about it," Dare agreed. "But you still need to do it."

He already knew he'd attend. "Not a problem. I'll just wear armor when I talk to her afterward."

"You know the reason she has issues with you, right?" Dare asked.

"She idolizes Ethan and hates me because I don't."

Dare let out a laugh.

"Not funny. I've done everything possible to win her over short of groveling at our oldest brother's feet."

Dare waved to Gina, motioning for a check. "No one expects you to grovel. Ethan knows damn well what he did to us was wrong. But we can't change the past," Dare said, his face growing suddenly dark.

Nash felt a chill whenever Dare's optimistic outlook took on unexpected shadows. He never knew quite how to react, and a helpless feeling crept over him, much like when Richard Kane had explained to Nash the boys would be separated.

He shivered at the memory.

"We just need to keep moving forward," Dare said, unaware of Nash's reaction.

"I'm doing the best I can dealing with Ethan's return," Nash said.

"I know. And when she gets older, Tess will too. In the meantime, just pick up Kelly at the house at seven and be at the school by seven thirty."

"Kelly?" Nash's mouth grew dry at the mention of her name.

Dare arched an eyebrow. "Did you think I was going alone? Of course Kelly wants to see how Tess is adjusting." His brother studied him, an amused grin on his face. "Or do you have problems with Kelly too?"

Nash frowned. "You obviously already know the answer. Who told you?" he asked, resigned.

Dare grinned, enjoying this. "Our baby sister wasn't too happy that you — and I quote — 'had your tongue down Kelly's throat.' "

Heat rose to Nash's face. "*That* was an accident."

Dare's belly laugh had other diners looking over at them. "Tess catching you was an accident or you kissing Kelly?" Thank God Dare lowered his voice. "I'm not sure what that was but you've wanted her from the minute you laid eyes on her."

Did not. The immature reply came to Nash and he squelched it. Why deny the obvious and prolong the conversation?

"It can't go anywhere," he said instead.

"Why not? It's not like you're married anymore. You just *act* like an overprotective husband."

Nash gripped the edge of the table. "She needs someone to help her," he said of his ex-wife.

"So let her find someone who's getting something from the relationship in return," Dare said, looking out for him like they always did for one another. "Look, ever since Ethan bailed, you've taken on the role of protector. You gave me your clothes, you even brought me extra food. But you can't spend your life making sure you never end up like *him*."

"Jesus," Nash muttered, never expecting

Dare to be so analytical and brutal at the same time. "I'm not having this discussion."

"Fine." Dare raised both hands in submission.

"We're friends," Nash said of his ex.

Dare rolled his eyes. "Fine. And what are you and Kelly?"

That was the problem.

Nash had no idea. But now, thanks to Dare's change of plans, he was obviously going to get a chance to find out.

Nash stood at the doorway of his brother Ethan's mansion. From seventy degrees the day of the wedding, the temperature today had just barely touched sixty and now it was a cooler fifty-something with a breeze that felt much more like fall. He wore the same sport jacket he'd chosen for work today and rang the doorbell, eager to get inside.

In seconds, the door swung wide and Tess stood on the other side. Her hair, once jet black, was now a lighter brown, and the purple streak was faded and almost gone. Even her gray sweatpants and imprinted T-shirt said *normal teen,* and he appreciated the change.

Until she opened her mouth, that is. "Oh,

it's you," Tess muttered, her standard greeting.

"I see some things haven't changed."

Tess folded her arms across her chest and remained silent.

"Are you going to let me in?" he asked, reining in all his frustration and maintaining patience and calm.

"Why are you here? I thought Dare was going to my parent-teacher conference with Kelly."

Here we go, Nash thought. "He had to work so I'm filling in."

"Swell."

He forced a smile. But he still stood outside on the welcome mat like a stranger she was unsure whether to trust. "Again, can I come in?"

Tess moved aside. He stepped into the house and shut the door behind him. He stared at Tess and she glared right back.

"How's school going?" he asked her.

"I guess you'll find out soon enough," she said with mock sweetness.

Nash gave up for now. "Is Kelly ready?"

Tess turned and shouted toward the upstairs. "Kelly, lover boy's here to pick you up!"

Nash winced. Normally he wouldn't let Tess dictate who he saw or what he did, but he understood how seeing them kissing had threatened her safe world. "Look, about that —"

"Save it." She held out a hand to stop him from speaking. "Anything you're going to say would just be TMI and I don't want to hear it."

He closed his eyes for a brief second. "Okay, what's TMI mean?" he asked, resigned to making an even bigger ass of himself in front of her.

She rolled her eyes in complete disgust. "Too much information." She pulled in a deep breath. "Kelly!" she yelled once more, even louder.

"I'm coming!" Kelly appeared at the top of the stairs and made her way down. Wearing black leggings and a long purple top, belted in silver, she looked every inch the sexy woman he couldn't stop thinking about.

He shook his head and reminded himself that not only wasn't this a date but he also couldn't allow himself to think about her in any way except Tess's sister or he'd destroy any chance he had with the kid. Not that he felt that he necessarily had any chance at all, but still, Tess had to come first.

"Hi! Dare sent me a text letting me know you'd be here instead," she said, padding down the stairs. "Tess, next time invite your brother inside and let him sit down!" she chided the teen.

"That's okay. We were just catching up." He met Tess's gaze, daring her to disagree and get herself in more trouble.

"Oh!" Kelly said, sounding surprised. "Well, that's good, then. I just have to get my shoes and I'll be ready to go." She opened the hall closet and pulled out a pair of high boots.

Sexy boots that covered her entire calf up to her knee and folded over at the top with buckles along the outside for effect.

He swallowed a groan. "So, what's tonight's agenda?" he asked Tess in an effort to distract himself from the sight of Kelly, bent over, back to him, pulling her boots on.

Tess shrugged. "How should I know?"

"Tess! Quit being so rude." Kelly grabbed a leather jacket from a hanger and shut the closet door, then walked over to where they were standing. "Every time I put my coat or shoes in my room near my suitcase, Rosalita hangs everything in the hall closet like I live here," she said, obviously embarrassed.

"That's just her job."

"I wouldn't know. I didn't have a housekeeper growing up."

Nash hadn't had a housekeeper when he'd lived with his parents either, but after moving in with the Rossmans, they'd had a woman named Consuela who'd run the house much as Rosalita appeared to do here. He didn't see the point in going into a long explanation.

Kelly merely shrugged at his silence and struggled to put on her jacket.

Reaching over, Nash grabbed the coat and helped, holding it out so she could slip her arms through the sleeves. Because Tess was watching, he pretended to be unaffected when Kelly flipped her hair from beneath the collar, giving him a whiff of strawberry-scented shampoo, and treated him to a smile that nearly knocked him on his ass.

"There. All set. Tess, Rosalita's here if you need anything. Be good," she said to the teen.

"I should be saying that to you two," Tess muttered.

"Relax. Go watch TV," Nash suggested.

"I have homework," she said icily.

"Then go do that."

"Ignore her." Kelly grabbed his hand and pulled him toward the door.

He followed, grateful to get away from Tess's moodiness only to realize once they were outside and the house door shut behind them, they were alone.

He'd jumped from one awkward situation right into another.

Since her arrival in Serendipity, Kelly discovered there'd been a lot of nevers in her life. She'd never had a maid, never lived in a mansion, and never gone to private school. She walked into Birchwood Academy and immediately wondered if her sister's discomfort with the uniform was more due to the atmosphere than the clothing. This was no public school with dimly lit halls, old metal lockers, and dingy commercial linoleum everywhere. Money elevated the look of the building and from what Kelly could see, affected the attitudes of the parents and teachers. But she was determined to keep an open mind.

"What's wrong?" Nash asked.

Surprised by the question, Kelly stopped walking toward the classroom where they'd been told Tess's homeroom teacher would meet them. "What makes you think anything's wrong?"

"You stiffened up the minute we walked into this place. Not to mention the fact that you talked about a million and one things on the ride here and you haven't said a word since we walked in." Hands in his jacket pockets, Nash leaned against one of the brightly painted metal lockers and studied her through perceptive ocean blue eyes.

"I chatted in the car to keep you comfortable," she lied. She chatted to keep herself level-headed and so that she wouldn't be tempted to coax him into kissing her again. The attraction was definitely there, but she didn't want to upset her sister's life by pushing for a fling with Nash. No matter how sexy she found him to be.

"And what changed now?" He probed for answers like the lawyer he was.

Kelly frowned. With his short, expensively cut hair, he looked every inch the rich boy who'd fit right in at this school. Only the fact that she'd seen him feeling awkward and out of place at his own brother's wedding had her considering leveling with him now.

"Well?" he prodded. "We're going to be late if we don't get a move on."

"Then let's go," she suggested.

"Not until you tell me what's bothering you."

The concern in his tone got to her. "This place just feels out of my league," she admitted.

He groaned. "Do you want to know the truth? It's out of mine too. If it weren't for the fact that the couple who adopted me had wealth and privilege, I'd be as uncomfortable as you are. I had to get used to it earlier, that's all."

Kelly blinked, stunned both by the revelation and the fact that he'd confided in her at all. She'd sensed his unease with many things in his life, but she never thought he'd let her in enough to explain. Ethan had once mentioned that he'd let his brothers down, but he'd been vague and she hadn't wanted to pry. Now she wanted to know more from Nash, but she had no time to ask.

"Just hold your head up high and believe you belong here. You'll be fine." He reached out and squeezed her hand, the unexpected reassurance causing a lump to form in her throat.

He hid himself so deeply that she hadn't known he could be kind. Now that she did, it only added to his appeal.

"Thanks." She smiled in appreciation.

"You're welcome."

"And don't worry. I won't tell anyone you're really a nice guy behind that gruff exterior," she said with a laugh.

He raised an eyebrow. "I *am* a nice guy!"

"Then try smiling more often. Maybe more people would know it." *Like Tess.* But she didn't voice the thought out loud. She already knew his strained relationship with her was a sore subject.

"Come on, wise guy." He placed a hand behind her back and led her toward the classroom.

Tess's homeroom teacher, a woman named Julie Bernard who looked to be in her midfifties with glasses, gestured for them to come in and waited for them to sit down across from her desk.

"So," Ms. Bernard said when everyone was settled.

"We're looking forward to hearing about Tess," Kelly said. "I'm her sister, by the way. Kelly Moss." She extended her hand and the woman shook it, her grip cold.

"I'm her brother. Nash Barron." Nash also shook the teacher's hand.

Julie Bernard treated them to a curt nod. "I understand Tess has a complicated family situation," she said through pursed lips.

Kelly tried not to read anything into the other woman's words. "Yes, but no more so than many kids today," she said with a smile. "Tess lives with her brother, Ethan. He's away on his honeymoon."

"So you're all related?" Ms. Bernard asked.

"Actually Tess and I share a mother," Kelly explained. "Nash, Ethan, and Tess share a father. It's complicated, as you said."

The woman clasped her hands together on her desk. "Well, that explains a lot."

Kelly narrowed her gaze, no longer so willing to assume the best about the woman. "I can assure you that Tess has a solid foundation behind her and people who love her. So perhaps you'd like to tell us what you mean by 'that explains a lot.' "

"Your sister has a bit of an edge."

So do you, Kelly thought. "So do most teenage girls."

Nash placed a hand on her arm, warning her to relax.

"Not most teenage girls here, Ms. Moss. At Birchwood, we place higher expectations on our students."

Could her nose reach higher in the air?

Nash leaned forward in his seat. "Is Tess acting out in class?"

Ms. Bernard met his gaze. "Not particularly."

"Mouthing off?" Nash asked.

Kelly bit the inside of her cheek, knowing firsthand how foul Tess could get.

She shook her head. "Not with the teachers or the staff."

"Then what's the problem? You just don't *like* her?" Kelly couldn't help but ask. Obviously this woman did have an issue with Tess.

She pushed her glasses farther up on the bridge of her nose. "As I said, she has an edge. She does what she's asked but often begrudgingly. Her work is completed on time but often looks rushed. She has an attitude that's not acceptable here."

What is acceptable? Kelly wondered. *Stepford children?*

"We'll definitely talk to Tess about her attitude, but I sense there's something more," Nash said, "another reason you don't like Tess, because based on your description, I have to agree with Kelly. Tess sounds like a typical teenage girl." He braced his hands on the desk, his knuckles white as he gripped the edge hard. "That you happen not to like."

Kelly had picked up on Ms. Julie Bernard's attitude, but she figured Nash would be the first one to jump all over Tess for hers. Instead, his perceptiveness surprised her.

Kelly folded her arms over her chest and waited for the woman to reply.

"Okay, fine. I'm well aware of the fact that Mr. Barron — Ethan Barron — wrote a large check to get his sister into this school. And if the institution hadn't been financially crippled by his wife's father, Martin Harrington, the school wouldn't have needed the influx his cash provided."

"And a child like Tess would have been turned away?" Kelly asked bitterly.

"Yes." Ms. Bernard didn't flinch as she replied.

"Shame on you," Nash said as he rose to his feet. He grasped Kelly's hand and pulled her to a standing position beside him.

She was too stunned to do anything but follow and admire as she watched him in action.

"Excuse me?" Ms. Bernard asked.

"I said, *shame on you.* As an educator, you're supposed to be tolerant and understanding of each child as an individual. All I hear now is bias toward an innocent kid who's had a rough life and whose brother cared enough about her to give her a second chance. Not to mention that he helped stabilize your school's financial situation at the same time."

Kelly wanted to applaud.

Ms. Bernard rose to her feet. Her diminutive height didn't help her cause. "I have colleagues who lost jobs because of Faith Harrington's father. Programs were cut. Children who were thriving here were forced to return to public school when their parents also lost their savings!" The older woman trembled with anger.

"So did my parents," Nash said to her. "My foster father had a heart attack and died not long after. But at least my parents placed the blame with the person on whom it belongs. You're taking your anger out on a child."

Nash turned to leave, but Kelly, stunned by Nash's revelations, still had one thing more to add. "You can be certain that Ethan Barron and his wife, who so generously provided money to this school, will hear about how his sister is being treated." Kelly stormed out of the classroom, breathing hard, Nash right behind her.

Once in the hall, she turned to him. "You were amazing! The way you stood up for Tess! Ethan and Faith will be so grateful you backed them up too."

Nash pinched the bridge of his nose and leaned against the wall, his breathing shallow. "I didn't do it for them."

"I know. You did it for Tess."

"Who wouldn't be in this position if it weren't for Ethan," Nash said.

Kelly reached out and placed her hand on his shoulder. "But she wouldn't have this opportunity, either," she gently reminded him.

He met her gaze.

In his eyes, she saw a pain that touched her deeply. “I want to help,” she said softly.

He drew a deep breath and nodded. “Okay, let’s go.”

“Where?”

“Someplace where you can learn all about the Barron brothers’ sordid history.”

THREE

Nash and Kelly drove through downtown Serendipity.

The sun hadn't set completely, but streetlights were on in readiness for the night. He wound through familiar back streets until they reached a small house at the end of a cul-de-sac. A house he knew as well as he knew his own name. He, Ethan, and Dare used to play in the yard and they'd learned to ride bikes around the circle. He glanced up at the old place he still thought of as home. Even the front windows still held the bright orange-red Tot Finder stickers on the room he'd shared with Dare. He wondered whether children lived there now or the owners were just too lazy to remove the decals.

"Where are we?" Kelly asked, breaking into his thoughts.

"I grew up here." He gestured to the home

he'd parked in front of. "Ethan, Dare, and I."

Kelly glanced over, then waited. She was smart enough to sense this story wasn't easy, and he appreciated her letting him tell it his way. His childhood wasn't something he revisited often and definitely not in front of someone else. He couldn't say exactly why he'd chosen to confide in her now. Though he was certain her relationship to Tess had something to do with it, his gut told him the reasons had more to do with Kelly herself. Her perceptiveness and quiet understanding made it easy.

"My brothers and I were close. All three of us, even Ethan," he said before she could ask. "As for my parents, my father traveled a lot, and when he was home they argued, mostly over his traveling and being away from home. The thing is, he provided for his family the best way he knew how. At least that's how I saw things until —"

"Until you found out about Tess."

He nodded, remembering how floored he'd been, standing in Ethan's kitchen and hearing about Tess, a sister none of them knew they had. The conclusion, that their father had had an affair, had been an obvious one. Nash had been in such denial he'd insisted they run a check on the DNA test results Kelly had given Ethan. He'd had a lot of time to think since then, to revisit his earlier years when they'd all been a family.

"I knew my parents had problems, but so did so many of my friends' parents, so I buried my head in the sand. I didn't want to think the fighting meant there were other things going on, like affairs."

Kelly nodded. "I can understand that. What kid wants to let his mind go there?" she asked. "I never wanted to think about what my mother did each and every night she left the house."

He met her gaze and realized how little he knew about her and his new sister. "What was it like for you and Tess?" he asked.

"Oh, no. No changing the subject to me. We're here in front of your childhood home. Let's just stick to the Barron boys for now," she said, an amused and knowing smile on her face.

For the first time, he hadn't forced the subject away from himself on purpose. He really had wanted to know more about her. "Okay, but that means you'll owe me," he warned.

She curled one leg beneath her and maneuvered into a more comfortable position. "That's okay. I don't welsh on my debts."

He laughed. "Good to know."

"So . . . ? What were you going to tell me next? You were close to both of your brothers — what happened?" She prodded him for more information about his childhood.

"Would you believe I was just thinking about how your quiet understanding made it easy to talk to you?" He shook his head, amused at her sudden change in tactics.

She grinned. "You already tried to ditch the conversation once. I'm just making sure you don't do it again."

He rolled his eyes, but he did enjoy how she joked and tried to lighten any subject or mood. Except where he had to go now in conversation . . . it was almost impossible to lighten.

"Ethan and Tess have a lot in common," Nash said, finding the easiest way to broach things.

"How so?"

He thought back to the tough, hard exterior his sister possessed when she'd arrived on Ethan's doorstep this summer. "He was a juvenile delinquent too. He ran with the wrong crowd, stayed out all night, drank, and literally drove my parents crazy."

Kelly blinked, obviously stunned by the revelation. "Ethan looks like the most upstanding kind of guy!"

"Which is exactly what drives me mad.

Everyone sees him as some sort of savior. I know the truth. Hell, I lived it," he said through clenched jaw.

Kelly reached out and touched his cheek. "Relax and tell me," she said softly.

He exhaled a deep breath. "It's not like Dare and I were angels," he said at last.

"But?"

He swallowed hard. "But Ethan was trouble. Then one night, he didn't come home. My parents were so used to it, nobody even bothered calling around until the phone rang at three A.M. He'd been arrested for joy riding. My parents went to bail him out and they were killed by a drunk driver on the way to the police station."

She sucked in a stunned breath. "I'm so sorry." She edged closer, until they were inches apart, separated only by the center console.

"There's more."

"I'm listening."

"The judge was understanding and gave Ethan a second chance, but instead of coming home to me and Dare, he took off for parts unknown and we didn't hear from him for ten years." Even as he spoke, Nash realized his entire body shook, taut with the rage that always consumed him when he allowed himself to both remember and feel.

"Where did he go?" she asked quietly.

"Does it matter?"

Kelly placed a hand over Nash's tightly clenched fist. "I guess not," she said for now.

In reality, where his brother had gone and why he'd made the choices he had might matter if Nash were ever going to get past his hurt and anger. That she wanted to help him in this mission told Kelly she was in trouble.

But first things first. "What happened to you and Dare?" she asked.

"Foster care." Without warning, he faced forward, shifted the car into drive, and put his foot on the gas pedal.

She knew without asking they were taking the next part of his tour. She was so grateful for the insight and his willingness to share, she remained silent on the drive, fearful any wrong comment would cause him to change his mind and withdraw instead.

She couldn't be any more surprised when he pulled up to a mansion like the house fairly close to where Ethan and Faith lived.

"This is the house I grew up in after my parents died," he said, speaking again at last.

She let out a low whistle. "Nice."

"You'd think so." He inclined his head, pressed his foot to the accelerator, and drove on, past the house, not spending time at this particular stop.

They circled around, passed through town once more, ending up in what had to be the most run-down section of Serendipity. The entire area made a mockery of the town's name. Streetlights were randomly out, graffiti marked the buildings and gangs of leather-jacket-clad boys, or maybe they were men, grouped together along the darkened street.

Kelly shivered.

And she waited.

He drove farther. Beyond the run-down apartments were equally shabby-looking houses. The occasional porch light illuminated a shattered window here and a broken wood railing there. Nash parked in front of a home that possessed both; the front window had been shattered, bound together with heavy-duty tape in a poor attempt at makeshift repair, and yellow ties crisscrossed the entry, preventing anyone from walking on the porch.

"Where are we now?" Kelly asked into the silence.

"This is where Dare grew up," Nash said.

"Wait. I knew you ended up in foster care, but —"

"You assumed we stayed together?" Nash let out a harsh laugh.

Kelly winced. "Well, yes."

Nash closed his eyes for a moment. When he opened them again, she could see he was lost in memories. "We didn't."

Therein lay the source of his anger and bitterness, she thought. He couldn't have been more than sixteen. He lost his parents, his older brother abandoned him, and then the state ripped his brother from him too. So, really, who could blame him for his resentment?

"What happened?" she asked softly.

"Richard Kane was the DA at the time. He told me that Ethan had taken off and Dare and I would have to go to foster care. He said he'd do his best to keep us together. We each stayed with a friend for a couple of nights, and one day Richard showed up and explained how he'd tried but couldn't find a family to take us both."

Despite having been warned of the outcome, Kelly gasped anyway.

He let out a rough laugh and she wished she could take back the sound.

"Why couldn't your family take Dare? It's obvious they had the money."

He shrugged. "To this day, I don't really know. Richard said there were reasons but that the Rossmans were good people. They'd lost their only son the year before."

Kelly shook her head, overwhelmed by the story, yet Nash had lived it and he'd only been sixteen years old at the time. "Did you know their son?" she asked.

He rested his arm on the steering wheel and shook his head. "He'd gone to private school. But the whole town knew the story. Rich kids let out of school early because of a freak power failure. They went to someone's house whose parents were out of town. They were drinking, one thing led to another, one guy threw a punch and hit Stuart Rossman. He fell and his head hit the patio. While he lay there, the rest of the kids panicked. Some ran, others cleaned up the evidence of alcohol before calling nine-one-one."

"That's awful!"

He nodded. "And a horrible mark on the town. I'm guessing since I was the same age as Stuart, the Rossmans wanted me. They'd never wanted two kids. When I got older, I tried to talk to them about it, but they always shut me down. It's ironic, really, since in all other ways we grew very close. They talked to me about everything else."

She didn't know what to say — or feel — so she could only imagine that Nash had felt the same way. "You must've been a mess," she whispered. "Guilty over your little brother's living conditions yet grateful for what you had."

He turned his head and met her gaze. "You should've been a shrink."

She shook her head. "It's not hard to figure out. I just put myself in your place."

"I was afraid Dare would hate me. I ran away a few times, hoping to make my point, but the cops would find me and bring me back. Eventually I accepted that I had no choice. Richard played a big role, talking to me and making sure I knew Florence and Samuel were good people. That they just couldn't have done anything differently. I still don't understand but I played the hand I was dealt."

Kelly's stomach had cramped in a tight knot. "How'd you manage?"

"Honestly? Dare made it easy. He wasn't angry at me or at the Rossmans. He was older at fifteen than I was at sixteen. I just did what I could for him. I brought him extra food when I could and gave him my not-so-older clothes."

Her heart swelled with emotion, for the kid he'd been and the adult he was now, who still so obviously held on to so much pain.

"You're a good man," she said, sensing he needed a reminder.

"A good man would've made sure his brother had it as good as he did."

"The man you are now, maybe. The kid you were then did everything he could." Kelly leaned across the car's center console so she could get closer to him. "It's time to let go of the guilt."

He turned his head and their faces were inches apart, their mouths so close, Kelly couldn't say who moved first, but the kiss was inevitable. Not hungry or urgent, this was more about comfort and understanding . . . and a sudden sense of caring that both shocked and frightened her. Because now she knew him better. Now the beginnings of emotion were involved. Hers, definitely. And if the gentleness in his touch was any indication, his feelings were now engaged too.

A sudden knock on the car window startled her and she jumped back with an unladylike yelp.

"What the —" Nash glanced over and opened the window, and a flashlight shone into the car, all but blinding her.

"I got a report of someone casing the area," a familiar voice said.

"Shut off the damn light, Dare," Nash muttered to his brother. "You know my car, so quit playing games."

Officer Dare Barron snapped the flashlight shut, braced his hands, and leaned down so he could look into the car. Then he grinned. "Can't you two find a better place to hook up?"

Caught again, Kelly thought, embarrassed. And this time they weren't even really making out, they were just . . .

"We were just talking," Nash said to his brother.

"Yeah, I saw the dialogue. Mama Garcia put a call in to the station," Dare said of his foster mother.

Nash groaned. "Tell her I'm sorry we scared her. I was just giving Kelly the Barron tour of Serendipity."

Dare nodded, his expression one of understanding.

Nobody had to tell the youngest brother that Nash had been reliving their family history.

"I'll let her know. Can I give you a suggestion?" A definite mischievous twinkle lit Dare's dark brown eyes.

"Could I stop you?" Nash asked.

"Next time you two feel the urge to lock lips? Go somewhere more private. You have a habit of making a spectacle of yourselves," he said with a laugh.

Dare straightened to his full height, tapped

the top of the car twice, and strode off, leaving Kelly mortified.

Baring his soul had left Nash more exposed than if he'd stripped naked and run through the street. Not even being caught kissing Kelly — yet again — bothered him as much as the fact that she now knew his deepest secrets. Okay, not secrets, since anyone in the town could repeat the Barron family history, but she instinctively knew exactly how circumstances had affected him.

And wasn't that why he'd told her? Because she made him feel less alone? Not even his ex-wife who'd been his best friend had understood him quite so well. Nor had he understood her. If he had, he wouldn't have been shocked when she'd asked for a divorce.

Kelly met his gaze. To his surprise, she remained silent and he wondered what she was thinking.

"Not as fun as the last one, huh?" Kelly asked.

"What?"

"That kiss — it wasn't as fun as the last. More serious."

He groaned. Leave it to her to not only speak first but get to the heart of the matter. "No, it wasn't fun," he agreed.

"Hey!" Clearly not expecting him to agree, she treated him to a mock punch in the shoulder.

"It was much more intense," he said, his voice gruff, even taking him off guard.

"Yeah. About that . . ."

Okay, so there'd be no ignoring *this* kiss as he'd tried to do with the last. She obviously wanted to *talk* about them. He hated discussing his feelings. Hadn't he done enough of that for one night?

"We can't keep doing this," she said, shocking him.

He thought she'd want more between them not less. "I agree," he told her, even though a part of him would rather ignore what was best, what was right, and go for what *he* wanted for a change.

"You do?" This time she sounded surprised . . . and maybe a little hurt?

They each had mixed feelings about their attraction and he took some comfort in the fact that he wasn't alone.

He cleared his throat and forced himself to continue this awkward conversation. "I do agree. We can't pursue this thing between us. Because of Tess." He latched onto the most obvious explanation.

Not the truth that she captivated him. More, she understood him. All of which had him putting up walls. His ex-wife might not have been as intuitive as Kelly, but he'd loved her and had been blindsided by her request for a divorce, her sudden need for independence and the chance to find something *more.*

He'd moved on but lesson learned. He had to protect his heart.

"Exactly. We can't do this because of Tess." Kelly exhaled hard, her expression one of disappointment. Because she'd hoped he'd try to talk her into a relationship, not out of one?

"I guess we'd better go before Dare gets another call about us being parked out here."

"Yeah."

He restarted the ignition. "So about Tess and school . . ."

"I was thinking I should talk to her about Ms. Bernard. See if there are more problems than she's admitting before we do or say anything else," Kelly said.

"Good idea, but I doubt she'd listen. But about Tess . . ."

Nash spared a quick glance over.

Kelly had relaxed in her seat, no longer uptight now that they'd ended their discussion about them.

"Now that I know what your issue is with

Ethan, I think it'll be easier to smooth things over between you and Tess. So maybe you'd like to come to dinner one night this week? This way Tess can spend more time with you in familiar surroundings."

He raised an eyebrow, surprised by the offer. "I'd like that."

"Good!" Kelly smiled.

An easygoing smile he'd come to rely on to ease the knots in his stomach that Tess caused. "I appreciate you trying so hard to help me forge a relationship with her."

"It's the least I can do."

He turned onto the road leading to the mansion. "And why is that?"

"That's easy. Because Tess needs a man like you in her life," she said as he parked the car in the driveway.

She already had Ethan, yet Kelly thought Nash would be good for Tess too. Something inside him warmed at the knowledge. Dangerous given the sudden emotional pull he felt toward this woman. Yet given how isolated he'd felt since Ethan's return, he couldn't deny having someone in his corner was nice for a change.

Nash came home to the condo he temporarily shared with Dare to find his brother already there. He'd changed from his uniform into a pair of old sweats and was drinking orange juice from the carton when Nash walked into the kitchen.

"Nice timing tonight," Nash muttered.

Dare opened the fridge and put the carton back before turning to face Nash. "Just doing my job. What were you doing?" he asked. "And don't give me that *just talking* BS."

Nash shrugged. "I was giving Kelly our family history. I thought a visual would be better than the narrative so I drove her by the places we lived, that's all."

"Huh."

"What's that supposed to mean?"

"You're the least talkative of the three of us," Dare said, leaning against the counter.

"And?"

"And you're opening up to Kelly."

"So?"

"Well, either you're making room in your life for one more lady friend, or there's more going on between you two than you want to admit."

Nash ran his hand through his hair. "Since you obviously know the answer, why push me to talk about something I don't want to admit to?"

"Because I'm your pain-in-the-ass younger brother, that's why."

Nash started for the doorway, intending to go to his room and turn in for the night.

"So, tell me, are you going to let a fourteen-year-old dictate your love life?"

Nash paused in the archway and turned. "I don't want to give Tess another excuse to push me away."

Dare nodded. "Understandable, except the kid doesn't need another excuse. She'll act the way she wants to act no matter what you do."

He'd never thought of it that way. "How do you know so much about bratty teens?"

"I grew up with two. And I run the drug and alcohol program at the high school, remember? I see my share of obnoxious adolescents every day. Want my advice?"

Why not? He hadn't been doing so hot himself. "Tess already knows she gets to you. If I were you, I wouldn't give the kid any more power."

Nash nodded slowly. "Good point."

"In other words, if you want to sleep with Kelly, you're both adults. I say go for it. Just be discreet around our new sister. She's a teenage temper tantrum waiting to happen."

Despite himself, Nash laughed at the description.

"Speaking of Tess, after meeting her

teacher and seeing that school for myself, I'm not sure it's the right place for her. And before you say anything, my feelings have nothing to do with the fact that Ethan picked the school."

"Relax. I've actually noticed Tess is more moody lately. You think it has something to do with school?" Dare asked, concerned.

Nash shrugged. "I'm not sure. But I think we need to be aware. We don't want her to spiral out of control. We already have one probation issue to deal with."

From the day she'd arrived at Ethan's, they'd been warned that Tess had a juvenile probation officer she had to answer to. While living with Kelly, she'd been arrested for breaking and entering, but owing to her age and circumstances, if she behaved for the next four months, the charges would be dropped. And if she stayed out of trouble until she turned eighteen, her arrest record would be expunged.

Dare was right. They couldn't afford for her to slip.

"Kelly said she'll keep an eye on her," Nash said.

Dare grinned. "And you'll keep an eye on Kelly."

His brother was a wise guy. But Nash was glad he and Dare were back under one roof, even if it was temporary. The condo belonged to Nash. Dare had moved in when the lease on his apartment was up, while he looked around and decided where he wanted to move next. Though he'd bought and was renovating an old house in town, he'd been thinking about selling it on spec and had listed the property. Instead of moving in himself, Nash had decided to take more time to figure out where he really wanted to live.

"I'm going to bed," Nash finally said.

"Me too. Just think about what I said. If you like Kelly, go for it. You don't need anyone's permission."

"Including yours," Nash said over his shoulder as he walked to his room and shut the door behind him.

He stripped off his shirt and sat down on the bed, thoughts of Kelly filling his head. Not thoughts of kissing her, though those recollections were never far away. Instead, he found himself recalling how fiery and defensive she'd become on Tess's behalf, how outraged she'd been on discovering that Nash and Dare had been separated by the state, and how her innate understanding and caring had affected him earlier tonight.

How memories of her affected him now. So maybe his brother was right. If they couldn't escape the attraction, maybe it was time to act on it like two adults, without letting a pint-size teenager dictate their actions.

Decision made, he finally settled in expecting a good night's sleep. Instead, he tossed and turned, the anticipation of how things between himself and Kelly would play out keeping him awake all night long.

Four

Kelly was frazzled. For the second day in a row, Richard hadn't shown up at work, calling in sick and asking Kelly to take care of things at the office. His receptionist had quit the week before and he hadn't yet found a new one, so she was answering phones and deflecting new clients until he was better. The one bright spot was that after work she was meeting Annie for happy hour at Joe's Bar.

She'd hesitated about saying yes, not wanting to leave Tess, but her sister had invited a friend over from school. Kelly realized she'd have time to come home from work, meet Tess's friend, and go out later while Tess was doing homework. As usual, Rosalita had no problem staying, so Kelly agreed to meet Annie at eight o'clock. And since her apartment was over Joe's, Kelly stopped there first to change into something fun for a night out.

She walked downstairs and met Annie at the door. It was the first time Kelly had been inside Joe's at night. According to Annie, the bar had been remodeled when Joe Lockhart had taken over the bar for his retired father. The atmosphere was inviting for customers, the walls covered in dark wood paneling and the fixtures casting an orangey glow over the bottles of alcohol lining the wall behind the bar.

The place was packed and they knew it'd take a while for them to reach the bar to order a drink. While they were waiting, Annie introduced Kelly to people she knew, some for whom she did work as an accountant.

Kate Andrews, Faith's best friend whom Kelly had met at Ethan and Faith's wedding, stopped to ask about Tess and how she was doing in school. Stacey Garner, a pretty bubbly blonde, stayed and talked to them for a while. A dentist, Kelly learned, and made a mental note to make herself an appointment. Everyone was warm and friendly, making her like this town more and more.

In between interruptions and hellos, Kelly and Annie caught up.

"How's your father?" Kelly asked Annie. "He only checked in with me once today."

And Richard was a hands-on boss.

Annie spread her hands wide. "I wish I knew. He says he's fine, Mom says he's having chest pains, but he claims it's a pulled muscle. Yet —"

"He's home from work," Kelly finished for her.

"Exactly. He has an appointment with a cardiologist tomorrow, so hopefully we'll know more then. I know he appreciates you keeping things running while he's out."

Annie's voice was touched with concern, and though privately Kelly agreed with her worry, there was no reason to panic her further. "Everything's fine at work. How are *you* feeling?" Kelly asked.

"I'm actually doing well, knock wood." Annie tapped the top of her head with her knuckles and laughed. "You never know what will happen, but right now I'm feeling okay."

"Glad to hear it."

Some people left the bar in search of tables and Kelly wedged her way through the slimming crowd until she finally arrived at the counter.

There she found Joe wiping the area with a towel before glancing up. "Good evening, ladies," he said in his smooth voice.

He cast an easy smile at Kelly. Then his

gaze lit on Annie and he leaned across the bar. "How are you doing, beautiful?"

Annie blushed. "Pretty good. And you?"

"Everything's perfect now that you're here."

Kelly raised her eyebrows. Joe had a way about him that made everyone comfortable. It was probably just one of the reasons his bar was such a success, that and the fact that his was the only game in town.

The day Kelly moved into her apartment, Joe had helped her, carrying boxes from her car. Since then, whenever she ran into him, he took the time to talk and get to know her better. She'd seen him smile at everyone, but he'd never had a gleam in his eye quite like now.

Hmm.

Kelly glanced between the two, Joe in his wrinkled T-shirt, faded jeans, and tousled light brown hair, and Annie with her petite body, perfect blond curls, and coordinated leggings and silky top. Outwardly they couldn't be more different, but appearances had nothing to do with attraction and Kelly wondered what kind of man Annie went for, because Joe clearly had a thing for her.

"How about you?" Joe turned to Kelly. "How's life treating you in that fancy house on the hill?"

"What could be bad?" she asked. "It's been kind of nice getting a break from doing everything for myself. Rosalita is an angel."

"Will you move back to your small apartment upstairs now that you've lived the good life?" Joe asked, teasing.

Kelly laughed. "Of course. All good things must come to an end."

Annie chuckled. "Not *all* good things."

"So, you're an optimist?" Joe asked, his gaze steady, as if studying her for answers to more than just that one question.

Annie shrugged. "It's not always easy keeping up the faith these days, but I do try."

He eyed her warily, obviously concerned. "Are you feeling okay?"

"I'm *fine.*"

"Good. But if you ever need anything —"

"I won't."

"You never know." He smiled, his dimples showing.

But Annie just shook her head and his shoulders slumped in defeat.

Kelly narrowed her gaze, surprised by Annie's obvious rejection.

"What can I get you, then?" he asked, pointing to the fountain.

"Just the usual," Annie said lightly. "You

know me, big night out and I order a virgin."

At the word coming from Annie's mouth, Joe seemed to freeze for a minute before he took a tall glass from behind the counter and filled it. "Seltzer for you." He placed the glass in front of Annie.

"What about you?" Joe asked Kelly.

"I'll have the same thing." She pointed to her friend's full glass.

Joe served up her drink, and with a lingering glance at Annie, he headed to serve other customers.

"You hurt his feelings," Kelly murmured. "He offered to help because he obviously likes you. And he's hot, don't you think?"

Not as hot as a certain Barron brother Kelly couldn't stop thinking about, but she didn't want to discuss her attraction to Nash.

"It doesn't matter what I think," Annie said. "Joe likes to be in charge. He's a born nurturer, like my ex-husband. They both like to be in control."

Kelly raised her eyebrows, wondering what was really going on with Annie. "You talk about your ex a lot. Are you sure you aren't still in love with him?"

Annie shook her head. "Of course I'm sure!" she insisted. Lifting her drink, she eyed Joe longingly.

Actually she eyed Joe's behind, but Kelly opted not to mention it. "You like him too," she said instead.

Annie let out a wistful sigh. "Let's just say I could be persuaded," she admitted. "But I know his history, how he cared for his mother after she had a breakdown while his father chased everything in a skirt. I feel for him, but he's another man who thinks he needs to overcompensate for his past by controlling everyone in his present."

"Just who is this domineering ex-husband of yours?" Kelly asked.

At the question, Annie looked surprised. "Nash Barron. I just assumed you knew since he's Tess's brother and you work for my father."

Kelly opened her mouth, then closed it again. "I, um . . . no. It never came up with Richard. I had no idea."

"Did I just hear my name?" a familiar masculine voice asked.

"Nash," Kelly said, still processing the shock of finding out her new best friend had been married to the man she dreamed about and wanted more than her next breath.

She hadn't admitted that to herself before. *Helluva time now,* she thought. And now that she had? Forget not getting involved or having a physical relationship because of her sister, her interest in Nash was even more wrong now that she knew he was Annie's ex.

Kelly's stomach churned and she thought she'd be sick.

She couldn't let herself get more emotionally involved with him than she already had. Tess's welfare connected them and that had to be it. Unable to think, the crowds stifling, she needed air.

Nash didn't know whether to be pleased Annie and Kelly had connected and were clearly friends or concerned because Kelly's face turned pale and she wasn't speaking. Kelly wasn't the speechless type.

"Hi, ladies," he said carefully.

"Hi, Nash." Annie treated him to a smile. "What are you doing out so late?"

"Very funny." He recognized her sarcasm because in their married days, he was the one who'd turned in earliest. "I didn't know you'd be here tonight."

Annie raised her glass. "That's the way it's supposed to be between divorced people. Kelly and I decided to enjoy Ladies' Night."

He glanced at Kelly, who remained quiet. "When did you two become friends?"

Annie grinned. "We're coffee buddies,

aren't we, Kelly?"

"Are you sure caffeine's good for you?" he asked his ex.

"I drink decaf." Annie visibly gritted her teeth. He knew she hated when he told her what to do, but someone had to make sure she was taking care of herself.

"I need some air," Kelly said suddenly.

"Are you okay?" Annie asked.

"No worries." Kelly smiled, one Nash recognized as forced.

"Okay, but come right back in."

"We'll see. I'll text you," Kelly said, turning and hurrying for the door.

Nash stared after her, wondering what the hell had just happened. "What was that about?"

Annie shook her head. "I have no idea. She was fine just a minute ago."

"Until?" Nash pushed her, unable to tear his gaze from Kelly's retreating form until she'd disappeared from view.

Annie shut her eyes a second, trying to remember. "Until she found out you were my ex-husband."

"Son of a bitch," Nash muttered, suddenly knowing exactly what was bothering Kelly. "I have to go talk to her."

Annie stared at him, surprised. "What's going on?"

"Nothing. I'll be back." He left his ex-wife standing with her mouth open wide, knowing he'd be in for a ton of questions when he faced her again.

Nash didn't care.

He pushed his way through the crowds to get to the front door, wondering when the hell life would cut him some slack. He'd just spent a sleepless night going over Dare's point that he didn't need Tess's permission to see her sister. He'd come to the conclusion that Kelly affected him too deeply to just ignore the attraction.

Now she ran at the sight of him.

He went after her. There was no way he'd let a little thing like his ex-wife come between them.

Annie stared after her ex-husband, dizzy from his sudden turnaround from concern about her to worry for Kelly. Nash was interested in another woman. The first one he'd shown serious interest in since their split two years ago, Annie thought, a sudden riot of emotions coursing through her.

She stood alone and attempted to process her feelings. She'd have thought that when Nash finally turned his attention to another woman she'd be completely relieved. And she was. She didn't want him hanging around, insisting she needed him when she didn't. But they'd been inseparable since they'd met when they were sixteen, and she'd be lying if she said she didn't feel a tug of possessiveness now. But that didn't mean she was still in love with him. And she definitely didn't want him back.

She'd divorced him so she could be free. Lately she wondered . . . free to do what? She never thought to leave town. She was too tied to family and too much of a home-and-hearth-type girl for that. She'd just sensed something was missing with Nash. Something she was still looking for now.

Nash's interest in Kelly meant Annie could finally have the freedom and independence she'd craved. She'd just have to get used to the new reality.

She breathed in deep and rotated back toward the bar only to find Joe directly in her line of vision. He provided a welcome distraction from her thoughts of her past, and she drank him in like she would a sweet piña colada — if her illness didn't stop her from drinking.

He'd changed a lot from when they were kids. He'd grown up and filled out, and the man was a vision, his light brown hair straggly like he'd come from the beach, his body so muscular beneath his bar shirt.

She placed her glass on the counter and smiled, hoping to make up for her rudeness earlier. "I'll have a refill."

"I aim to please." He pulled out the soda dispenser and filled her glass.

"How are you with forgiveness? I shouldn't have shut you down like that earlier."

"Really." He sounded skeptical.

"Yes. I'm sorry."

"Because you mean it or because your ex ran after another woman and I can soothe your bruised ego?" Joe asked.

Annie winced and placed her hand over her heart. "Ouch."

"I just call 'em like I see 'em, sweetheart."

"I know." He didn't pull any punches, something Annie had always liked about him. Actually there was a lot she liked about him. She braced her elbows on the bar and leaned over. "I said I'm sorry because I am. As for Nash, I divorced him, remember? I'm over him."

"Then prove it," he said, a sparkle of a challenge in his gaze.

"How?"

He also rested his elbow on the bar, his face inches from hers. "Go out with me."

Adrenaline began flowing through her veins and Annie exhaled hard. She hadn't been out with anyone since her divorce. Saying yes to a confident, sexy man like Joe would be like jumping into the deep end of the pool without wading first.

She wanted to dive in so badly. After all, wasn't that why she'd ended her marriage in the first place? Because being diagnosed had taught her that life was short and unpredictable and she shouldn't live it being safe. Nash had been her refuge since they'd met when she was sixteen. But there wasn't a spark anymore and hadn't been for a while. She wanted to experience life fully and sensed Joe felt the same way.

The only problem was her illness. She had relapsing-remitting multiple sclerosis and she didn't know when she'd be hit by an episode, which could last anywhere from twenty-four hours to a week or more. She didn't want to be a burden to anyone, especially not to a vibrant man like Joe.

It was hard enough dealing with Nash's overprotective nature. But him she understood. Joe, she didn't. And the last thing she wanted was his pity.

Still, she *wanted.* Butterflies kicked in her stomach as she stared into his mocha-colored eyes. "*Why?* Why do you want to go out with me?"

"Are you kidding?" he asked her. "I've

been sucking up to you for the last six months. You have to know I'm interested."

His words gave her ego a much-needed boost. "And I need to know why because I'm not looking for another guy who has a need to take care of me. I can take care of myself."

"Good." He rose to his full height and folded his arms across his chest. "Because there's a big difference between wanting you and wanting to babysit you," he said bluntly. "Happy now?" he asked her.

"I most definitely am," she said, smiling, surprising even herself. "So yes. I'll go out with you. What did you have in mind?"

His grin was wide and equaled hers. "That would be a surprise. Saturday night work for you? My manager can watch the bar."

She nodded. "You can pick me up."

"Be ready at eight."

"I think I can manage that."

"Looking forward to it, gorgeous." Joe winked at her before turning his back on her completely and focusing on another patron.

Alone again, Annie looked around for Kelly, but she hadn't returned. She didn't see Nash, either. A part of her was glad. She would much rather head home and savor the anticipation of her upcoming date.

■ ■ ■ ■

As Joe watched Annie leave the bar, he gripped the cleaning rag tighter in his hand. In order to get a date with the woman he'd had a thing for since he'd seen her coming out of Gillman's ice-cream shop when he was fifteen, he'd had to lie. Hell, yes, he wouldn't mind taking care of her. Somehow he'd gotten an overabundance of the protective gene his father had been lacking.

His old man, who had turned the bar over to him, had used this place as his personal playground, picking up women and discarding them when he was through. His mother had been the first in a long line of females, the only difference being he'd married Joe's mom. Frank hadn't done his wife any favors since he often came home reeking of booze and other women, ignoring her and whatever she needed out of life. He and his sister both resented the old man, and when he'd died, all Joe had felt was relief.

Joe had had a crush on Annie since high school. He wanted to get to know her better now that she was single and open to it. He had to be careful not to step over the line and act like Nash, the ultimate take-over-and-do-what-he-wanted kind of guy. Joe told himself he could handle not looking out for Annie to the point of driving her crazy. He'd already done his share of caretaking for his mother. Though Ilene Lockhart was better now, Joe knew what it was like to be a caretaker for an emotionally fragile woman. Though his sister had helped, it hadn't been easy and he wasn't sure he'd want to repeat his teenage years.

He respected Annie for wanting equality and independence. But equality required trust and she didn't know him well enough to have that kind of faith. Coming off a marriage and recent diagnosis of a serious illness, she wanted fun and no strings.

He wanted *her.*

He could give her exactly what she needed right now. They'd have fun together and he had the patience required to win her over.

Kelly couldn't get out of the bar fast enough. No sooner had she found out that her new best friend had once been married to Nash than she'd had to watch him fawn over Annie and worry about her welfare. The jealousy had bitten her hard and she hated everything about the situation she suddenly found herself in. Kelly had had enough of awkward triangles to last her a lifetime.

Once in the parking lot, she looked for her Ford Fiesta and realized she had the bad luck to be parked beneath a broken light. Instead of emitting a steady glow, the light merely flickered and she had to fumble for her car keys inside her purse. Finally she pulled them from her bag.

"Kelly!"

Startled by Nash's voice, she dropped the key chain on the ground.

"Why did you run out?" he asked, coming up beside her.

"I already told you. I needed air."

"Why?" Little lines of disbelief crinkled around his eyes, making him even more sexy than usual.

She tipped her head to one side, wondering why he was questioning her over something so trivial. "Because it was hot in there. Why else?"

"Because you just found out that Annie and I had once been married."

"Well, you don't pull any punches, do you?" she asked, embarrassed.

He propped an arm on top of her car. "Not when it comes to something — or someone — I want." His hot, serious gaze bore into hers.

At his words, the air left her lungs in a rush, his implication clear. "And since when do you want me?"

He laughed suddenly. Not a light chuckle but a deep laugh that came from someplace inside him she'd never seen before.

"Since when have I *not* wanted you?" He reached out and grabbed a strand of her hair, twirling it between his fingers.

The pull was strangely erotic and she felt the tug low in her belly. She swallowed hard and licked her dry lips. "Maybe I should rephrase. Since when have you wanted to act on it? Just last night we agreed *we* can't go anywhere because of Tess."

He nodded. "And I've done nothing but think about Tess since." He paused. "But this thing between us. It's electric and undeniable."

His husky voice sent tremors of awareness darting through her veins.

"Are we really going to let a fourteen-year-old dictate how we act?" he asked.

Kelly blinked, stunned not just by his change of heart but at the rationale behind it. "I hadn't thought of it that way."

"Neither did I until Dare pointed it out." An embarrassed grin lifted his lips.

"You and Dare talked about me?" God, could this night get any more mortifying?

He shook his head. "We talked about *us*." He gestured between them. "Don't forget

Dare's the one who interrupted last night."

"Don't remind me," she said on a groan.

"He's also the one who made me see reason. I mean, what he said about not letting a fourteen-year-old dictate our decisions makes sense."

Kelly nodded slowly. "It does," she agreed. "Unfortunately, it doesn't change the fact that nothing more can happen between us."

He blinked, obviously stunned. "Why not? We're both adults. We can trust ourselves to act like it before, during, and . . . after things end."

Well, that was an optimistic summary, she thought. But at least he was honest — he was looking for something short term. So would she. If she allowed herself to get involved with him. Which she wouldn't.

"I've already been through a relationship with someone who swore their marriage was over, and there is no way I'll put myself through that again." She folded her arms across her chest, protecting herself with her words and her actions.

Nash placed his hand on her shoulder. She tried to step out of reach, but her back hit the car. She couldn't go far and he liked having her in his personal space. "Annie and I are divorced. She's the one who initiated the damned thing. Trust me, she won't hold it against you if you're with me," he promised Kelly.

Was the man obtuse? "Exactly my point! She may be over you, but *you're* not over her. All any observant person has to do is watch how you treat her and it's obvious you still have feelings for her."

"Of course I care. She's sick and she needs a friend who's aware and who understands. But that's all we are. Friends," he insisted. "Platonic friends."

"Nash —" Kelly held out a hand to keep a barrier between them.

"Kelly," he mimicked gently. "You and I are nothing like me and Annie." He threaded his fingers through hers, slowly raising her body temperature. "Not once did Annie and I ever generate heat like this."

Before Kelly knew what hit her, he'd pulled her forward. Her chest collided with his and their hips pressed together intimately. She found herself locked between his waist and the car, the hard ridge behind his jeans deliciously obvious, and her body responded, melting for him. Molten liquid fire flowed through her veins.

Heat exploded between them and he sealed their lips firmly together. He was hungry, his mouth nibbling on hers, tasting, demanding until finally he slipped his tongue between her lips. She moaned and wrapped her arms around his neck, enjoying the sensations. Knowing this was all she could take from him, she eased her fingers through his hair and let him deepen the kiss. After all, how far could they go in a parking lot, but as she wondered, her stomach curled with growing need and an awareness of wanting more.

Which made her regretfully pull back. "You're right. We're explosive," she murmured. "But you're still emotionally connected to your ex, which puts you off limits for me."

Still shaking, she knelt down, picked up her keys, and over his argument, unlocked the car, opened the door, and slid inside.

"I'm stubborn," he told her as he helped her shut the door.

Then she'd just have to be *more* obstinate than him.

FIVE

Kelly woke up with a splitting headache and a full day of work ahead of her. For once, Tess beat her to the kitchen and was eating a bowl of Cap'n Crunch cereal. Knowing what she planned to ask of her sister, Kelly didn't mention the lack of nutrition in Tess's breakfast choice.

Kelly made herself a bowl of oatmeal in the state-of-the-art chrome kitchen, amused as she compared her surroundings now to the tiny space she called a kitchen in her small apartment. It was hard to believe half the week was over. Ethan and Faith would be back Sunday night and she'd be moving back to the still-new place she needed to make feel like home.

The microwave beeped and she took out her bowl, settling in beside her sister at the table. "I liked your friend Michelle." The girl had been unlike Tess, soft spoken and more girlie. Odd that Tess would choose her as a friend, but she seemed nice.

Tess shrugged. "She's okay."

Kelly narrowed her gaze, sure there was more to this friendship of opposites. "What aren't you saying?" Kelly asked.

"That she's the only girl who'll hang with me. Happy now?" Tess snapped.

Kelly waited until Tess reluctantly met her gaze. "Are *you?* Happy at Birchwood, I mean?" Every time Kelly had brought up Ms. Bernard this morning, Tess had shut down, not that Kelly blamed her. The woman was a bitch.

Tess shoveled a spoonful of cereal into her mouth. "Does it matter?" she asked while she crunched.

"Of course it matters! Ethan didn't put you in Birchwood for you to be miserable. He thought it would be good for your art. He thought you'd be happy."

Tess banged her spoon into the bowl. "And he paid a shitload of money to get me in. I couldn't bail even if I wanted to." With that, she stood, grabbed her bowl, and placed it in the sink.

"Thanks for cleaning up," Kelly said, pleased.

Tess ran water into the bowl and spoke over her shoulder. "If I didn't, Rosalita would rip me a new —"

"Language!" Kelly finally said, drawing the line. "Have you given any thought where you'd *want* to go to school?"

Tess nodded eagerly. "Maybe public school where the kids don't have so much money they stink of it."

Where there was also a greater chance of Tess falling in with the wrong crowd again, Kelly thought. But she was convinced a happy Tess would seek to please, not act out. Not to mention she was still in therapy. She had to believe they had her situation under control enough to take the risk.

Kelly drew a deep breath. "I'll tell you what. You go back to the sweeter personality you had at the end of the summer, and when Ethan gets home I'll talk to him about switching schools."

Since their mother had bailed, Kelly had de facto if not legal custody of her sister. From the time Kelly had moved to Serendipity, she'd agreed to let Tess live with Ethan where she was flourishing, but Kelly and Ethan shared in decisions affecting the teenager's welfare.

"You'd do that for me?" Tess asked, her eyes wide and hopeful.

"If you watch the language and remember to behave."

The truth was, Kelly would do whatever it

took to keep Tess safe and happy, but her sister didn't need to know what a pushover she was. Letting Tess think her future hinged on her behavior could only benefit Kelly.

"Deal!" Tess held out her hand to shake on the deal.

"Deal," Kelly agreed, grabbing her sister and pulling her into a hug.

Tess squirmed but hugged her back.

"Now I need a favor," Kelly said.

Tess stepped back and eyed her warily. "Were you just buttering me up?"

Kelly laughed. "I wish I'd been that smart. I was going to ask you to do this no matter what."

"Uh-oh." Tess folded her arms across her chest. "What is it?"

Kelly pointed to her sister's cell phone. "Call Nash and invite him for dinner tonight at six."

"You're kidding," Tess said, horrified.

"Nope. Invite him. Then I'll let Rosalita know we're having a guest." Kelly met Tess's defiant glare and waited, prepared to stare her down until she made the call.

A definite pout formed on her lips. "I don't want to."

"I know." Kelly bit the inside of her cheek in an effort not to grin. "But you will. One, because you just promised me you'd behave; two, because he's your brother; and three, because you're judging him based on how he feels about Ethan."

"So?" Tess asked on a prolonged whine.

Kelly exhaled hard and propped her hands on her hips, determined not only to be the adult in this confrontation but to make her point as well. "So his issues with his brother have nothing to do with you. They're also none of your business."

"But —"

Kelly shook her head and held up one hand to stop Tess's imminent tirade. "I bet if you got to know him, you'd understand him a little more. And you'd even like him."

"Like *you* do?" Tess shot back at her.

Man, the kid was quick. "Yes, like I do." *Better to go with it than to argue,* Kelly thought. "I think Nash is a solid, upstanding guy."

With sex appeal in spades, with whom she shared an incredible attraction. If he was so upstanding, then why was she pushing him away? Kelly asked herself. The answer was obvious. Because Ryan Hayward had been upstanding too. In her heart, Kelly knew Ryan had believed himself over his ex-wife and was finished with his marriage. He hadn't deliberately set out to cheat or hurt her. But he had and the fallout wasn't over yet.

So lesson learned.

Kelly glared at Tess, pushing thoughts of Ryan and relationships out of her head.

"Fine!" Tess grabbed her cell and called Nash. "Kelly said to invite you for dinner tonight. You busy?"

As invitations went, it sucked, Kelly thought, but at least she'd made the overture.

"Fine." Tess ended the call and glanced at Kelly. "He's coming and said to tell you he's looking forward to it." She made a face that let Kelly know she was disgusted by the message.

"I'm sure he meant he's looking forward to seeing you. He's just thankful I invited him." Then why did those stinking butterflies begin to kick around in her stomach at the thought of seeing him again?

She shook off the thought and ordered Tess to get ready to leave for school. Tonight would come soon enough.

Kelly glanced at the clock on the microwave in the kitchen. Six thirty P.M. The table was set, and dinner was heating in the oven, the apricot chicken Rosalita had prepared probably shriveling while they waited for Nash.

At six fifteen, Kelly had excused Tess and told her she could go on the computer and chat with her friends until he arrived. She thought he'd be the punctual type as he'd been for the parent-teacher conference. She hadn't thought he'd stand up Tess, not without good reason and definitely not without calling to explain.

She looked at the clock again and frowned.

"I used to think Mr. Ethan a bad man," Rosalita said. The other woman stood by the sink, rinsing off a dish. She dried the plate and placed it on the counter.

"You don't think that anymore?"

The plump housekeeper shook her head. "No. But I no tell him that. I like to keep him on his toes." She smiled at her private joke. "Mr. Dare is a policeman, so I always think, he's a good man."

Kelly bit the inside of her cheek. "And Nash? What do you think about him?"

Rosalita walked around the center island and joined Kelly in a seat by the table. "He's not around enough for me to decide."

Kelly didn't want to speak about Nash behind his back or share his secrets. "I'm sure you'll get to know him better tonight," she said, and once again looked at the clock.

"Maybe he's delayed at work and forgot to call?" Rosalita asked.

If he was, it was damned inconsiderate.

"He's not coming, is he?" Tess asked, suddenly appearing in the doorway.

"We don't know that." Kelly finally picked up the house phone and dialed Nash's number, but the call went straight to voice mail.

She waited for the beep, and forcing a lightness into her voice she didn't feel, Kelly spoke for the answering machine. "Nash, it's Kelly. Tess and I are waiting for you. Dinner's ready and smells delicious . . . I hope you're on your way over here. See you soon."

Disconnecting the call, she looked hopelessly at Tess. "I'm sure he has a good explanation," Kelly said in an attempt to give Nash the benefit of the doubt and still look like a good guy to his sister.

That had been the point of this dinner, after all. Otherwise, why would Kelly want to look at him across the table and wish for things she couldn't have?

A glance at Tess's angry expression, an obvious facade for the hurt she was feeling, quashed Kelly's desire for the man. If he hadn't been in an accident, God forbid, she'd kill him first and ask questions later.

A few minutes later, her cell phone rang. A quick glance told her it wasn't Nash and she shook her head at Rosalita. "Hi, Annie," Kelly said, answering.

"Hi. My father's in the hospital and he needs immediate bypass surgery," the other woman said, her voice trembling. "Quadruple."

Kelly winced. "I'm so sorry."

"Thank you. He wants to talk to you before he's willing to go in. I hate to bother you, but can you get to University Hospital right away?" she asked.

"Of course! Are you okay?" Kelly asked her new friend.

"I'm numb. But thank you."

Kelly nodded, thinking what a stupid question it had been. Annie's father was having serious surgery. Of course she wasn't okay. "I'll be right there." Because Richard had asked, which she figured had everything to do with instructions on what he wanted done in the office, but she'd also be there for Annie.

After Annie explained where to meet her, Kelly said good-bye and hung up the phone. She called Tess downstairs and explained the situation to Rosalita and to her sister, who wasn't interested in anything except being angry at Nash.

Kelly didn't blame her. She glanced at Tess, who'd changed into a pair of navy sweatpants and an oversized hooded sweatshirt, always a sign the teenager was upset. Kelly acknowledged the silent signal, grateful it was just her lounge clothes and not her old army surplus jacket and other rebellious items she'd worn on her arrival in Serendipity.

Kelly sighed. "You might as well eat dinner."

"Fine," Tess muttered. "But I'm finishing it all. Every last bite. So if he does show up, there's nothing left."

Kelly bit the inside of her cheek. "Save me some at least. We'll talk when I get back." With a last glance at the set table, Kelly walked out, all the while thinking of ways to strangle Nash.

Once in the car, she paused to process where she had to go. She recalled passing hospital signs on the highway, the exit before Serendipity. She had a good sense of direction and was able to backtrack herself and find the place with little problem.

She parked out back and rushed inside the main entrance. Annie had promised to meet her by the front desk. She glanced around, but other than an older woman in a wheelchair with her nurse behind her and a couple checking in with the guard, she didn't see Annie.

Until Kelly turned toward the gift shop and caught sight of Annie's familiar blond curls. She stood near the window filled with balloons and stuffed animals, and she huddled close with none other than Nash. A strong prick of jealousy pierced her heart as she watched them together. She hated it, wasn't proud of it. But it was a reminder of why she promised herself she wouldn't get involved with the man.

Breathe, Kelly instructed herself. His ex-wife's father was here. An ex-wife he worried about constantly. Of course he'd come here instead of showing up for dinner . . . but he could have called. His preoccupation with Annie had hurt his relationship with Tess and he'd been rude to Kelly, building on her hurt.

She glanced at the exit, torn between leaving and waiting. She really didn't want to interrupt them and she couldn't be more uncomfortable standing alone in the lobby like a lost child.

"Kelly!" Annie had caught sight of her and was heading her way in purposeful strides.

"Hey. I just got here," Kelly said.

"Thanks for coming." Annie pulled her into a brief hug, which Kelly returned.

She just couldn't bring herself to dislike the woman, who she believed had been honest with her about her feelings for Nash. It was Nash's feelings for Annie that concerned Kelly.

"Hi," Nash said.

Speak of the devil, Kelly thought.

"I'm sorry about dinner. Annie called me when I was on my way over." He shot her a look filled with regret.

Kelly merely treated him to a curt nod. Now wasn't the time to argue or remind him of etiquette. "How's your father?" Kelly asked, turning to Annie.

"The doctors performed a stress test and basically threw him off the treadmill. He can't exert himself at all or they're afraid he'll have a massive coronary. They want to operate immediately. He just wants to talk to you both about his business," Annie explained.

Richard wanted Nash here. For some reason, that eased the anxiety filling Kelly's chest.

"Let's go," Annie said. "The nurses are prepping him in his room. As soon as the surgeon gets here, they'll be ready, so I need to get you two in and out quickly."

Kelly nodded and with Nash by her side followed Annie to the large bank of elevators and up to her father's room.

■ ■ ■ ■

On the elevator ride up to Richard's room, Nash grew frustrated. Kelly wouldn't look at him, wouldn't let him whisper a word in her ear. And he needed to talk to her because he'd seen her walk into the hospital and knew exactly how intimate he and Annie had appeared. He'd just been comforting her and getting an update on Richard's condition, but Kelly already had preconceived notions of him and Annie as a couple.

So far he hadn't done anything to ease her mind or dispel that idea.

Little did Kelly know the only woman he could think of was her. He'd driven to the mansion, so distracted by thoughts of Kelly and how he'd handle dinner tonight with her and Tess that he'd nearly run a light that had turned red.

Then Annie had called, catching him halfway to Ethan's house. In a shaky, breathless voice, she'd told him about Richard and asked him to come see her father before his surgery.

His palms immediately grew damp and he'd broken into a sweat, a familiar gnawing fear overtaking him. Since his own parents' sudden deaths, emergency calls panicked him, taking him back in time. Once he reached that place, everything in the present disappeared.

Annie stopped them outside Richard's room. "Wait here. I want to make sure he's decent before I let you in."

He and Kelly nodded.

Annie knocked, waited for an okay, then pushed open the door and walked inside.

Nash knew he had limited time so he turned to Kelly. "Talk to me. You're angry. What you saw with Annie —"

"Is none of my business. But Tess is and you stood her up. Don't get me wrong, I understand the emergency. But you should have called her."

He ducked his head. Of course he should have called. He'd just been so thrown by the news about Richard and then his past had crashed in on him. He'd forgotten, plain and simple. The reasons didn't matter or excuse his behavior.

Still, Nash noticed she hadn't mentioned being stood up too. She was making this all about Tess, distancing herself and her feelings. That he'd deal with later.

"You're right. You and Tess deserved better and I'm sorry."

"I wasn't upset for me, I was upset for Tess."

"Maybe you should have been upset for yourself. Or at least admit that it bothered *you* too." He braced one hand on the wall behind her and leaned in close. He inhaled her now-familiar, intoxicating scent and wanted her to let him in.

A pink flush stained her cheeks and she straightened her spine. "Now isn't the time for this."

"I agree. But the subject's not closed," he warned her.

"You know Tess isn't going to make it easy for you to apologize," Kelly shot, changing the subject.

He nodded. "I already have my work cut out for me with Tess." Apparently with Kelly as well. "What's one more roadblock?" he asked only half sarcastically.

"You can come in," Annie called out.

At the same time a nurse walked out the door and paused. "Be quick and don't agitate him. He needs to stay calm until his surgery."

At the mention of surgery and the thought of entering the hospital room, Nash's fear and anxiety immediately returned. His feelings for Richard were complex, his emotions invested much more than if he were just an ex-in-law. Nash respected his legal abilities, loved Richard like a father, and most important, owed him for stepping up and handling Barron family matters when Nash had been a teenager, unable to control either his destiny or his brother Dare's.

Richard had done the best he could, and some debts could never be repaid. Still, Nash would sure as hell like many more years with the man in order to give it a try.

Kelly walked into the room, and her gaze settled on Richard. He lay in the hospital bed, his salt-and-pepper hair messed, his face pale. Used to seeing the older man in a suit and tie, she was upset at the sight of him in a hospital gown awaiting surgery. Though she'd only worked for him for a few weeks, she'd grown to like him enormously in a short time. And he'd been good to her in the past, which had bonded her to him in some small way.

"What's the matter? You weren't getting enough attention at home?" Nash stepped closer, a forced smile on his face adding to his fake, light tone of voice.

Taking her cue from him, Kelly moved forward, pausing at the foot of the bed.

Richard frowned. "You just wait until you're older. You won't be making jokes when age catches up with you," the man grumbled.

"Dad, behave," Annie's said lightly, but her voice trembled. She was obviously more nervous than she wanted to let on in front of her father. She fidgeted with the water cup on the table, then turned her attention to the covers and smoothed them over and over again.

"You're going to be fine," Nash said with steel in his voice, as if willing it so.

"That's what my wife tells me." Richard's voice spoke of a love that had lasted for years, and Kelly couldn't help but envy them both the emotions they shared along with the longevity.

"Well, Mom's the boss, so that's that," Annie agreed.

"Amen," Richard added.

"Where is Mary?" Nash asked.

"I sent her to get coffee so I could conduct business." The older man waved toward the door with one hand.

Now that sounded like the Richard that Kelly knew.

"Dad, you are not conducting business. You have five minutes to tell them what you need to. No stress, remember?" Annie placed her hand on her father's shoulder and squeezed.

He patted the top of her hand indulgently. "I could say the same for you. Now quit your worrying and go check on your mom. I'll see you before surgery. I promise."

Annie didn't leave immediately, unable to stop staring at her father. The bond between the two was obviously strong, and Kelly couldn't imagine the fear Annie felt at the thought of losing her father.

Kelly swallowed hard, the pain of not having what Annie did washing over her. She couldn't remember her own father all that well and she recalled enough of her mother to miss the parent she'd once been until Kelly had turned sixteen and life had changed forever. Just like Nash's life had been permanently altered by the accident that killed his parents.

He couldn't be having an easy time with Richard's condition, either, since the man wasn't just his employer or friend — he'd also once been family.

Kelly glanced over and the tense set to his jaw proved her right. With everything in her she wanted to reach out and stroke his cheek, ease his pain. His ex-father-in-law in the hospital bed prevented her from acting on impulse.

"I love you, Dad," Annie said. "I'll be back in a few minutes." With a lingering glance, Annie walked out of the room.

"Thanks for coming on such short notice,"

Richard said when his daughter was gone.

"Of course!" Kelly said.

"What can we do for you?" Nash asked.

Richard cleared his throat and pushed himself higher up in the bed. "This isn't something I'd admit in front of Annie or Mary, but today's operation is serious. Four bypasses isn't something to sneeze at, even though they tell me they perform this kind of surgery every day."

Kelly clenched her fists at her sides.

"You'll be fine," Nash said again.

Kelly nodded in agreement.

"Maybe. But if I'm not —"

"No talking like that," Nash said.

Richard frowned. "Come on now. You're as pragmatic as I am. I need to plan . . . just in case. So if something happens, I need to know you'll step in and take over my practice," he said, meeting Nash's gaze. "You're the only lawyer I know and trust. Actually, despite the divorce, you're like the son I never had, and I still wish you'd have gone into practice with me after you graduated."

All of this was interesting news to Kelly. She already knew Richard had stepped in when Nash was a kid and helped him out after his parents died. Now she saw firsthand just how close their relationship really was. Could that be another reason he didn't want to end his connection to Annie? No matter, it only complicated his ties to the woman and her family.

Nash smiled indulgently at his ex-father-in-law. They'd had this conversation many times over the years. "I wanted to make it on my own," Nash said, feeling the need to explain his reasons again.

Richard inclined his head. "That independent streak of yours is another reason I respect you so much. And you certainly accomplished your goal. So you'll take over if you have to?"

Nash immediately nodded. "Of course. You're like a father to me too," he said gruffly.

"Good. Now to the more palatable alternative. I'm going to be in this place for the next week and out of commission for four to six."

Torture for an active man who liked to be in the middle of things, Nash thought.

"I can do the basics while you're out of the office," Kelly assured Richard.

She'd been quiet for most of the visit, but she was obviously visibly shaken by seeing her boss laid up and talking death. Nash didn't know much about her legal skills, but he had no doubt she could hold down the fort while Richard was gone.

"She can refer any new cases to me," Nash offered. "I'm happy to step in while you're out of commission and hand things back over to you when you're ready to return."

Nash had been considering making Bill Manfredi, an associate who worked in Nash's office, a junior partner. The influx of work would just speed up the process, something Nash was comfortable doing.

Richard visibly relaxed against the bed. "I knew I could count on you two."

"Anything to put you at ease and speed up your recovery," Kelly told him.

"One more thing. Just because I won't be coming to the office doesn't mean I want to be out of the loop," Richard said in a firm tone.

"I never assumed any such thing," Kelly said with a light laugh.

Like Nash, she obviously held a great deal of fondness as well as respect for the older man. Not that Nash was surprised. Everyone liked Richard. In turn, if Richard sensed a need in someone, he tried to step in and assume a father-figure role. But he had to focus solely on himself and his recuperation for the next couple of months.

"I think Mary will have a thing or two to say about you trying to do too much too soon," Nash warned him, knowing his former mother-in-law and deflecting his own concern.

"I most certainly will," the woman under discussion said, walking into the room, followed by Annie.

Nash stepped over and said hello to Mary, kissing her on the cheek. "Call me if you need anything," he said to her.

"Thank you." Her smile was understandably strained.

"Now, everyone out." Mary pointed toward the door. "Richard needs his rest."

"Do you see what I have in store for me?" Richard grumbled. But nobody knew better than Nash how much the older man loved his wife.

He'd always envied them their relationship. Richard and Mary represented the marriage neither his parents nor he himself had accomplished. Even the Rossmans, though they tried, suffered from the strain of losing a child. They never seemed to share the elusive connection Richard and Mary did. He thought he and Annie had, but looking back Nash realized it was more of an intersection of lives. Richard and proximity had put them together. Teenage physical attraction had done the rest. Neither had been able to sustain the needed emotions for the long haul. The end of his marriage had seemed like the end of the world as he knew it, and he'd kept his liaisons casual ever since.

Even with Kelly, he wasn't thinking about relationships in the long-term sense, or so he'd told both himself and Kelly.

How had he phrased it? They were adults who could act like it *before, during, and . . . after things ended.* The ending was an implied presumption.

But wouldn't it be nice to look forward to something more? he wondered for the first time.

"Nash. I asked if you're ready to leave," Kelly said.

He glanced up, shaken to suddenly find her by his side, hand on his shoulder.

"Yeah, sure." He'd spaced out, lost in his own thoughts.

He followed her out. As soon as they hit the hallway, Kelly turned toward the elevators, but Nash grabbed her hand. She surprised him by not pulling away. She let him lead her to a private corner of the hall without resisting.

"This is getting to be a habit," she said once they were alone.

"Stop avoiding me and I wouldn't have to push you into conversation. It's not like you don't *want* to talk to me."

She let out an annoyed huff. "Talk about ego."

"Are you going to argue the point?"

She bit her bottom lip and hesitated before answering. "Okay, no. But I haven't changed my mind."

He couldn't stop the smile. "Then I intend to change it for you."

"Nash —"

"Kelly —"

She ran what he realized were shaking fingers through her hair.

"What's wrong?" he asked.

"Nothing —"

He pinned her with a warning glare. He wouldn't let her deflect her emotions.

"Fine. I'm hungry, that's what. I didn't eat so I'm dizzy. So can I go now?"

He let out a groan. He was such an ass. Between his not showing up and then Annie's call, she'd missed dinner. "Come on."

"Where?"

"We're going to eat. Give Tess a call on the way to the car and tell her we'll pick her up on the way."

"Tess already ate. Every last bite, so if you did show up, there'd be nothing left," Kelly said, unable not to grin.

"Brat," he muttered with a shake of his head.

"Her or me?" Kelly asked, and this time they both laughed, breaking the tension.

He used the opportunity shamelessly. "So we'll go eat. It's the least I can do."

"Yeah it is," she said at last.

"Good." He tried not to let his surprise show. "Elevator?" he asked, knowing when to retreat.

"Yes. Let's go."

Together they headed downstairs and out to the parking lot. When she started for her own car, he called her back.

"Kelly."

She turned to him. "What?"

"You're dizzy. I'm driving. You can pick your car up later."

She perched her hands on her hips and he found the pose damned sexy.

"You know, I'm beginning to see what Annie means. You're bossy and controlling," she said.

"It's not the same thing with you, and you know it." And Nash didn't like her bringing Annie's unreasonable issues with him into their relationship.

And, he realized, they did have a relationship. What that said about his earlier thoughts, he hadn't a clue.

"Now are you going to let me drive so you get there safely?" he asked, gentling his voice because he was determined to get his way.

Kelly met his gaze and held on until he wondered who was going to break first.

"Fine," she said at last. "But only because I'm starving. Not because I think it's necessary."

"Understood." He would not gloat, he told himself, despite the fact that he'd gotten his way twice in as many minutes. Still, he couldn't help but grin as she ducked inside.

He finally had Kelly alone and he wouldn't be choosing a restaurant where they could run into people he knew. Instead, he picked one close to the hospital but far enough from Serendipity so they'd have plenty of the one thing he craved — complete privacy.

Six

Exhaustion pulled at her very bones, hunger gnawed at her stomach, and the events of today completely stressed her out. For all those reasons, Kelly had agreed to come to dinner with Nash. Then there was the fact that she just plain wanted to be with him. He clearly felt the same way because instead of taking a seat across the table, he slid into the booth beside her. She didn't have the strength to fight him tonight. She blamed it on being tired and hungry because it made her feel better. Again, she just plain wanted him there.

He seemed to read her mind, asking the waitress for the bread basket before she could formulate the words and ordering her a soda for her empty stomach. She ate and drank in silence until her hands stopped shaking and she was breathing easily again.

"Better?" he asked when she leaned back against the booth, relaxing for the first time.

She smiled. "Yeah. Thanks. Actually, now that I have something in my stomach I'd like a glass of wine."

He nodded. "Red or white?"

"White. Dry."

"As you wish." He placed that order too, and they both told the waitress their dinner choices, then settled in.

"I wish this weren't happening," Kelly said.

Nash nodded. He knew she meant Richard and his surgery. "There's nothing we can do now but wait. I'm sure Annie will call when she knows something, but the doctors said the surgery could take hours."

Kelly swallowed hard. "I know."

Their server returned a few minutes later with her wine and Kelly took a grateful sip. "To relaxing," she murmured.

He picked up his glass of club soda. Because he was driving, he'd said. "To relaxing." He casually slipped one arm behind her.

She wasn't sure if he'd also inched closer, but suddenly his body heat surrounded her. She hadn't meant to get in over her head at an impromptu dinner . . . or had she?

"What are you doing?" she asked him seriously.

"Spending time with someone I want to

get to know better." His tone was equally solemn.

They weren't playing games anymore. She sensed that right now — if she pushed him hard enough, he'd leave her alone. And this time it would be for good.

But was that what she really wanted? It was what she'd been telling herself was the right thing to do. But these feelings between them just wouldn't be denied.

Warning bells went off in her head, but she didn't want to listen to them. She wanted what he wanted.

"I want to get to know you too," she admitted.

"I think you got to know me plenty during our tour of Serendipity. How about you return the favor?"

She laughed, but she wasn't about to be as much of an open book as he might like. She had too much self-protection ingrained, too much fear of rejection she couldn't let go of. Sometimes the people who left didn't mean to, like her father. Sometimes it was a selfish choice, like her mother had made. Other times, it couldn't be explained. Ryan Hayward had sworn he loved her and he'd chosen his almost ex-wife over her. The pain was still fresh a year later and she wouldn't put herself in the same position again.

Her past prior to Ryan? That, however, she was more than willing to share. "It's a pretty sad story, actually," she told Nash.

"How so?" While he spoke, he played with her hair, sifting a strand between his fingers.

Distracting her. She cleared her throat. "You already know most of it. I tried and failed to raise Tess well. And here we are."

He raised an eyebrow. "Do you really think you're getting away with that?"

"It was worth a shot." She peered at him over the top of her wineglass, then took a large sip for fortification.

"Let's start with you, not Tess," he said gently.

She inclined her head. His soothing voice urged her to explain. "I actually had a pretty good life until my father died. Heart attack," she added before he could ask. "After that it didn't take my mother long to hook up with her boss. Your father." She ducked her head in shame over something that though already out in the open embarrassed her anyway.

She drew a deep breath. "But as wrong as that was, it seemed to keep her stable." Another sip of her drink was in order, and to Kelly's relief, Nash seemed content to wait.

He toyed with her hair and let his fingers

brush her shoulders, a light skitter over her silk shirt she felt straight through to her bare skin.

"Whenever you're ready," he said in that reassuring voice.

"Your dad died, my mom spiraled downward. She moved us to New York City where she indulged in a random succession of booze and men."

"So you raised Tess."

She squirmed at the admiration she heard in his voice.

She didn't deserve it. "The landlady and I shared most of the responsibility. I had school and then later work. I couldn't let myself give up my path or I'd have ended up just like my mother, thinking I couldn't survive without a man in my life."

He nodded and treated her to a warm smile. "I always sensed you were smart."

Not smart enough, she thought, remembering the last few years. "I try."

"What about men?" he asked, taking her off guard.

"What about them?"

He shook his head and laughed. "You already know my romantic history. Now I want to know yours."

Not likely, she thought. A man like Nash valued integrity and intelligence. What were the chances he'd understand her choices or forgive the results if somehow the scandal blew up in her face?

"I have men in my past." She sipped at her wine, careful not to overindulge and repeat yet more of her mother's mistakes.

"Anyone serious?" he asked, pushing.

"No one that matters now." At least that much was true. She hoped he'd just drop the subject.

"Hmm. I guess I can live with that."

Thankfully the waitress arrived with their meals and he did let the topic drop, allowing her to finally focus on filling her stomach.

Except, sitting next to him, all she could think about was his hard thigh pressing into hers. And though she ate, she could barely taste her meal. How could she when she found herself solely focused on him — his strong hands lifting his food to his mouth, his masculine scent enticing her more than the penne alla vodka on her plate.

They ate in silence, comfortable on the one hand, sexually charged on the other. For the life of her, she couldn't imagine how she could be experiencing both emotions. She did know the combination had lowered her defenses, making her vulnerable to needs she'd been pushing away and ignoring for too long.

He paid the bill despite her suggestion to split the check. And as they walked back to his car, when he slid his hand into hers, she didn't argue.

He opened the car door and she turned to face him. He met her gaze with his and she sensed this was it. The point of no return.

"Come home with me," he said, his voice gruff and deep, his longing obviously matching hers. Clearly she read him well.

She could go home and begin *something* between them or say no and probably end things right now. For good. A man like Nash wouldn't come back for more if she rejected an outright invitation to sleep with him.

Bottom line, though, she wanted him. She wanted this. And she'd deal with tomorrow when it came.

"Yes," she murmured, swayed by forces beyond her imagining a mere hour ago.

They drove to his place, Kelly's nerves in high gear by the time they reached his town house complex. Her past might seem sordid, but *seem* was the operative word, and though she had some experience, going home with a man wasn't something she did often.

Or ever.

But here she was, walking into Nash's

house, his hand on the small of her back, the object of her desire waiting for her to reach out and take.

"You're trembling." Nash helped ease her coat off her shoulders.

"You do that to me," she said, finding herself at a loss for a witty reply. There was nothing funny about how she was feeling now.

His sexy smile sent her heartbeat skittering and she looked away, glancing around instead. The decor was strong and masculine, dark wood furniture, overly large, soft-looking beige cushions on the couch, and basic landscapes on the walls. It definitely looked as though he'd bought the showroom set, she thought, amused and yet strangely warmed by the thought.

"How long have you lived here?" she asked.

"About a year." He hung her jacket on a coat rack in the front hall. "Can I get you a glass of wine? A beer? Soda?"

She shook her head. "No, thanks." She drew a deep breath, then reminded herself that she wanted this man, and when she decided on a course she barreled straight ahead.

Enough with the shy, embarrassed girl routine, which wasn't truly a routine. She spent so much of her life hiding her real emotions and putting on a tough front to get through the day that she was surprised at how easy she found it to be herself around him. To be open and real. But to let him see her vulnerability exposed too much of herself and of her heart.

"I can't get you anything?" he asked.

She shook her head and smiled. "Just you."

"Now that I can give you." He stepped forward, pulled her into his arms and all her anxiety dissipated in a rush of heat.

She tipped her head back, expecting him to lower his lips to hers as he'd done before. Instead, he slid her shirt off one shoulder and pressed his mouth against her skin. She shivered and her entire body responded, her breasts grew full, her nipples puckered, and flutters picked up deep in her belly.

Nothing that felt this good could be wrong and she tilted her head, giving him better access. The smart man took advantage, trailing his tongue over the sensitive flesh of her neck. He was gentle, which somehow caused every nerve ending she possessed to come alive under the arousing strokes of his tongue. A soft moan escaped her lips and she felt a responding shudder go through him as well.

"Let's go somewhere more private," he said roughly in her ear.

"I thought Dare was working." She hadn't seen him around the apartment.

"He is. But haven't we been interrupted enough?" he asked, winking at her and thereby easing her anxiety.

What was it about him that he calmed her as easily as he often agitated her? She didn't know, but right now she wanted to find out as much about him as possible. Every part of him.

"Lead the way," she said in a husky voice she barely recognized.

She shed her shoes and followed him upstairs, making her way down the carpeted hall and into the master bedroom. Once inside, she had no second thoughts, no hesitation.

She sat down on the bed's navy comforter, making herself at home. She glanced at him standing by the door, silently watching her, looking sexy in his dark khakis and long-sleeved shirt, unbuttoned just low enough to give her an enticing peek of his dark chest hair.

She wanted to see so much more.

"What are you waiting for?" she asked, leaning against the pillows and patting the space beside her.

With a wolfish grin, he stepped closer, unbuttoning his shirt as he approached the bed.

Inspired and feeling braver by the second, she followed his lead and undid the buttons on her blouse too. He slowed his steps, giving him more time to undress. Garment by garment — pants for pants, her bra, his socks, her panties, his boxers. By the time he reached the bed, they were equally naked.

Beneath the polished clothes was a magnificent male body. He clearly worked out. His shoulders were broad, his upper arms muscular. His chest was also a treat, hard and toned for her viewing pleasure. Below the waist . . . well, that defied description and made her want to do more than watch and admire.

He devoured her with a hungry gaze. A hunger she hoped he found reflected in her own eyes. Just in case, she crooked a finger and he joined her on the bed.

His thigh brushed hers and his body heat caused a rush of warmth to envelop her and a sweet feeling of anticipation to course through her veins.

He leaned back against the pillows, propped up on one arm. "You're beautiful," he said as he brushed her long hair off her shoulder.

She shivered and knew without glancing down that her body flushed at the compliment. "Thanks." She shivered and he pulled her close.

"So, tell me, are you having second thoughts? Or wondering why we fought these feelings so hard?" he asked in a husky voice.

"Wondering," she murmured as he rolled her onto her back and came down on top of her.

Her soft body fit perfectly against his rock-hard one, and his erection nestled between her thighs. He felt delicious. "I'm definitely wondering why we were so stupid," she said, as liquid heat lit a fire inside her and she arched against him, enjoying the intimate contact.

"As long as we make up for lost time, I think we can go easy on ourselves."

She had no time to reply.

He lifted one breast in his hand, then lowered his head and pulled her rigid nipple into his warm mouth. Heat slammed through her like wild fire. Though he started slowly, letting her acclimate to his touch, he quickly accelerated his pace. His tongue flickered over her breast, fast and furious licks that had her thrusting her hands into his hair and pulling him closer to her body, not wanting him to stop.

He sensed her need, and while he worked at one breast with his lips, his tongue, and his teeth, he grasped the other with his free hand. Using his thumb and forefinger, he rolled that nipple back and forth, creating exquisite friction that pulled like a never-ending band between his fingertips and the dampness that pooled between her legs. He was eternally patient, relentlessly determined.

Her throat filled with need and her body bucked beneath his, searching for more of what he was giving her, needing to be filled by the hard ridge pulsing with life and desire against her mound.

She curled her fingers into his back and moaned. "Now — you — inside me," she managed between gasps.

Suddenly he released her breasts, allowing the sensations to ebb and the yearning for him to be inside her to grow. She forced her eyelids open and discovered him going down. Down her stomach, trailing soft kisses over her rib cage and her belly until he reached the place that throbbed with emptiness.

Being naked with him was intimate, having sex with him was too, but letting him do *this* created an even deeper connection between them than she was ready to face. But he wasn't asking for her permission and when he settled himself at the apex of her thighs and kissed her *there,* thinking was no longer involved at all.

Almost reverently, he licked her with his tongue, and the crescendo of need began to build all over again. He braced his hands on her legs and pried them apart, pausing long enough to look up, meet her gaze, and show her with his clouded blue eyes and taut expression how much *he* wanted this too.

"Relax," he said, rubbing his thumbs along the sensitive skin of her thighs.

He then returned to his mission, which she immediately understood by the caress of his tongue along her inner folds. Long, loving laps of his tongue alternated with short nibbles of the tiny bud that brought her closer to climax. Strokes followed by delicious nibbles, ending with the thrust of his tongue deep inside her, and Kelly lost track of reality.

All she cared about was the pleasure that lay just out of reach but so close she could almost taste it, and she lifted her hips and allowed him deeper. Obviously sensing her need, he parted her, and between the plunge of his tongue and the sudden pressure of his fingertip on exactly the right spot, Kelly's world flew apart.

She shattered, her orgasm sending her into a never-ending roller-coaster ride of pleasure. Pleasure Nash seemed determined to continue because he didn't stop, deep glides of his tongue and perfect circles against her mound that allowed wave after wave to rock her to her core.

And when the pleasure finally wound down, her body too sensitive for more, she heard the ripping of a condom, felt the rustle of movement, and suddenly Nash thrust deep into her body, filling her exactly the way she'd imagined during that long, intense climax. *He fits,* she thought when she could think at all, *fits so perfectly,* and she shut her eyes and let go.

Pure pleasure coursed through Nash, as Kelly surrounded him in damp heat. Need slammed into him hard.

"Open your eyes," he said roughly against her ear. "I want to see how I make you feel." Because in his wildest dreams, he'd never experienced anything like this — anything like her — ever before.

Nash watched as Kelly forced her heavy eyelids open and met his gaze, and there he found the same intensity, the same shock, the same desire as the physical and emotional yearnings inside him.

Knowing she shared those feelings helped now, in the moment. Later, those same emotions would come back to haunt him. But right now all he could do was concentrate on how good it felt to be buried inside her, her inner walls still contracting from the climax he'd given her.

As he began to rock his hips from side to side, her eyes opened wide, her expression one of utter surprise.

"What?" he asked, unable to keep still, sliding in and out of her body, reveling in the unbelievable friction they created together.

"I didn't think I could . . . That is, I just . . ." Her voice trailed off. "And I was so sensitive, I didn't think I could. Again."

He slid all the way out, then drove back in and a low groan reverberated from her throat.

"But I was obviously wrong. You *must* be that good."

In other words, she'd never come twice in one night? There was a boost to his ego that was as unexpected as it was satisfying. "You know how to give a compliment, sweetheart."

She grinned and he was lost. Lost to her smile, lost to her blissful expression, lost inside her tight sheath.

Beside himself now, he began to thrust into her, a steady rhythm she obviously enjoyed because her breathing came in harsher shallow gasps. She grew damper beneath him as she met his movements with equal force. Each time their bodies collided, she seemed to come closer, her pants and moans keeping him going. She dug her nails into his shoulders, the pain nothing compared to the pleasure building higher and harder until her body contracted around him and she cried out, telling him she was ready.

And damn but so was he.

She curled her legs behind his back and he levered himself up on his hands and pushed harder and higher, sure he was hurting her, but her screams were good ones and he couldn't stop even if he wanted to. But she begged him not to stop and he didn't, not until he came in the most intense explosion he'd ever experienced.

And with the way she twisted her hips and ground herself into him, she was still coming too.

Nash didn't know when he came back to himself. He just suddenly became aware of his surroundings — the warm body beneath him, her harsh breaths in his ear, his entire body still shaking in reaction.

Sure he was hurting her, he rolled to his side, giving her room to breath, space to process. "You okay?" he asked.

She reached her arms over her head and sighed. "Better than okay."

He smiled at her, enjoying her feline-like stretch, the flush in her cheeks *he'd* caused.

"But I'd better get home before Tess starts wondering where I am."

He didn't want her to leave but couldn't argue the point. "I'll take you back to the hospital for your car. Are you up to driving home?"

She nodded. "Not a problem. I definitely got my second wind." She rolled to her side and sat up in bed.

Even from behind, she was a treat for his senses. Her long hair falling over her pale skin, her trim figure and narrow waist . . . He shook his head to stop from staring.

He had to get moving too.

They dressed in silence. Somewhat awkward but, all things considered, not too bad. Even the car ride back to the hospital was comfortable all things considered.

He pulled up near her car. Before she could get out, he turned and placed his arm behind her seat. "I'd like to see you again."

A whole host of emotions flickered across her face, none of which he could read.

"I didn't mean more sex," he added when she didn't reply. Of course he *wanted* to sleep with her again, but he sensed she was suddenly thinking too much and he'd do anything to keep her cemented somewhere in his reality, whatever it took.

She laughed suddenly, breaking the tension. "Okay, then what did you mean?"

He grinned. "I want to be with you. How about dinner on Saturday night? We can take Tess to this great Mexican place I know."

"Using your sister to get to me again?" she asked, clearly amused.

"You know as well as I do that I want to spend time with Tess. Being with both of you at the same time is a bonus."

He trailed his fingers over her arm and she bundled her coat tighter in her hands.

"Okay, Saturday night with Tess sounds great." She was out of the car before he could speak or open the door.

She definitely needed time and now that he was alone in his car and overwhelmed with emotions, he realized he needed some space of his own.

SEVEN

The next morning, Kelly slept through her alarm and by the time she woke up, she was late for work, with no time to rehash last night in her head. Which was fine, since she'd spent her dreams doing just that. Her body tingled deliciously in some places while she was equally sore in others. Her sex life had been nonexistent since Ryan, and that had been okay with her.

Until Nash.

But she had no time to dwell on what she'd done, what it meant, or how she felt. With Richard in the hospital, it was up to Kelly to run the office. Still, she was so frazzled, it took two wardrobe changes before she could walk out of the house, and running late, she couldn't even stop for coffee before work.

The minute she stepped into the office, Annie called with an update on her father's condition. At the sound of her friend's voice, Kelly's stomach cramped as she remembered that she'd spent the night with Annie's ex-husband. Kelly forced herself to remember Annie insisted she was over Nash and she'd wanted out of the marriage. Kelly had come along long after.

"How's your dad?" Kelly asked, sticking to what was most important.

"The surgery was long, but the doctors said it was successful." Annie sounded exhausted. "Dad made it through the night and he's in CICU — cardiac intensive care," Annie explained. "I'll keep you posted as I know more, okay?"

"Okay. And if you need me for anything, just yell."

"I will. Thanks."

Kelly bit the inside of her cheek, then asked, "Do you want me to let Nash know?"

"I already did, but thanks. I told him I'd be calling you next."

"Great!" Kelly said, hoping her voice didn't sound as awkward as she felt. "Go take care of *you*." Though Annie tried not to focus on her MS, Kelly was worried about her anyway.

They said good-bye and Kelly hung up, letting the good news flow through her. Richard wasn't just a good boss, he was a truly decent man and she was so thrilled he'd come through surgery.

To her surprise, work was quiet except for people checking on Richard. Apparently in a small town, business came to a halt out of respect, so she fielded those concerned calls from business acquaintances and accepted that nobody she spoke to wanted to work on anything that would involve Richard's office today.

Unfortunately, lack of work gave Kelly way too much time to think about herself, herself and Nash, and having slept with him last night. She hadn't planned it, and if anyone had asked her earlier in the day, she'd have said the idea was absurd. And now?

Now, with free time on her hands, the memories came flooding back. He was phenomenal. They were explosive. But the biggest surprise of all was just how tender and caring he could be. She hadn't seen that side of him before and that was the part of him she was falling for.

Hard.

And oh, wasn't that just her typical MO? Though she didn't have many relationships in her past — she'd been too busy in school, at work, and caring for Tess — that when she allowed herself to get involved, Kelly fell too hard too fast, walking blindly into emotional danger without thinking things through.

Not this time.

Though she'd slept with him once, she had to pull herself together and take things slow. She exhaled deeply, surprised to find herself actually wringing her hands.

"Caffeine withdrawal," she muttered to herself.

Since today was a slow day, she turned on the answering machine and headed to Cuppa Café, hoping if she flooded her veins with coffee, she'd feel better and more able to function.

Instead of the usual teenager at the counter, Kelly found the owner, Trisha Lockhart, taking orders and working the register. Trisha was Joe's sister, and by all accounts the two had a close relationship. Trisha liked to say that her job in opening this place was to sober up the people her brother served alcohol. But she knew the two were close anyway.

Kelly ordered her drink and, since there was no one behind her in line, talked to Trisha while she waited for her drink to be made.

"So, what has you working the register?" she asked the owner, who was usually in the back or walking through, talking to customers.

Trisha sighed. "Carrie was a no-show. Which is what I get for hiring minimum-wage labor." She frowned and wiped down the counter as she explained. "Lissa Gardelli used to work here before she made it big as a reporter, and though she had an attitude, she always showed up ready to work." Trish looked as stressed as she sounded, having pulled her normally lustrous brown hair into a messy ponytail, no makeup on her face, and her expression tense.

"The hazards of owning your own business," Kelly said, commiserating.

Trisha nodded. "I was surprised when I didn't see you this morning, but then I heard about Richard and figured you were holding down the fort."

"I was. But nobody seems to want to work until Richard's completely out of the woods. So here I am."

Trisha leaned closer. "I'm glad you came in today. Something odd happened yesterday. Odd for around here, anyway, since everyone knows everyone else and a stranger asking questions is unusual."

The hairs on the back of Kelly's neck literally stood on end. "What do you mean, a stranger asking questions? About who?"

"You," Trisha said softly. "Some guy was hanging around the shop, nosing around for information. I finally asked him to stop bugging the customers and leave."

Kelly swallowed hard. For all the trouble she'd left behind, she wasn't surprised. "What kind of questions?"

Trisha shrugged. "Where you live, who you hang out with, things like that. Don't worry. I didn't tell him anything. But I can't vouch for other busybodies. By now you've been here long enough that folks know who you are, where you live and work, things like that."

"I know. And thanks," Kelly said, grateful. But her stomach began to clench painfully in response to the news.

Trisha put down the rag she'd been using to clean the counter and leaned closer. "Are you in some kind of trouble?" she asked quietly.

Kelly shook her head. "Not the kind anyone else has to worry about." Just the personal kind that could send her own life spiraling.

The other woman nodded in understanding. "Well, if there's anything I can do, just let me know. I'd like to think that here in Serendipity, we take care of our own."

Trisha smiled in an attempt to put her at ease.

"Thanks. Again." Kelly offered Trisha a genuine smile, appreciating the sentiment.

More important, she valued how Trisha had grouped Kelly into the *our own,* as if she already belonged here. It had been a while since she'd had a place where the people surrounding her cared about her and she cared for them right back. Mostly because she'd spent her formative years in a large city, taking care of herself.

Serendipity was a place she'd quickly grown to love, a town where she was beginning to feel at home. The last thing she wanted was for her past and her mistakes to come back and haunt her, make staying here impossible.

A customer strode up behind her and cleared her throat. Kelly stepped aside and waved a silent thanks and good-bye to Trisha. Kelly headed out the door, feeling both edgy and angry because someone was lurking around, determined to find out information instead of just confronting Kelly.

Ryan? she wondered, then immediately discounted the idea. A vice president at a major brokerage and financial services firm in Manhattan, Ryan Hayward was nothing if not direct; and if he had something to say, he'd come to her himself. Even if he needed her to testify about their relationship during his divorce proceedings, he'd just ask. He wouldn't send someone sniffing behind her back.

Someone his ex had hired to find out more about her?

Frustrated and in no mood to return to the too-silent office, Kelly turned around abruptly, planning to go to her apartment over Joe's instead.

She bumped into someone and quickly stepped back. "I'm so sorry," she mumbled, and glanced up only to realize she'd walked directly into Annie. "Oh, hi!"

"Hi! What's the hurry?" Annie asked. One glance at Kelly's expression and she asked, "What's wrong?"

Kelly exhaled a deep breath and replied, "Just about everything," immediately regretting the admission. The other woman had more things to worry about than Kelly's life problems.

"Talk to me. What's wrong?" Annie asked again.

Kelly shook her head. "It's okay. I'm fine. How's your father?"

"Status quo, which the doctors say is a good thing. My mother basically threw me out of the hospital. She told me either I go home and get some sleep or she'll bar me from visiting him permanently." Annie scowled at the threat.

Kelly smiled. "She's just looking out for your health. That's a mom's job, isn't it? Can't stress and lack of sleep exacerbate your condition?"

"Yeah, yeah," Annie said, sounding annoyed. "But I'm not the one who's sick right now and I want to be at the hospital in case Mom or Dad need me." Annie's eyes filled up, her frustration clear.

The other woman clearly needed a break as badly as Kelly did. "How about this. I was just going to go upstairs to my place for a little while." Kelly explained how nobody wanted to discuss their legal affairs with Richard just out of surgery, so she'd decided to take a few hours off. "Let's go and hang out."

A warm smile replaced Annie's earlier angst. "Sounds good. Just let me get a cup of coffee." She gestured her head toward the café.

Kelly nodded.

A few minutes later, they were upstairs in Kelly's apartment. "It's still a little sparse," Kelly said as a way of apologizing for the bare walls and lack of warmth. "I haven't had a chance to really unpack the little things or shop for what I need here."

Annie laughed. "You're worried about what I'll think? Please. Half the time I have a sink full of dishes when I have unexpected company. Today is what? Thursday? I'm losing track of things since Dad went into the hospital. Anyway, when Ethan and Faith come home on Sunday, you'll have all the time you need to fix things up here."

Kelly nodded, sliding her hand over a table that had once sat in her mother's apartment. After her Mom left, Kelly had kept a few cherished things, but with the price of storage rentals these days, she'd had no choice but to get rid of everything else. She blamed her mother for forcing her to make such a difficult decision about that too.

Annie glanced around the small apartment. "I like the place. It's cozy."

"Thanks. I felt the same way the first time I saw it. The timing was perfect, what with Faith getting married and me needing a place to live."

Annie settled onto the couch and stretched her legs out in front of her, avoiding the cocktail table. "Luck is something we could all use a time or two."

"Amen."

"So what had you so preoccupied earlier? You practically ran me down back there outside Cuppa Café." Annie raised an eyebrow in curiosity.

Kelly slumped into her small sofa and curled her legs beneath her. She'd wanted a friend here in Serendipity and now she had one. But friends exchanged confidences and secrets, and though Kelly definitely had some of those, was she ready to open up to someone about them?

She glanced at her more delicate friend. Annie had already admitted she had MS, which showed a definite kind of trust in Kelly. And Kelly needed someone to talk to, both about Nash and about her past — otherwise she'd turn into a mass of anxiety and worry. Then Tess would sense something was wrong and the life she was building here would crumble.

"I won't judge, you know," Annie said.

"I know. It's just that you have so much on your plate right now, between your father and your —"

"My condition is part of who I am, so don't mention it, okay? And I can definitely use a break from thinking about heart monitors and machines and all the things that can possibly still go wrong back at the hospital."

Kelly bit the inside of her cheek. "What if some of it's about Nash?" After all, she'd slept with this woman's ex-husband.

Annie focused her honest gaze on Kelly. "If you're telling me you will be distracting him and keeping him out of my personal business, I'm all for it." Annie laughed. "Seriously. I'm fine with the idea of you and Nash. Besides, if you talk to me about your love life, I'll talk to you about mine." She stared at Kelly, obviously waiting for her to go first.

"Okay." Kelly decided to take Annie at her word. "I slept with Nash last night," she said, and held her breath, waiting for a reply.

Annie's eyes opened wide, but she nodded slowly, a smile easing onto her face. "I can't say I'm surprised," she said at last. "I've never seen him bolt after someone the way he did with you the other night. He cares about you," Annie said, sounding sure.

Kelly's heart did a flip at the thought that her friend might be right.

"But? What's really going on? You're upset and it can't be about that. You've got this rosy glow when you talk about him."

Kelly tilted her head back and stared at the white ceiling she'd debated painting a different color. "You're right. It's not about him, it's about me." She forced herself to meet Annie's gaze. "I don't have the best track record when it comes to relationships," she admitted.

"And I'm the poster child for them?" Annie laughed at her own joke. "What matters is what's in your heart. Just do the best you can. At least that's what I tell myself about this date I have with Joe."

Kelly stared in surprise. Joe the bartender? She'd agreed to go out with him? "Okay, we definitely have to talk about that."

"Not until we're finished with you. What's this bad track record?" Annie asked.

This time, Kelly looked down at her polished nails. She'd managed to do them herself each week despite her busy schedule because she liked having fresh colors on. This week's choice was a deep, soothing purple. She knew she wasn't being fair to Annie, finding first the ceiling and now her nail polish to focus on instead of answering a direct question.

Kelly let out a sigh and decided it was time to dive in. "I was in a serious relationship with a man back in Manhattan. When we got involved, he was married but separated. I was sure I wasn't breaking up a relationship or involved in cheating. I even insisted on seeing proof that he was getting divorced before I agreed to get involved."

She drew a deep breath and continued. "I saw the divorce papers he wanted his wife to sign, and I knew he wasn't living at home, but they had a child and there were some sticking points. I shouldn't have let things get so far, but the chemistry was so strong, the feelings were so real . . ."

"So far it sounds like you were only being human. What happened?" Annie asked.

"Is it possible to say he cheated on me with his wife?" Kelly shook her head, still finding the situation hard to believe.

Annie frowned. "In technical terms, I guess it is."

"Well, his wife got pregnant, he decided he had to try and make it work for the sake of his kids, and that, as they say, was that." She rubbed her hands, as if wiping him out of her life. Kelly only wished it had been that easy.

"What happened next?"

"About eight months later, all the things that drove them apart the first time resurfaced and they separated again, except this time things got ugly and I got drawn into it."

Annie propped her head on her bent knees. "I'm still listening."

"Right." This was the hardest part to admit to anyone. "Ryan and I didn't meet in a traditional way." And that was the kicker — the one thing she was running from because even the truth sounded ickier than it really was.

She twisted her hands together, forcing out the story. "I was just starting out as a paralegal when a friend came to me about this great opportunity to make extra cash. Gayle and I met in school and we both had student loans to pay back plus other expenses, and she'd started working nights for someone who owned an escort service, the type that provides dates for wealthy businessmen. Gayle swore there was no sex involved and I believed her." Kelly bit the inside of her cheek and waited for Annie's reaction.

Her friend's eyes opened wider, obviously fascinated with the story. "Did you . . ."

Kelly shook her head. "Not at first. The whole idea wasn't my thing. But then one night, Gayle came down with a nasty stomach bug and she asked me to fill in for her at the last minute." Kelly still remembered how sick she'd been over the idea of going out with a stranger in exchange for cash. "I didn't want to go, but Gayle was in a bind and afraid she'd be fired if she were a complete no-show. I knew how important the job was to her, so I said yes."

"And that's how you met Ryan?" Annie asked, thoroughly enthralled.

Kelly nodded. "It was instant attraction." Or at the very least lust, she acknowledged now. A slightly older, extremely good-looking man showering her with attention and compliments he swore had nothing to do with the fact that she was hired to accompany him.

"Did you sleep with him that night?"

"No. I was too uncomfortable with how we'd met, but he wasn't deterred. He kept calling and showing up with flowers. I mean, really persistent." She shrugged. "What can I say?"

Annie grinned. "Like I said, you're only human. So now fast-forward to his second separation from his wife."

"You're following this like a pro." Kelly sighed. "Their divorce got ugly, and last time I heard from Ryan, his wife was threatening to expose to the world the fact that he used an escort service while they were still married."

"But legally separated."

"Yes. But the firm where he's a vice president won't care. If word gets out and negatively impacts the firm's reputation, Ryan could have major problems. And if my name is linked to the scandal . . ." Kelly shivered and wrapped her arms tightly around herself. "Here I am preaching good behavior to Tess while I'm hiding this? Can you imagine what kind of hypocrite she'll think I am? I'll lose all credibility with my sister. And if the kids at school find out, Tess will be mortified! You have no idea what she was like when she came here."

"Ex-wife, remember? Nash told me all about Tess." Annie reached out and placed a comforting hand on Kelly's arm. "But it sounds like this Ryan has a lot to lose too. That means he'll do all he can to keep his wife quiet, right?"

Kelly hoped so. "You would think. But after today . . ."

"What happened today?"

Kelly swallowed hard. "Trisha told me that someone was hanging around the coffee shop yesterday asking other customers questions about me."

Annie waved away the issue. "The coffee shop is gossip central. Who was it?" Annie asked.

"I wish I knew. But what's worse is that Trisha didn't know either, and she knows everyone in town." Kelly shook both hands in frustration. "Trisha said she told him nothing and asked him to leave."

"What's your best guess?" Annie asked.

Kelly frowned. "It's not Ryan. He'd just come talk to me himself."

"Mrs. Ryan?" Annie asked, only half joking.

"His last name is Hayward," Kelly said. "And yes, it's possible she's sending someone to see what I'm up to now."

Annie scrunched up her face in confusion. "Call me naive, but I don't understand why what you're doing now would impact her divorce case," Annie said.

"Because you had an amicable split from your husband. Mrs. Ryan, as you called her, seems to live for angst and drama. And I think that if she can add to my already-*sordid* résumé, she'd love to squeeze even more money out of Ryan."

"What a bitch!" Annie exclaimed.

"She very possibly is. Especially if I'm right."

"What in the world can she find here?" Annie wondered aloud.

Kelly's stomach cramped at the answer. "Only that the onetime escort of her soon-to-be ex handed off her sister to her millionaire half brother, then used her connection to said brother to move into his mansion?" Kelly groaned. "Sounds like one helluva story to me! The worse she paints me, the worse Ryan's judgment looks."

"There's not one person in this town who'd agree with that perception of you! Especially not Ethan or Nash!"

"Oh no. *They* can never know." Kelly jumped up from her seat, nearly knocking over her small end table in the process.

Annie rose too. "Calm down. They won't hear it from me, but can we at least talk about this?"

Kelly nodded. "I'm sorry. It's just humiliating. And I don't want anything I've done to reflect on Tess or how the Barron brothers will feel about me sharing custody of Tess." To Kelly's embarrassment, her voice cracked as she revealed the fear she had never voiced aloud, let alone admitted to herself.

"Oh, honey, no! Do you even know Ethan's history?"

Kelly nodded.

"Then you must realize he'd be the last person to judge anyone!"

"Maybe. But considering how Nash refuses to forgive Ethan, let alone even listen to his side of the story about why he left, he'll be the first to judge me." And find her lacking.

So Kelly intended to keep him from discovering a part of her past that deserved to stay dead and buried considering how innocent it actually was.

Annie blew out a long breath. "I see your point. *But* Nash's feelings about Ethan are personal. He was the one hurt and left behind. I'm sure he'd understand anything you told him about yourself."

"The way he understands when you ask for independence?"

"In that case he hears what he wants to hear . . ." she trailed off. "I still think you should tell him."

"Not unless I have to. For all I know Ryan will pay his ex-wife off and none of this will come out. But if I'm subpoenaed to testify or give an affidavit in their court case, or if it looks like this mess will come out, I'll tell him myself first."

Annie pursed her lips. "I don't like it."

"But you won't say anything?" Kelly asked, determined to hold on to her pride and dignity as long as possible.

"Of course not," Annie said. "Are you just going to wait around and see what happens next?"

"Oh, no. I'm going to go directly to the source and find out for myself." Though she didn't relish the idea of talking to Ryan after all this time, she wasn't about to sit back and be a target, either. *Proactive* was the word of the day.

"I'm glad to hear that. I'm curious, though. You're upset someone's in town asking questions. That much I understand. You're worried your new family will find out about your past. I get that too. What I don't get is where that leaves you and Nash now."

Welcome to the club, Kelly thought.

"You said you don't have the best track record with relationships," Annie said, as if Kelly needed reminding. "But you two already . . . *you know.* So what are you going to do about you and Nash now?"

Kelly shrugged, her exhale sounding more like a groan. "I only wish I knew." Half the day had gone by and Kelly hadn't heard from him.

She might be confused about herself, but she knew exactly how combustible they'd been and how he'd rocked her world. A phone call of confirmation he'd felt the same way would be nice. She bit the inside of her cheek, determined not to admit her pathetic neediness to Annie. Kelly was never going to be like her mother, wailing to the world and her liquor bottle how much she needed whichever man at the time.

"Tell me about your date on Saturday!" Kelly said to Annie, ready for a change of subject.

A slow smile slid across Annie's face. "I'm excited."

"Where are you going?"

Annie shrugged. "When he asked me out, he said dinner, but he wouldn't say where. He wanted to surprise me."

Kelly grinned. "Sounds exciting."

"It is. But Joe's not without his issues too."

"Do tell." Kelly nodded toward the sofa and they sat down once more.

For the next twenty minutes, Annie explained about Joe's family history in Serendipity, his ladies' man father, and the reasons and ways he was too much like Nash for Annie's peace of mind. "But the attraction? That's everything I've been looking for," Annie admitted.

Kelly smiled, understanding exactly what Annie meant about *that.* Memories of last night were never far from her mind and her body tingled at the mere thought of Nash Barron.

"But Joe did say he's not looking to be anyone's babysitter." Annie's smile grew wider at the admission.

"That doesn't sound very nice to me."

Annie shook her head. "No, I know exactly what he meant and it's more than okay."

Kelly merely stared at her friend. "If you say so."

"I do. But . . ."

Kelly tipped her head. "What?"

"Do you ever worry about jumping in too fast?" Annie asked.

Kelly couldn't hold back a laugh. "After what I just told you about myself, do you really need to ask?"

Annie grinned. "Well, I'm nervous. What if I'm making a huge mistake, going out with Joe despite the fact that a part of me is worried he'll be that overprotective guy I don't want?"

Kelly sighed. "Another thing I wish I had the answer to. But I'm going to keep your advice in mind and you should too."

"Remind me?"

"You said that what matters is what's in your heart. Just do the best you can," she said, repeating what she still thought were wise words of wisdom.

"Right. Gotcha." Annie shot her a wry look.

Kelly definitely understood Annie's sarcasm. It was one thing to give advice, another to take it. Kelly was afraid she was already in over her head emotionally with Nash Barron. If she followed her heart, she might end up with it broken again, except this time there was much more at stake.

EIGHT

Nash didn't call Kelly the next day. He couldn't because he didn't know what to make of the thoughts rioting through his brain. Thoughts about Kelly, last night, and how different it'd been from anything he'd experienced before.

He'd married Annie young and had been with her since he was sixteen. Yeah there'd been other women since the divorce but not many. This was Serendipity, and the single women here wanted commitment, and if not, gossips would hook you up as a couple whether you wanted it or not. Leave your car outside someone's house, the neighbors were sure to know it, and the people at Cuppa Café would hear about it soon after.

Nash had found a few out-of-the-way places in neighboring towns to hang out when he wanted female company, and a lawyer's convention also gave him the chance to meet out-of-town women. Sure, he'd gotten his share following in Ethan's footsteps beginning when he was fifteen — like his brother, he'd started young — but damned if he'd count *that* as an active love life.

Now he had to deal with the fallout of what he clearly hadn't thought through. He knew what he felt for Kelly was more. He just hadn't anticipated how much more. And he didn't know what to make of it. Of her.

He finally picked up the phone from his office after calling the hospital for a check on Richard. Status quo, Mary had informed him. Kelly's cell rang once and immediately went to voice mail. The second he heard her recorded voice, his gut clenched and he regretted not calling earlier, feeling like a selfish ass.

"Kelly, it's Nash." *Last night was spectacular,* he thought. "Just wanted to say hi. Looking forward to dinner Saturday," he said, and disconnected the connection. Then he got back to business, staying late to finish up and keeping his mind occupied.

Because by the time he turned into bed at midnight, Kelly hadn't returned his call.

After hanging out with Annie, Kelly made her way to the office, returned some phone calls, and compiled a list of cases and questions to discuss with Richard when he was ready. But she made sure to be at the mansion when her sister came home from school. Knowing Kelly would be moving back to her apartment in a few days, they had an unspoken agreement to spend their free time together. Though Tess had a lot of homework, they sat in the family room, Tess doing her work while Kelly read a book. And before bed, they shared chocolate-chip ice cream and hot fudge like they used to do on special occasions when Tess was young.

Once her sister headed for her bedroom around eight thirty, Kelly wanted to try Ryan again but she'd left her cell upstairs. She picked up the house phone. She still had Ryan's private number memorized, and though she'd hoped to never use it again, she had no choice. She refused to be used as a pawn or caught by surprise in his ex-wife's bid for more money in their divorce settlement.

Drawing a deep breath, she dialed.

The phone rang and rang . . .

"You've reached Ryan Hayward," the familiar voice said. A voice that she once thought the world of. "Leave a message and I'll call you back." A loud beep went off in her ear, startling her despite expecting it.

Nerves, she knew.

"Hi, Ryan. It's Kelly," she said, her voice firm. "I need to speak to you as soon as possible. Call me."

She hung up without saying good-bye, and when she was through, she was breathing hard, unable to relax. She ended up staying downstairs for an extra couple of hours, reading and drinking a warm cup of tea to calm herself down.

When she finally walked into her room around midnight, she picked up her cell on her nightstand. A quick look told her Nash had actually called and she played the message. Short and simple. He'd called to say hi and he looked forward to dinner. On hearing his voice, she was once again reminded of how amazing they'd been together, how much she was beginning to feel for him, and her stomach flipped in sweet anticipation. Until she remembered all the things that could come between them.

To make matters worse, Ryan hadn't returned her call, and the idea of some unknown guy asking questions around town and eventually getting around to Nash made her sick.

She ran a shaking hand through her hair, wishing she were baggage-free to enjoy the newness of the affair.

But she wasn't.

And she was grateful it was too late to call him back now.

Kelly left another message for Ryan on Friday and another on Saturday. Now she was beyond nervous. She was angry and frustrated and barely able to conceal her emotions. When Tess asked to go to the mall with Michelle and her mother, Kelly was grateful for the break from having to hide her feelings.

Richard had been moved to a private room and though he was asking to see visitors, Mary and his nurses had him on lockdown, as they called it. Kelly took it as a sign of progress and laughed, thinking of the hell he had to be giving the nurses, even in his weakened state. She couldn't send flowers or food. Instead, she sent her love in the form of a card and a letter to Richard's wife promising to relieve her when she was overwhelmed with his home care. It was the only thing she could think of doing for them at the moment.

Unable to sit still, Kelly drove downtown, parked, and took a walk down Main Street. Though the temperatures were cool, her down vest, scarf, and a pair of gloves gave her enough warmth, and the crisp air felt good against her skin and cleared her mind, letting her just *be* for a little while.

She walked aimlessly, weaving in and out of the side streets, checking out the various stores for the first time. She passed by Faith's interior design shop. Inside, she caught sight of Faith's mother, also her newest employee. A peek in the window revealed Lanie Harrington was about to lock up for the night, which was for the best, Kelly decided. Call her a coward, but Kelly planned to steer clear until Faith was back. She'd seen her mother in action at the wedding, heard clients in the office talking about losing money to Martin Harrington, and the interview that Faith had given to Lissa Gardelli, detailing her life growing up the Ponzi schemer's daughter. It was all Serendipity lore by now. As family of sorts, Kelly knew Faith had a strained relationship with her mother, a difficult woman to say the least. Though Kelly was dying to go inside and view Faith's shop firsthand, next week would be soon enough.

Along the same strip of stores was a bakery Kelly had heard of but hadn't yet tried and a place called Consign or Design. When Kelly had complimented Faith on one of her jackets, Faith had told Kelly about the shop. The owner was both a consignment store operator and a designer, creating and selling unique pieces of clothing. Thanks to Faith's closetful of now-unused couture pieces, April Mancini, the owner, was making them both a profit by deconstructing her old clothes and creating new designs. Since it was a little after 5:00 P.M., Consign or Design was already closed for the day, but Kelly promised herself she'd check the place out soon.

Realizing the time, she headed back to the mansion. Tess was due home at six and Nash was supposed to pick them up for dinner at seven.

Nash.

She wanted to see him as much as she needed to cancel. Until she had her answers from Ryan and understood where her life was headed, she couldn't go out for dinner with Nash and Tess and pretend everything was fine. And though she could send Tess alone with her brother, Kelly wasn't up to the argument Tess was sure to give her.

It was easier all the way around to call Nash and promise to reschedule dinner.

Joe rang Annie's doorbell, daisies from the local florist in his hand. She didn't strike him as a roses kind of woman, and with her father in the hospital he didn't want to pressure her or come on too strong. With everything going on in her life, he was just happy she hadn't canceled.

He waited, taking in the small house at the end of a tree-lined street. She and Nash had sold the place they'd bought when they got married and Annie now rented from a couple who'd moved to Florida to be nearer to their children. Joe had been friendly with Nash back in school, but they hadn't been close. For one thing, Joe was a year older, and for another, Nash had run in a tougher crowd, at least until he'd left for private school. Annie, on the other hand, was Nash's age and had gone to the same private school with him. Joe used to watch Annie in the afternoons, when she'd come to town with her friends, always thinking how gorgeous she looked in her preppy uniformed skirt.

He inhaled, taking in the cooler fall breeze and the scent of leaves and knocked again. Stepping back, he studied the place where she lived. The outside of the house was white, painted with a blue trim and black clapboard shutters. The lawn was well manicured and autumn mums were planted out front. But the shades on the front windows were drawn closed, and the house appeared . . . sad.

He frowned, and when nobody answered, he rang the bell and knocked again, even louder this time.

Still no Annie.

Not deterred, Joe pulled out his cell and dialed her number, standing on the porch while it rang and rang. Finally the front door cracked open and Annie appeared in the doorway behind the screen. She didn't look like a woman ready to go out on a date. In fact, he thought he'd woken her up. Her normally perky hair was matted against her head and her face pale.

"Joe?" she asked, sounding confused as she ran a hand through her curls. The action did little to give them their normal bounce. "What are you doing here?"

He slipped his cell back into his jacket pocket and narrowed his gaze. Now he was really worried.

He stepped closer and held out the flowers wrapped in paper. "You, me, date?" He waved the bouquet in front of the storm door.

"Oh! I forgot!" Her hands flew to her mouth and she unlocked the door, letting him inside.

"Should I be insulted?" He followed her into the small foyer.

A full blush stained her cheeks. "I . . ."

"Is it your father?" he asked. "Is Richard okay?"

She nodded. "Improving steadily."

If it wasn't her father that had her out of sorts . . . "Are you sick?" He put a hand to her forehead.

"No." She stepped back, out of reach. "Look, I'm really sorry and I should have called you, but —"

"You forgot," he finished for her, still not understanding.

His gaze swept downward from her hot pink tank top that had KISS ME emblazoned in silver across her breasts, to her low-cut drawstring pajama pants with red hot lips scattered all over them, to her equally pink bare toenails.

Swallowing a groan, he asked, "Did I wake you?"

She shook her head, oblivious to his perusal. "I was just resting."

She wasn't sick, but she'd forgotten their date. And she sure as hell didn't look well. Suddenly he remembered her MS and he all but slapped his hand against his head. "You're having an episode."

"Can we just reschedule?" She looked away, obviously embarrassed.

Joe didn't know what having multiple sclerosis entailed and he sure as hell hadn't thought it through when he'd pushed her for a date. Clearly he was going to have to read up. For now, though, he'd have to muddle through because he wasn't leaving her alone.

When she swayed where she stood, his decision was confirmed. He sure as hell wasn't abandoning her to take care of herself. He placed the flowers on the credenza and wrapped his arm around her waist at the same moment her legs gave out and she sagged into him, feeling tiny and frail yet so warm and good against him.

"What are you doing?" she asked, her voice too weak to sound like she was really putting up much of a fight.

"Taking you back to — where? Bed?" he asked, his voice thick thanks to both the womanly feel of her in his arms and the faint scent of strawberry teasing him with every breath he took.

Silence followed his question and he could almost imagine her internal fight. This proud, independent woman did not want him taking care of her.

Well, too bad. He lifted her into his arms, shocked at how light she felt. "Where to? Bed or couch?" he asked, not planning on taking no for an answer.

"Bed," she said, closing her eyes, obviously embarrassed. "Up the stairs, first door on the right."

The stairs were four short ones that led to a landing, her bedroom on the right.

"I thought you weren't anyone's babysitter?" she asked, her arms tightening around him.

As if he'd let her fall, he thought wryly.

He wanted to tell her he'd lied, that he'd watch out for her as long as she'd let him, but his stomach cramped at the notion. He'd thought his care-taking days were behind him. Besides, Annie wouldn't let anyone close enough to become her keeper. Once she was better, she'd run far and fast if he tried, and that was the thought that eased his mind.

"Who said anything about babysitting? I'm helping you out for a little while. And when you're back on your feet, I plan on letting you make tonight up to me." He laid her on one side of the bed, realizing she hadn't yet been underneath the covers. Too tired to even crawl under, he'd bet.

He strode to the other side and turned down the eyelet comforter, pushing the pillows into what he thought was a more comfortable position. Then, without asking, he walked back, picked her up again and tucked her in, pulling the covers up over her.

She mumbled something incoherent, rolled over, and fell fast asleep, not giving him a chance to ask when she'd eaten last.

Good thing he'd had plenty of practice cooking for his mother. As long as Annie had a few staples in the kitchen, he'd make do.

He glanced down. Her breath was slow and even, her eyelashes surprisingly long and dark against her paler skin. Unable to stop himself, he brushed her hair off her cheek before turning and heading for the kitchen.

Kelly might have canceled, but Nash didn't plan to take no for an answer. She claimed to have a headache and not to be up for dinner at a restaurant, throwing in too that Tess said she wanted to spend her last night at home with her sister. But there was every possibility Kelly was avoiding him.

He'd know soon enough. If it was a headache, he wouldn't stay long. If it was something else, something related to *them,* he intended to find out. Either way, he'd come prepared. If he was going to surprise two women, he'd arrive bearing gifts.

He rang the doorbell, grateful this was the

last time he'd have to visit Ethan's to see Kelly, since his brother was coming home tomorrow. But that also meant that when he wanted to see Tess, he'd have to go back to dealing with his oldest sibling and their issues.

The door opened wide, sparing him from that depressing thought, and Rosalita greeted him, eyes narrowed. "I thought Ms. Kelly say she cancel her plans with you tonight."

"Hello to you too, Rosalita." He treated the always-wary woman to a smile. "Since Kelly's not feeling well, I thought I'd surprise her and Tess with dinner. I hope you like Mexican because there's enough for you too."

He gestured to the bags at his feet. It had taken a few trips from the car to bring everything to the front door.

"Oh, Mr. Nash. I didn't know you were a charmer." Her expression softened.

"There's a lot you don't know about me," he said, feeling ridiculously pleased to have made any inroad with the gruff woman.

"Let me help you."

Nash took the heavier things and left the bags of food for Rosalita, following her into the house. From upstairs, he heard the sound of loud music blasting from what he assumed was Tess's room.

"How do you live with that racket?" Nash asked the housekeeper.

"Oh, Miss Tess like her music. But a little lower music now than when she first moved in. Back then the walls shook. Now? Not so bad." She laughed to herself.

That wasn't so bad? Nash shuddered at the noise from upstairs.

"Rosalita, are you talking to me?" Kelly called out from another room.

Without warning, the older woman turned to face Nash. "You go surprise her. I'll put dinner in the kitchen. Miss Kelly was about to order takeout. She told me not to dare cook since I'm supposed to leave early tonight. You're going to make her very happy." She nodded to herself, as if she were certain.

Nash liked this new, friendlier side of his brother's housekeeper. "Why don't you leave when you're ready? I'll be more than happy to clean up around here, since Kelly's not feeling well."

"Oh, Miss Kelly, she's fine. Pacing around the family room and staring at her cell phone a lot, but fine. I'm telling you, you'll be a nice surprise."

Feeling fine, huh? Nash had a hunch he wouldn't be as welcome a surprise as Rosalita thought. Obviously Kelly wasn't sick — she was avoiding him just as he thought.

"But if you're sure you don't mind, I'll be leaving in a few minutes. I appreciate you helping Miss Kelly. You tell her I'll be here early tomorrow to make sure the house is spotless for Mr. Ethan and Miss Faith's homecoming." With an oblivious smile, Rosalita headed for the kitchen with the bags of food, leaving Nash to surprise Kelly on his own.

Grateful that Tess was upstairs and hoping she'd shut the music off so he'd have warning before she barged in, he walked into the family room and was surprised to see Kelly sitting on the couch, flipping through a magazine. From the way she quickly turned the pages, he could tell she wasn't really concentrating on anything between the pages. She'd even appeared to have forgotten she'd called out to Rosalita.

"How's the headache?" he asked as he walked into the room. He had the biggest, heaviest gift, the one for Tess, tucked beneath one arm and was happy to unload everything onto the floor.

"Nash!" Kelly jumped up from the couch. "I wasn't expecting you."

"That was the point of surprising you." He made sure Tess's surprise wasn't going to topple over before turning to Kelly. "When you said you weren't feeling well, I thought I'd bring dinner to you."

No longer distracted by his packages, he took in her appearance. Her hair was up in a high ponytail, her face makeup-free, and her outfit . . . left him breathless. Even at her most undone, she was breathtaking. She wore a pair of pink low-cut sweats rolled down at the waist, revealing her pale stomach, while her bare feet with matching hot pink toenails peeked out from the bottom of the pants. Her matching T-shirt was as form-fitting as the pants, the word PINK appropriately scrawled across her chest. And she wasn't wearing a bra.

"All these bags are dinner?" Kelly asked, her gaze on the bags and the obvious painting easel for Tess, while he couldn't tear his attention away from her.

"Dinner's in the kitchen. Rosalita said to tell you she'd put the meal on the table and then she'd be leaving for the night. I promised to clean up . . . since your head hurts and you're not up to going out." He looked her in the eye, daring her to deny she'd lied to get out of seeing him tonight.

"Sorry about that. I had . . . have a headache."

"Which is why I brought dinner to you."

He wasn't about to debate whether or not the headache was real.

"And what's all this?" She pointed to the various items on the floor.

"This is an easel and art supplies for Tess. It's collapsible and I thought if she already has one here I could bring this one over to your place. So she could use it when she was there."

"Oh, Nash. That's fantastic! She'll love it."

He'd prefer it if his sister loved him, but he was resigned to baby steps.

"I also brought something for you." He bent down and pulled flowers from one of the bags. He was relieved to see he hadn't mangled them too badly while bringing everything in at once. "I should have called you earlier yesterday." He held out the long-stemmed roses.

"Pink!" Kelly exclaimed, the excitement in her voice clear. "Thank you," she said softly.

"My pleasure. So was the other night and I wanted you to know that." His heart beat harder in his chest.

"Same here." The words seemed pulled from her. She leaned in close and he expected her to kiss him. Instead, she touched her forehead to his and sighed.

He had the distinct sense she wanted to say something else, something important. He held his breath and waited.

And a cell phone rang, destroying the chance and the moment.

She flinched and turned away, heading to the phone she'd left on the sofa. She glanced at the number. "It's about time," she muttered before meeting his gaze. "Excuse me a second. I have to take this."

"It's about time," she said into the phone. She walked across the room and through the door leading to Ethan's private office, preventing him from hearing anything more.

He paced the floor and waited for her to return. He didn't have to wait long for company.

His sister bounded into the room, stopping short when she saw him. "Oh. It's you."

Her usual greeting.

"Rosalita said we had company," Tess said. "She didn't say who."

Nash laughed. "Smart woman." She got Tess down here without argument.

"I thought Kelly canceled dinner." Tess, dressed in a similar sweat outfit to Kelly's, looked young and wary as she studied him.

"She canceled dinner out, so I brought dinner to you." He drew a deep breath. "I also brought this." He gestured to the easel, which lay on the floor. "It's an easel — do you have one?"

Her eyes opened wide as she shook her head from side to side. "I usually just use sketch pads."

A feeling of accomplishment swept through him. "Well, I also asked the person at the art store to pick out beginner supplies. I think there are things like canvas, paints, brushes . . ."

"That's freaking awesome!" She knelt down and began looking through the various bags.

"Tess, how about a thank-you for your brother?" Kelly appeared in the doorway, looking paler than she had minutes before.

Tess glanced up from her excitement, her eyes big and wide. "Thanks, Nash," she said, the first genuine sentiment she'd given him since they'd met.

Warmth rushed over him. "You're welcome. I'd say we could set it up after dinner, but I think Ethan and Faith need to tell you where they want it."

"Aww —"

Kelly nodded. "Nash is right. But they'll be back early tomorrow, so you don't have too long to wait," she said, coming up beside Nash.

Tess let out a frustrated groan. "Fine.

Then I gotta go video-chat with Michelle and tell her about my new stuff!"

Kelly smiled. "You two are different, but you do like Michelle, don't you?"

Tess shrugged. "Yeah. She's quiet but kinda cool in her own way."

"Go ahead. We'll eat in about fifteen minutes." Kelly waved Tess out the door.

She streaked from the room and Kelly turned to Ethan. "Sorry about before." She raised the phone in her hand.

"Business?" Nash asked her.

She paused then shook her head. "Personal."

He waited, hoping she'd confide in him, but she remained quiet.

"How's your head?" he asked.

"Better." She glanced away and blew out a long breath. "I'm sorry. I didn't have a headache. It's just that . . ." She paused. "It's nothing. I needed time and space to process the other night."

She obviously wasn't telling him everything and he was forced to admit her refusal bothered him. Not because she wasn't entitled to privacy but because his instincts screamed that something was off tonight. Something more than her needing time. From her canceling dinner to how reticent she suddenly was around him.

Nash hated secrets because they reminded him of how duped he'd felt when Annie had asked for a divorce. He hadn't seen it coming because she'd never told him she was unhappy. Just like he hadn't known Ethan would leave town the minute he walked out of jail.

So, yeah, he disliked surprises and things left unsaid.

But he was sick and tired of being the most cynical Barron brother. He'd gone into this thing with Kelly determined to enjoy it for whatever it was. So, despite the nagging gut feeling that something more was bothering her, he was too involved to walk away now.

Nine

Nash was shocked at the pleasant dinner he shared with Kelly and Tess. His sister was actually nice to him. He hated to think he'd bought her off and rather believed he was making progress in letting her see she could like being around him. Either way, he enjoyed the feeling of being around family in a peaceful setting.

Kelly and Tess told stories about growing up in the city, lighter tales about Kelly's habit of burning breakfast, including toast, and how Tess once snuck a kitten home and tried to keep it a secret from everyone.

Kelly's cheeks flushed pink at the memories, her laughter so real and genuine it made his heart ache in some strange way. *This* was what he'd missed out on after his parents died, the warmth, the feeling of belonging.

"Nash, did you have a pet growing up?" Tess innocently asked.

Kelly's eyes opened wide, obviously sensing the potential for disaster.

"I did actually. A mutt named Lucifer."

Tess wrinkled her nose. "Why Lucifer?"

Nash grinned. "Because he was the devil dog. Always knocking over the neighbors' garbage and digging up their rosebushes." He shook his head at the memory. He hadn't thought of Lucifer in years.

"What happened to him?" Tess asked.

Nash's breath caught in his throat. "I don't know." Hence the reason he hadn't thought of Lucifer in years. Hadn't let himself.

"Huh? How is that possible?" Tess pushed.

"Tess, let it go," Kelly said quietly.

"No, it's fine." It had to be if he didn't want to shut Tess out and find himself back at the starting line. "You know how our father — my parents — died?"

Tess looked at him, wide-eyed, and nodded. For once her smart mouth was silent.

"And you know Ethan left town." He swallowed the bile that rose to his throat.

Again, Tess nodded.

Beside him, Nash was aware of Kelly's silent support as she waited to hear the end.

"Well, Dare and I went to live in separate foster homes."

"And Lucifer?"

"I'm not sure. I think he went to the local pound." Nash pinched the bridge of his nose.

He didn't have the heart to tell her the dog who'd slept at the end of his bed and licked his face had probably been put down. The place he'd gone to was what people today called a kill shelter. For that Nash blamed himself. He hadn't asked the Rossmans to take Lucifer in. Nash hadn't had the nerve to ask for more than they'd already given him, a roof over his head and food to eat. Especially when they hadn't taken his brother.

"That sucks," Tess said at last.

Neither he nor Kelly reprimanded her for her choice of words.

They finished their meal in silence, Lucifer's story pretty much killing everyone's appetite.

Kelly rose and started clearing the table and Nash helped, Tess pitching in without being asked. Though they were all more somber, the comfortable atmosphere remained and soon they were back to giving each other a hard time and laughing.

"Can we have a welcome-home party for Ethan and Faith?" Tess asked just as Nash had tied up the garbage. He should have known the peace was too good to last, and every last nerve in his body tightened at the mention of his brother's return.

"I think that's a great idea!" Kelly said, shooting Nash an apologetic look. "Why don't you go upstairs and start a list of what we'll need and I can pick it up tomorrow morning."

"Cool!" Tess darted for the door, suddenly turning. "Nash?"

"Yeah?" he asked, surprised.

"Thanks for my art stuff."

He smiled. "You're welcome."

"You'll come to Ethan and Faith's party, right?" She hung on to the molding along the doorframe, waiting for an answer.

Like she'd given him a choice? "Yeah. I'll be here."

She treated him to her biggest, most genuine smile, making his sacrifice almost worthwhile.

"Go make the list," he said gruffly. Who knew her approval could make him so happy.

" 'Kay. Oh, one more thing?"

He braced himself for heaven knew what. "Yeah?"

"I'm sorry about your dog." And then she was gone, disappearing from view, her footsteps pounding farther and farther away.

He turned to Kelly. "Where should I put

this?" He held up the trash bag.

"Just leave it. I'll take care of it later. Nash —" She stepped toward him.

"We really don't need to rehash it," he said.

She walked up to him and ran a soft hand down his cheek. "That's your problem, you know. You don't need to talk, you don't need to share, you just need to do . . . for others." Her hand lingered on his face. "What about you?"

"I'm fine." But a muscle twitched in his jaw, making his words a lie. "Okay, how about this? You tell me what's really behind you canceling our dinner tonight and I'll talk all you want about my dog, my past, even my brother."

She dropped her hand. "I told you. I had a headache."

"And that phone call?"

"I told you it was personal."

"As in you don't want to discuss it?" he asked pointedly.

She let out a frustrated breath. "I get your point."

"Good."

"But I don't have to like it," she muttered, her pout making him want to kiss those lips.

"Me neither." He wanted to make that point clear.

She was the one holding back. His past — hell, his present — was out there for her to know. And like he thought before, secrets made him uneasy. "Listen, I should get going. With that headache, you should get some sleep."

He wouldn't stand here and banter with her when in reality her withdrawal since last night was making him mad. He turned to go when she reached out and touched his arm.

Heat seared his skin. He spun around and without thinking backed her against the counter, bracing his hands on the cold granite. "You make me crazy."

One minute he wanted to throttle her, walk away without looking back, the next he couldn't keep his hands off her, needing to taste her and knowing even that wouldn't be enough.

She licked her lips and he was even more turned on. But his sister was upstairs and the sting of her canceling was still strong.

"Just so you know . . ." His hips bracketed hers, his erection pressing into her belly, his need for her strong.

"Yes?"

"When you move back into your apartment and we can be alone? We have unfinished business, you and I."

"This kind of business?" She rolled her hips against his and swallowed a moan.

If sex was what she wanted, sex was what he'd give her. He didn't know why she was playing hot and cold, canceling and withholding one minute, dropping her wariness around him the next. It could be something as simple as the fact that relationships scared her. He didn't know. And that bothered him.

So he'd do the one thing he'd planned to do from the start — guard his heart. Because the one thing she clearly didn't want to give him was the truth.

Kelly walked Nash to the door, her body still tingling from his teasing in the kitchen. They weren't finished. He'd made that clear and despite herself, she was glad. She enjoyed him too much to let things go after one night. She loved watching him grow closer to Tess, and he needed someone to help him through his conflicting feelings for Ethan and his past. Kelly wanted to be there for him. She wanted to be with him while she could.

As for Ryan, he'd claimed he had his ex-wife under control. He hadn't known about the private investigator but he'd get her to call the man off. Kelly knew he believed what he told her, but she was smart enough to be cautious and wary. In the meantime, she had a life to build, and for now she wanted Nash to be part of it.

Kelly and Tess hit Target early the next morning. The family room, which Faith had tastefully decorated in taupe and cream with beautiful abstract paintings on the walls, was now accessorized with WELCOME HOME balloons and purple and black streamers. Though the teenager no longer sported purple in her hair, her favorite colors hadn't changed. And that was okay with Kelly, since her attitude had.

Not only was the family all together on Sunday afternoon, including Nash, Dare, Tess, and Kelly, but Tess had included Faith's best friend, Kate, a pretty woman with auburn hair, and to Kelly's surprise, Faith's mother, Lanie.

When Kelly had asked Tess why she wanted the older woman there, Tess had met Kelly's gaze and said simply, "Because she's Faith's mother." *So much expressed in that simple statement,* Kelly thought.

So, though Kelly had avoided Faith's shop the other day, she'd welcomed Lanie Harrington a few minutes before Faith and Ethan returned. To Kelly's surprise, Faith's mother was more pleasant than she'd been at the wedding. More sober too, which probably helped. Faith and Ethan arrived a short time later, completely surprised and overwhelmed by the welcome-home party. Looking tanned and happy, the couple radiated marital bliss.

And Kelly found her gaze drifting across the room to Nash, his mood decidedly different from the happy couple's and so much different from the last few times Kelly had seen him. The night they'd spent together had been intense and special, and last night had ended up being sweet and pleasant. Now he greeted his brother and Faith with a tense smile and an attempt at civility, but his mood radiated tension and strain.

Yet he was here and making an attempt, all for Tess.

Suddenly Kelly realized she was in over her head with this man. Each time Nash revealed a piece of his past, and with every sweet gesture he made for his sister, Kelly understood how much it cost him and she lost a little piece of her heart to him every time. She *had* to protect what was left, but he made her care, chipping away at her reserve.

Which was why she now found herself walking toward him.

"Did I thank you for holding down the

fort while I was gone?" Ethan waylaid her, treating her to a grateful smile.

Kelly smiled at the oldest Barron brother. Ethan was broader than Nash, with chocolate eyes and jet-black hair, where Nash was lighter with blue eyes. Though Ethan had reformed his bad-boy ways, she still saw the twinkle of mischief in his gaze and knew many women would fall under his spell like Faith had. But Kelly still preferred the middle, more somber Barron brother.

"Kelly?" Ethan called her name, unaware she was running a direct comparison between him and his sibling.

She shook her head and laughed. "Sorry. I was distracted."

"I see that." Ethan's gaze drifted toward Nash, indicating he knew just where her mind had been, and Kelly struggled not to blush.

Nash, meanwhile, watched them from hooded, unreadable eyes.

Kelly rubbed her damp hands together and focused on Ethan. "Yes, you thanked me for holding down the fort and there's no need. It was my pleasure, though this is hardly some small fort." She swept her arm around the large area, which was one of many big rooms in the mansion.

Ethan laughed. "Well, you're welcome

here anytime. You know that."

"Thanks. Tess and I really needed the time together, you know?"

He inclined his head. "Glad my honeymoon came at a good time for us all. Speaking of Tess, what's going on?"

Kelly shook her head. "To be honest, I'm not sure. I think she's having a tough time with some of the kids in school and one teacher in particular." She summed up the parent-teacher conference and Ms. Bernard's attitude and the reasons behind it. "I think Tess wants to go back to public school, and before you say anything, yes, I understand the different element of kids she'd be exposed to and the chance we'd be taking of her falling back in with the wrong crowd. But I also think we're taking an equal chance of her acting out if we don't acknowledge her feelings."

Ethan's face reflected a complete understanding of the situation. "Let me get settled back home, talk to her, talk to the teacher, see what's really going on. We'll revisit this again, okay?" He reached out and touched her shoulder, clearly wanting her to know she had a say in the final decision.

Kelly nodded, grateful. "Sounds good. Now, how was your honeymoon?"

A broad grin spread across his face.

"That good, huh? Well, spare me the details," she said, laughing.

"Don't worry, I will." He looked over at Faith, an expression of wonder crossing his features, as if he couldn't believe *he'd* been lucky enough to end up with *her.*

Like Nash, Ethan tended to underestimate himself and his worth to those around him. Kelly wondered if the two men realized how similar they actually were and whether they'd ever get close enough to find out.

Before she focused on Nash, she had something else she wanted to talk to Ethan about. "There's one more thing I wanted to ask you."

"What's that?"

Kelly drew a deep breath. "Any luck finding our mother?" she asked of Leah Moss, her and Tess's runaway parent.

Ethan had promised to put a private investigator on her trail so they could both formalize custody and rights over Tess and her welfare.

Kelly had tried not to think too much about her mother. She told herself she'd grown used to not having one, but the truth was more complicated than that. Leah was the most selfish person Kelly had ever known, the one Kelly did her best not to emulate. It was better to put her mother out of her mind, but ever since Tess had made that comment about inviting Lanie Harrington today just because she was Faith's mother, Kelly wondered if Leah's absence weighed on Tess more than they knew. She explained as much to Ethan now, hoping he'd understand this was a sensitive issue for their teenage sister.

Ethan listened to the story and frowned. "There was no news before I left, but I'll follow up first thing in the morning. I want to find Leah, but I'm not giving Tess up," he said, adamant in tone.

Kelly swallowed hard. "I agree. But don't worry. I don't see my mother wanting her," she whispered sadly, though Tess stood across the room in no danger of hearing. They were words that should never have to be uttered about any mother and child. The sad fact was, Leah hadn't cared any more about Kelly and her life than she had about Tess.

A tingle suddenly ran through her and Kelly glanced up in time to meet Nash's stare. It was as if he knew just when she needed to feel his presence most.

"Ethan, can we talk more later?" Kelly asked.

He followed her line of sight to his brother, who despite a room full of family, stood alone. "Would you mind if I spoke to him first?" Ethan asked, tilting his head toward his middle sibling.

Kelly bit her bottom lip. "Umm, sure," she said warily.

"Nash is lucky to have you looking out for him." A knowing smile etched the corners of Ethan's mouth.

This time, at the mention of Nash, Kelly blushed. "Been talking to Dare?" she asked, figuring the youngest brother had blabbed all he knew.

"Nope." Ethan shoved his hands in his pants pockets. "But thanks for confirming the obvious." Ethan smiled and headed over to where Nash stood by the stone mantel.

Too near the fireplace pokers for Kelly's peace of mind.

Jealousy, anger, frustration, much of it irrational, some of it justified, churned in Nash's gut as he'd watched Kelly talk to his oldest brother. Now Ethan walked over to him, a determined expression on his face.

Son of a bitch, Nash thought. Wasn't it enough that he was here, smile plastered on his face — most of the time, anyway.

"Hey," Ethan said, coming up beside him.

Nash nodded. Aware Tess stood not far away and Kelly watched from across the room, he forced himself to make conversation. "Welcome back. Good trip?"

Ethan nodded. "The best. I recommend you try it some time."

"Turks and Caicos?" Nash asked, grateful for the benign topic of conversation.

"No, the honeymoon part. With the right woman, I mean," Ethan's gaze traveled to Kelly.

And everything inside Nash tightened in anger. "You aren't going to tell me to stay away from her."

Ethan let out a low growl of frustration. "That's it. We need to talk."

Nash raised an eyebrow, not sure he wanted to have any kind of conversation with his brother.

Ethan's expression turned cold and stony. "Unless you want to do this in front of everyone, I suggest you follow me." Without another word, he turned and strode out of the room.

Knowing this conversation was inevitable, Nash stormed out behind him, ending up in Ethan's study. Nash didn't like being on Ethan's turf, in his office, where his brother was comfortable and had the advantage. If Nash had given in earlier and had this private talk Ethan had been pushing for since his return, maybe Nash could have chosen the time and place. Now he was stuck.

Ethan shut the door to give them privacy, which was smart. The last thing Nash needed was Tess overhearing this argument.

"Hit me," Ethan said without preamble. He got into Nash's face. "Go ahead. Get some of that damned anger out. Hit me."

Nash bit the inside of his cheek and tasted blood, telling himself he had no desire to hit his brother. Or maybe he was afraid if he threw one punch he wouldn't stop.

Nash looked away and his gaze fell to Ethan's desk — to a small framed photo of Ethan, Nash, and Dare as kids, taken in front of the house they grew up in.

Next thing he knew, Nash's fist connected with his brother's jaw.

Ethan stumbled back, then righted himself, and Nash braced for a return blow. Instead, Ethan shook his head and rubbed his already bruising face.

Nash's own hand hurt like hell.

"Feel better?" Ethan asked.

"Fuck you."

Ethan's gaze darkened. "You're talking. At least now we're getting somewhere."

He wanted to talk? Fine. They'd talk. "How the hell could you do it?" Nash asked the question that had haunted him for years.

Bile rose in his throat, this conversation a decade in the making and one Nash would never be ready to have. "How'd you get on your bike and hightail it out of town without a thought to what you left behind?"

"You really think so little of me?" Ethan asked, disgust in his voice. "I thought of you and Dare every fucking day."

Nash narrowed his gaze. His heart beat so hard it threatened to launch out of his chest. "Yet you didn't come home."

"That's right," Ethan said, his voice rising. "Because *I* was the reason our parents were on the road that night. They were coming to the police station to bail *me* out." He slammed his hand against his chest. "Instead, they got hit by a drunk driver and died. So no. I didn't come home because I thought you and Dare were better off without me!" Ethan shouted at him.

Suddenly it was clear: what sounded like anger at Nash was really a burning self-hatred for his own actions. The notion, one Nash had never considered before, deflated some of his own anger. Some but not much.

A brief knock sounded on the study door. Without waiting for a reply, Faith opened it and poked her head inside. "Everything okay in here?" She stared at Ethan, love and concern in her eyes, making Nash wonder what his brother had done to get so damned lucky.

And question why he'd never been the focus of *that* kind of caring from the woman in his life. Faith wouldn't walk out on her husband. Ever.

"We're fine," Ethan said, his low growl bringing Nash back to the present.

"Your jaw!" Faith pushed the door open farther, and Nash caught sight of Kelly behind him, *her* gaze on Nash, a similar warmth and concern reflected there.

Or maybe that's what he wanted to see, since he'd been wishing for it from someone seconds earlier.

Ethan held up a hand, stopping Faith before she could launch herself across the room to check his injury. "We need more time."

She stopped short and nodded in understanding. "Okay, but I don't want to have to redecorate this room," she informed him, turning to Nash as well, including him in her warning.

In other words, no more fighting.

Nash and Faith hadn't gotten off to a good start; her father's actions had caused consequences for Nash's adoptive family too tragic for him to just welcome her back to town with open arms. It didn't help that she'd immediately aligned herself with the one man Nash nursed a simmering hatred toward. But her loyalty toward his brother showed a strength of character he hadn't given her credit for before now. Maybe she really was nothing like her criminal father or narcissistic mother. After all, Faith was the first person Tess had trusted when she'd arrived. Ethan had been the second.

The door shut behind Faith. Ethan turned to Nash and spread his hands out in front of him. "Well? What now?"

Nash ran a hand through his hair. Damned if he knew.

"As much as you don't like it, we're brothers. I was wrong back then, but I can't change the past."

"So what do you want from me?" Nash asked.

Ethan shrugged. "Get to know me. Judge me for who I am today, not who I was or what I did."

"That much, huh?" Maybe Nash could give him a kidney too.

Ethan nodded in understanding. "Yeah. I'm asking for that much." He let out a dark laugh. "You never know. You might just like me."

Nash rolled his eyes. "Don't hold your breath, big brother." Despite himself, a smile edged the corners of his mouth as he followed Ethan out of the office and back to the party.

Sunlight streamed through the window, hitting Annie's face and waking her in an instant. She rolled to get away from the offending glare and immediately hit a warm body. Her eyelids flew open and she found herself staring at Joe.

Oh my God.

She shut her eyes again tight, letting the reasons he was here come back to her. The tingling in her extremities reminded her that she was having a relapse — hence the name relapsing-remitting MS. These bouts consisted of severe exhaustion along with extreme discomfort in her hands and feet, accompanied by an inability to do little more than lie in bed until it passed.

She never knew what would bring on an episode, but this time she was certain her father's sudden illness, his being rushed to the hospital, her staying up all night when he'd had his surgery, and then the stress and worry of whether he'd be okay had all gotten to her. Yesterday she'd gone straight from Kelly's to the hospital, ignoring the warning signs, the tingling numbness and sudden tiredness telling her she'd better slow down and relax. Only after she'd seen her dad had she listened to her body and her mother and come home to nap.

Annie had barely been able to change into something comfortable before collapsing on top of her covers, her planned date with Joe gone from her mind.

Forgetfulness, another sign of an imminent relapse, she thought in disgust. She couldn't control the symptoms but she didn't have to like them — or who they made her become. Since being diagnosed over two years ago, she'd put on a brave front for the world, saving her pathetic routine for when she was alone.

Except she wasn't alone.

Joe was here.

TEN

"Ready to admit you're awake?" Joe's deep voice reverberated in Annie's ear.

She remembered him banging on her door, dragging herself off the bed, and yes, collapsing into his arms. The rest was a blur, so she assumed she slept through the night.

Forcing herself to face him, she rolled over and met his amused gaze. Sexy bedroom eyes stared back at her.

"I don't know what to say first. I'm sorry about the date? Thank you for staying?" She swallowed hard. "Or I'm okay now, so you can go without feeling guilty?"

He exhaled and shook his head. "No problem about the date, I should have called to make sure we were still on. You're welcome. I wasn't going anywhere. As for guilt, that's the dumbest thing I ever heard."

She blinked. "Okay, sorry for being dumb."

"Did you ask me to stay? Take me away

from something? No," he answered for her. "So, no guilt. How are you feeling?"

"Less exhausted," she said. At least that was honest. She was tired, not up for running a marathon, let alone simple errands, but she wasn't in danger of passing out.

"That's good." He hesitated, then asked, "What else are you feeling?" He propped himself up on one arm, looking into her eyes as he waited for an answer.

Joe's voice was calm and steady, and she forced herself to talk about the thing that had changed her life. "It starts as tingling, sometimes in my hands, my feet, or both. Like a warning. Combined with the absolute exhaustion, I can become pretty useless."

She glanced away, knowing she'd ended any chance of anything with this man and being more disappointed than she would have thought at the notion. She expected him to bolt. If not for Nash's commitment to her through marriage and to her family, she was sure he'd have run far and fast too.

"Does it hurt?" Joe asked, his voice tinged with curiosity and compassion.

Not pity, she realized, and that had her meeting his gaze. "Depends on the severity. Pain's a weird thing. It's subjective, you know?"

He nodded.

"And how long until you feel better?"

"Should be soon," she said lightly.

From experience, she knew it could be a day or two, or even weeks. It was the reason she'd quit her job at a large accounting firm in the neighboring town to work her own hours. But he didn't need to know how debilitating the disease could be.

"Joe, I'm grateful you're here. I am. But you didn't sign on for anything more than a date, and I slept — probably snored — through it. I'm sure you have more important things to do this morning." More fun things.

Her stomach chose that moment to let out a growl, reminding her she hadn't eaten since lunch yesterday.

"Hungry?" he asked with a devastating grin.

"Yeah. And I'm sure you are too, which is another reason you should leave. So you can go get breakfast." She rolled over and pushed herself to a sitting position, fighting the tiredness with everything in her.

"Where are you off to?" he asked.

"To wash my face and brush my teeth," she muttered, and headed for the bathroom. In all probability he'd be gone by the time she was finished and she could make herself a bowl of cereal slowly and in peace.

Except when she finally washed up, changed into fresh lounge wear, and made her way down the stairs, the smell of bacon assaulted her senses along with that of French toast.

She stepped into her kitchen to find a sexy man standing at her stove. "What are you doing?"

He raised an eyebrow and grinned.

Stupid question, since he was using a spatula to put delicious-looking pieces of crisp bacon on her plate.

She'd told him to leave and he hadn't listened. She should be mad, but her stomach was so empty that all she felt was extreme gratitude. Besides, how could she be angry at a man who'd made himself at home in her house so he could take such good care of her?

Despite having told herself she didn't want a caretaker, the sight of him sent warm happy feelings spiraling through her.

Ten minutes later, she'd devoured everything on her plate and was licking her sticky fingers when she caught him staring. Her hunger for food was gone, only to be replaced by a hunger of an entirely different kind.

"What would you have done if I hadn't been here?" he asked seriously.

She didn't want him to think she was too needy. "If I'd thought to call, my mom's housekeeper would have come over and helped me out," she admitted.

That was the agreement she'd made with her parents after her divorce. If she didn't want to move home, she'd admit whenever she couldn't care for herself. She'd hated it as much as she understood the necessity and so she'd agreed.

He nodded, as if glad there was a plan of action. "But what if you hadn't called at all? And I hadn't shown up?"

"Enough." She held up a hand to cut him off.

"Okay, then, what's on today's agenda?" he asked, readily accepting her change of subject.

"You're looking at it," she said. Surely now that he understood just what a burden she was, he'd take off.

Sure enough, he rose and she clamped down on the disappointment churning inside her. She liked having him here way too much.

To her surprise, he picked up her finished plate and cleaned up quickly and efficiently.

She released a pent-up breath. "I could have done it, but thank you."

He nodded. "I have to get over to the bar

and see what's going on."

Now he was leaving.

Pasting on a smile, she rose and walked him to the entryway and opened the door. It was for the best. No man would want to deal with her illness and issues for the long haul, so why pretend otherwise.

"Thanks for staying."

His dark eyes bore into hers. "My pleasure."

From his tone, he didn't sound the least put off. In fact, her entire body suddenly throbbed in response to his husky voice.

Before she could process or reply, he slipped one hand behind her neck, pulled her close, and kissed her. Not a quick good-bye kiss, either, but a hard, demanding *I want you* kind of kiss that had her nipples puckering beneath her tank top.

"What was that for?" she asked, dazed and surprised.

"Your shirt last night said 'Kiss Me.' I was just waiting for the right time."

"Oh." She ran her tongue over her damp lips and tasted him. "Oh." This time she smiled. "Mind if I ask why now?" He confounded her, this man.

A slow, easy grin eased up the corners of his mouth. "Because I know you think I'm saying good-bye for good. That was my way of telling you I'll see you soon."

He let himself out the door, leaving her alone, every inch of her body pulsing and aching for his touch.

Monday morning, Nash was on his way to the hospital to visit Richard when a nagging feeling he couldn't explain compelled him to drive by Annie's first. On Saturday, her mother had told Nash she'd sent Annie home from the hospital to rest. Later that day, and on and off yesterday, Nash had called the house to make sure Annie was keeping up her strength, resting when she should, and eating despite the stress in her life, but he'd gotten her voice mail. She hadn't called him back and he'd put it out of his mind.

This morning, Nash had called the hospital to make sure Richard was up to his visit, and when he'd asked about Annie, Mary said she hadn't heard from her daughter yet this morning. And Annie was normally an early riser — unless something was wrong.

So Nash drove past Annie's house and was about to slow down and park on the street when Joe Lockhart walked out the front door. Joe, the bartender. Joe, the guy who'd had a thing for Annie for as long as Nash could remember.

Nash's hands automatically gripped the steering wheel harder, an instinctive response to realizing the woman he'd been married to was obviously seeing another man. Nothing else could explain Joe being there this early. Instead of slowing down, Nash hit the gas, driving past before Joe or Annie realized he was there.

Sorting through his feelings wasn't simple or easy. It should have been, considering he'd been divorced for a while now, and he had to force himself to think about why Annie and Joe as a couple bothered him. It sure as hell wasn't about still having feelings for Annie because he didn't. Not in the way he had feelings for Kelly, he thought, another completely different set of emotions rising in his throat.

It was ego, he forced himself to admit. Annie had rejected him, broken his heart, and though she'd taken longer than him to move forward with someone else, she finally had. And it cemented the end of his former life in a way nothing else could.

Apparently Dare and even Kelly had been right. By insisting Annie needed him to look out for her, Nash had been holding on to the past. In reality, he'd been watching over Annie because doing so kept her in his life, which in turn allowed him to pretend Annie wasn't yet another person who'd disappeared and let him down.

He shook his head and focused on the road, discovering that he'd driven toward the hospital, but lost in thought, he'd passed the exit on the highway and had to circle around and come back again. Nash finally reached his destination and headed inside. Richard had been moved to a private room, but seeing him after the operation was still a shock. Paler, less robust, and definitely in pain, the other man had at least held on to his upbeat mood and spirits. He wanted to be back to his old self in no time, but the fact remained he had a long recuperation ahead of him and some cardiac rehab to follow. But he was alive and Nash was grateful.

He didn't stay long because Richard needed his rest. And Nash left the hospital, still thrown by both this morning's revelation about Annie and seeing his mentor and friend looking so old and frail.

In the aftermath, Nash could only think of one thing that would make him feel better. The only person he wanted to confide in now and the single woman who could help lighten his current mood. But given everything he had to say, would Kelly even want to see him?

■ ■ ■ ■

Kelly spoke to Richard for a quick few minutes, and though he sounded weak and in pain, he was as focused as ever. Obviously realizing real work would have to wait, he instructed her to archive old files and arrange for them to be put in storage. What she hadn't realized was how many huge stacks of boxes were in a back room, covered with dust and waiting for someone to sort through. She buried herself in the storage area, deciding that tomorrow she'd stick to jeans and a T-shirt for this particular job.

She didn't know how long she'd been absorbed in her task. Starting with the oldest documents, she'd gone back in time to the early 1980s. Without warning, the office door slammed shut and Kelly realized someone had entered.

"In the back," she called out, too settled on the floor and surrounded by boxes to get up and see who was there.

When Nash walked in, she couldn't have been more surprised. She hadn't spoken to him since they'd said good-bye late afternoon yesterday. He'd seemed to be in a passably good mood after his private talk with Ethan and since he hadn't offered up information, she hadn't asked. And when the time came for her to leave, she'd picked up her bag, climbed into her car, and headed back to Joe's.

She stood up and tried to brush the dirt and dust off her skirt before walking over to him. "Hey! What are you doing here?"

He remained silent for a few long seconds before meeting her gaze. "I needed to see you."

"Okay." She treated him to a warm smile.

He didn't seem to notice. Odd that he said he wanted to see her when he appeared so preoccupied with his own thoughts. "Come sit," she said into the silence.

He shook his head, expression thoughtful . . . and distant.

"Is everything okay?" she asked, growing concerned. "Richard? Tess? Ethan? Dare?" She named his family members, thinking maybe he didn't know how to express bad news.

"They're all fine." But a small line furrowed deeper between his brows. "Something happened this morning. You're the only one I wanted to talk to about this, but —"

Her heart clenched as his voice trailed off. "But?" she prodded, at this point unsure of anything, let alone him.

"But I think you'll take what I say the wrong way."

She swallowed hard. "Why don't you just tell me and I promise to reserve judgment until you explain." She curled her hands into fists at her side, waiting, not wanting to do anything that would make him change his mind about talking.

He blew out a long breath. "On the way to the hospital, I decided to drive by Annie's. Because her mother mentioned she wasn't feeling well yesterday, and when I called to check she didn't answer the phone."

Annie's. She should have known.

"I see," she said. Clearly this was the part Nash thought she'd have issues with.

And she did, but she also understood they were born of her own past and insecurities, which she was trying to live with and overcome.

"I already know Annie's an important part of your life," she said rationally.

After all, Kelly had slept with him knowing he was still heavily invested in his ex-wife's welfare. So his stopping by Annie's this morning didn't shock her. She couldn't say it thrilled her either. She was human and feeling a little insecure despite his past promises that he and Annie were just friends.

But Nash was here, she reminded himself, and she'd promised to hear him out. "Is Annie okay?"

Nash shrugged. "I don't know. When I got there, Joe Lockhart was walking out the front door, so I drove right by."

Kelly nodded, not all that surprised. Well, she was surprised Annie had let Joe stay over, but considering the chemistry she'd witnessed between them at the bar the other night, Kelly figured nature had taken its course.

"You knew?" Nash asked, obviously catching on to the fact that Kelly wasn't as stunned by the new couple as he'd been.

"I knew they had a date last night, that's all." She paused, trying to read his expression and unable to do so. "I'm guessing you're upset Annie's with someone else?" she asked, forcing herself to release the nails that were biting into her skin.

Given how shell-shocked Nash appeared to be, Kelly guessed it was the first time he'd been on the receiving end of Annie's dating another guy. Kelly blew out a deep breath, coming to the only conclusion she could — that seeing Joe leave Annie's made Nash realize just how much he still loved his ex and he wanted her back.

Why else would he have sought Kelly out? Told her she was the only person he'd wanted to see if not to untangle himself from their relationship before he went after Annie. Deep hurt settled in her chest, but she wouldn't make a scene.

"I understand." Reaching out, she put a hand over his, attempting to reassure him while ignoring the heat blistering her palms when she touched his skin.

"You do?"

She nodded. "And I'm not going to make this difficult for you. Go. Tell Annie how you feel." Kelly withdrew her hand and waved him away, forcing a smile she didn't feel, waiting for him to leave so she could give in to the pain slicing through her heart.

Nash shook his head. "That's not what I want. It bothered me that Joe was there, but not for the reasons you think."

Confused, Kelly held her breath.

"I was keeping Annie in my life even if she didn't want the same thing, claiming I just wanted to make sure she was okay and healthy. In reality, I was protecting my ego, not Annie."

"I don't understand."

"I hung on to Annie because that meant I didn't have to face the fact that yet another person in my life had walked out on me."

Kelly stared, unable to believe Nash was baring his soul this way.

"Seeing Joe leaving Annie's place made me ask myself the same question you've been asking me. How do I really feel about Annie moving on?" He spread his hands in front of him, as if begging her understand.

She didn't. Not yet. "And? How do you feel? Or should I ask, *what* do you feel?" Kelly asked, barely able to speak. She was afraid of the answer.

Nash lifted her chin in his hand, gently forcing her to look at him.

"Breathe," he murmured.

She hadn't known she'd been holding her breath. "What are you saying?" she asked.

"That faced with the reality of Annie and Joe, I didn't care." A sexy smile curved his lips as he said, "And the only person I wanted to be with was *you.*" He then slid his hand behind her head and pulled her in for a kiss.

And this was no ordinary kiss. It held everything he'd been trying to express, the emotion and the feeling, along with a new honesty he'd just now accepted. This kiss let her know that not only did he want her, but that she came first.

Kelly might have other concerns about

this relationship and there might be other things that would come between them in the future, but not his feelings for his ex. More than Ryan's unsigned divorce papers, this kiss assured Kelly that Annie held no romantic place in his heart.

Until her past collided with her present, she wanted to revel in being that only one. While she had him, he was hers.

She threaded her fingers through his hair and kissed him back, passion overwhelming common sense. He backed her to the nearest desk and she ended up sitting on the hard surface, Nash coming between her thighs, never breaking the kiss. His hands came to rest on her waist and he slid her silk shirt out of her skirt so his fingertips brushed the sensitive skin on her waist.

Her breath hitched and his fingertips moved upward until his thumbs grazed her nipples through her bra. She moaned and arched back. Taking the hint, he eased her onto the desk until she lay prone before him. Dark eyes never leaving hers, he unbuttoned her blouse, one tiny button at a time with painstaking slowness and care, teasing her. Tormenting her, since he remembered to skim the pads of his thumbs over the sensitive peaks of her aching breasts each time he worked a button through the loop.

When he was finished, he separated the blouse and pressed a warm, wet kiss to her stomach. Her muscles contracted, her skin rippled beneath his lips and a wave of sheer pleasure rushed over her.

But it wasn't enough.

And he knew it.

He braced his arms on either side of her shoulders. He didn't have to ask. She lifted her legs, locking her ankles around his back, forcing his erection into the juncture of her thighs. His hard male flesh pressed insistently against her skirt. The damn material had no give and she couldn't feel him, not enough of him anyway, and she shifted her hips from side to side in frustration.

In a flash, he lifted her skirt upward until it bunched around her legs. She'd worn a pair of pumps she'd left beneath her desk, and instead of panty hose, a pair of thigh-high stockings covered each leg and when she arched into him, there was nothing between them except her damp panties and the roughness of his slacks abrading her sensitive flesh beneath.

Soft moans and little cries escaped from her throat as he kissed her lips, all the while rocking into her, his hard ridge gliding over her, grinding into her, causing swells of need to crest inside her, building higher and higher.

Suddenly he broke the kiss and his amazing mouth suckled her breast through her bra. He nipped her playfully with his teeth, lapped her lovingly with his tongue, and finally pulled her aching nipple into his mouth once more. The heat and suction he generated combined with the friction of his erection and without warning, she exploded, coming apart as he jerked against her, his hips mimicking rough sex, thrusting against her over and over until her orgasm slowly faded.

She watched through heavy lids as he released the button on his slacks, let them fall to the floor, and shucked them aside.

His thick erection swelled behind the boxer briefs and that quickly she was ready for him to fill her. "Protection?" she remembered to ask.

Just barely.

"Shit." He sucked in a deep breath, but his body still shook with unslaked need.

Kelly processed their options and decided. "I'm on the pill. And safe." She glanced up at him, waiting.

He inclined his head, a warm smile her answer. "Same."

She believed him. If there was one thing about Nash, she knew he had integrity.

She grinned and crooked her finger at him. "Then what are you waiting for?"

Those briefs ended up on the floor in a heap too. And then he was coming toward her, naked and erect, a perfect male specimen who wanted only her. She sighed as he spread her thighs with his strong hands and pressed the tip of his erection into her pulsing, waiting heat.

She expected him to start slowly, carefully, deliberately. Instead, he shifted his hips and with one thrust, buried himself completely inside her. She sucked in a startled breath, thought she'd need to wait, to accommodate him. She didn't. He fit perfectly. And it was different, she realized immediately. No condom really did mean skin to skin and, as he leaned over her, heartbeat to heartbeat.

Warmth and emotion flooded her and a lump filled her throat. But the last thing she needed to do was focus on feeling and emotion, that much she knew, and his movements meant she didn't have to.

He slid out, teasing her, thrusting back in, his fathomless gaze never leaving hers. "You feel so damn good," he said gruffly, his eyes closing as he absorbed the intensity.

"I know." Just as she knew she'd never forget this moment, and she tightened her inner muscles around him, wanting to imprint herself on him too.

"God." The word exploded from deep inside him and though he slid out of her slowly, he returned quickly, driving into her harder and faster than before.

She didn't want soft and careful, she wanted him to take her and make her forget any messy feelings that might try and slip past her defenses. He did, picking up a rhythm that felt too damned perfect. Hands on her waist, he pumped his hips, making sure she met him thrust for thrust, making certain she felt him each time his body slammed into hers. She felt everything, more than she wanted to and reveled in it, panting at first, close to screaming the harder he took her.

Suddenly he bent forward, eased over her, his mouth coming down on hers, his tongue demanding entry inside, and she found herself reaching for an orgasm that was just out of reach. She arched her back, pressed her pelvis up against him, drawing him deeper until he ground into her, his insistent thrusting taking her up and over the edge.

She thought she screamed or tried to, but he was still kissing her, taking his pleasure and pronging hers, thrusting his hips until a low groan told her he was coming too. And somehow, impossibly, her body's contractions started over again, taking her on what felt like a never-ending ride.

Holy shit. Nash pulled out of Kelly, his head pounding along with his body, the reality of what he'd just done crashing around him. They'd had sex in Richard's office, the front door unlocked so anyone could walk in and see.

She deserved so much better. He turned and somehow they dressed quickly. Words weren't spoken. What was there to say? He'd shown up here with a hell of a lot on his mind and he'd lost himself inside her.

The fact that it had been the only place he wanted to be didn't make it better. And then he turned around to see her. Face flushed pink, her chest reddened as she buttoned her shirt, and a wide satisfied smile on her face. Maybe it was marginally acceptable after all, he thought with a grin.

He opened his mouth to speak when his BlackBerry alarm went off. Annoyed, he pulled the phone from his pants pocket to shut it off when the reminder flashed in front of him and he groaned.

He dismissed the reminder and tossed the

phone onto the desk.

Where they'd just . . .

"Is everything okay?" Kelly asked him.

When he turned back, she was completely dressed. But he could tell what they'd done by looking at her. Her face was still flushed and glowing, her hair tangled and her skirt wrinkled.

He definitely liked what he saw.

"What are you grinning at?" she asked.

He shook his head. "Which question do you want answered first?"

"You choose." She folded her arms across her chest, which was a good thing because her damp bra was showing through the light silk.

"Okay, I'm smiling because you look like you just had sex on the office desk and enjoyed it a whole lot."

Her eyes opened wide.

"And that beeping was my calendar reminder. Tonight's my mother's birthday and I have to be there for dinner at seven."

The mention of his adoptive mother reminded him that there was much more going on in life than just them.

"Do you see her often?" Kelly asked.

"Once a week or twice if it's planned, more often if we run into each other." He loved Florence in his own way; he was just torn by the past, still struggled with those feelings because of loyalty to his younger brother.

"Come with me tonight," he said without forethought.

She tilted her head to one side, wary and as surprised as he was by the invitation. "Why?"

He stepped closer, invading her personal space, feeling her heat. "Why not?" He threw the gauntlet back at her.

If he wanted to bring a woman home to meet his adoptive mother, he would.

Kelly bit down on her bottom lip. "Who will be there?"

"Nervous in front of a crowd?" he asked. That didn't sound like her.

"No, nervous in front of your mother. What if she doesn't like me because I'm nothing like Annie?"

"She'll love you," he assured her. "Besides, *I* like you, and isn't that what matters?" He leaned over and swiped his tongue over the lip she was nibbling on.

She shivered but didn't back away. Just one of the things he liked so much, Nash thought. "Did it ever dawn on you that the reason I like you so much is *because* you're nothing like my ex?"

"Explain."

"You're bold, daring, and you protect the people you care about." They both knew he was referring to Tess.

What she didn't know was that Nash suddenly wanted to be on that list of people who deserved her loyalty.

"That's sweet," she said with a grin.

He cringed. "Not the word I'd choose. Now back to you. You're also honest about things — when you couldn't handle Tess, you said so. When you didn't want to get involved with me, you told me why. You put things out there and that's something I value." More than she knew or understood.

"Nash, I —"

"Shh." He placed a finger over her mouth. "The only thing I want to hear now is you'll come."

"Again? So soon?" She teased him, wriggling her hips against his abdomen, making him groan.

"Not that kind of come. Little witch." He lightly swatted her backside. "Come to dinner, Kelly. It's just me and my mother, so please. Join us."

In case she needed incentive, he wrapped his arm around her and pulled her against him. "Please."

"Okay."

"Thank you." He grinned, not because

he'd gotten his way but because he'd be seeing her again tonight. "What do you have planned for the rest of the day?"

"Work, why?"

"Because I suggest you go home before someone else walks in that door and figures out what we've been doing."

Her embarrassed groan reverberated through him, heightening his anticipation for the night to come after they celebrated Florence's birthday, and he and Kelly could be alone once more.

ELEVEN

Kelly had been a sucker for the word *please* coming from Nash's mouth. That and the feel of his hard body pressed against hers, reminding her of the heaven she'd found in his arms. It could all be so good — if only she weren't hiding her past. And if honesty weren't so important to him.

But because it was, she'd come *this close* to telling him the truth about herself, but he'd silenced her with a touch. He'd wanted one thing from her and she'd given it to him. So here she was, his hand at her back, ready to walk into his adoptive mother's home.

The sun had begun to set, but it wasn't as dark as the night Nash had taken her on a tour of Serendipity, and she received a better view of the house now. Though not as grand as the Harrington mansion, the Rossman home was definitely an estate, an immense structure set back on a rolling lawn with an aura of wealth attached.

She stiffened before she even walked over the threshold.

"Breathe," he whispered in her ear, and memories of this afternoon immediately came flooding back. Earlier, "Breathe" had been followed by "The only person I wanted to be with is you." At which point, she'd done the most unprofessional thing she could imagine.

And didn't regret it one bit.

"Florence Rossman has no bite," he assured her.

Just then the door opened wide. "Nash!" the woman, obviously his adoptive mother, exclaimed. "I'm so glad you're here!"

"As if I'd miss your birthday?" He handed her a small gift box that even Kelly recognized as the distinctive blue of Tiffany's.

"You're all the gift I need," Florence said, pulling him into a hug.

Her love for Nash, adopted son or not, was so obvious. Never having been the recipient of that kind of affection, not that she remembered as a teenager or adult, it hurt Kelly to watch. It also saddened her to see how uncomfortable the warmth and caring made Nash, who squirmed in the older woman's embrace.

"Mom, I want you to meet Kelly Moss.

As I explained to you, Kelly is Tess's half sister."

"Happy birthday, Mrs. Rossman. Thank you for letting me intrude on your celebration." Kelly held out the flowers she'd bought late this afternoon.

The other woman smiled, inhaling the scent of the bouquet. "Nonsense, you are not intruding. I love having company." With a welcoming wave of her hand, she gestured for them to follow her inside.

Kelly glanced at Nash and together they walked inside, Kelly's thoughts on Nash's adoptive mother. Kelly didn't know what she'd expected, but the tiny woman with straight blond hair and a tanned face, who wore casual black slacks, Chanel ballet slippers, and a cardigan sweater, wasn't it. She exuded warmth and inclusion, and Kelly was astounded this same woman had refused to take an orphaned Dare in as well.

Florence Rossman seated them in a family room decorated in warm powder blues and cream. She talked, asking Nash questions about his life and his work. She asked him about Richard and said she would be sending a fruit basket when he was released from the hospital. She was warm and animated, and Nash seemed to relax as they talked, his face softening, his feelings for the woman clear. At least to Kelly. It was only when he was alone and his memories of his real parents intruded, when thoughts of Dare's foster care reminded him of how lucky he'd been in comparison, that Nash shut down.

During dinner, a delicious chicken dish Florence had made, she told stories about Nash as a teenager, and she continued with fond memories when they'd returned to the family room after the meal.

Kelly loved hearing about the boy he'd been. She'd never thought to get such an inside look at who and what had shaped the man he'd become, and she was grateful for the insight, hanging on Florence's every word.

"And you should have seen his face when he realized he had to wear a uniform to private school." Florence smiled at the memory.

Beside Kelly, Nash shook his head and groaned. He obviously still had issues with the uniform. *Just like your sister,* Kelly thought to herself, suppressing a laugh. It always amazed her when she found something Tess and Nash had in common. It almost explained their intense antagonism. They were actually too similar.

"The arguments over the blazer were

almost enough to make me send him back to public school."

Yet she hadn't.

Thinking of her sister, Kelly leaned forward. "Why didn't you send him back to pubic school? My — I mean our sister, Tess — is having a rough time in private school too. I'm not sure what to do," Kelly admitted.

Florence nodded, her eyes full of understanding. "As the adult, it was up to me to look to his future. I knew that in taking Nash from his public school friends we were hurting him. Especially after all he'd just lost," she said, her voice soft. "But if he stayed where he was, hanging out with kids, most of whom lacked ambition, we were worried he wouldn't take advantage of the opportunities his new school could give him. So we asked him to give it a chance."

"And I did," Nash said, remembering. He'd felt an enormous sense of obligation to these people who'd taken him in.

"Happily?" Kelly asked, obviously still thinking of Tess.

Nash leaned back in his seat. "Not at first," he admitted.

His first months both at the Rossmans and at the academy where they'd sent him had been horrific. He'd missed his friends, he'd missed Dare, and he was angry at the world for taking everything he'd known and loved away from him.

"But if I'd stayed at my old high school, I probably wouldn't have cared enough to study or think about the future. And in the end I went to both New York University and then NYU Law." He shot a grateful glance at his adoptive mother.

"I'm happy to hear you say it," Florence said. "I never was sure how you felt about . . . So many things."

Nash shifted uncomfortably in his seat. He'd always given the Rossmans mixed signals about his emotions because he'd always been conflicted. He realized now that he hadn't had it simple or easy and so he hadn't made *their* lives easy either.

He didn't like seeing himself as ungrateful, but there were times he probably had been, he thought, not liking himself much for it.

"Listen," Florence said, bringing his thoughts back to the present. "I know it's easier for you to give in to Tess when she's unhappy, but perhaps you should push her to stick it out a little while longer."

Maybe he could talk to her, Nash thought. They had made small headway the other day and she might at the very least hear him out.

Kelly nodded in agreement with his mother. "Wise words." Her smile hit Nash in the gut.

Everything about her hit him that way. Hard and in the solar plexus, stealing his breath.

"You know, I think Ethan feels the same way," Kelly said.

As she spoke, Nash felt her eyes on him, sensed her wondering if he'd blow up over her mention of his brother.

"How is your relationship with Ethan?" Florence asked, unaware of the new undercurrent.

"Still unresolved," Nash said. "But . . . I think we turned a corner."

Kelly's eyes opened wide. Though he'd seen her since Sunday at Ethan's, they hadn't discussed what happened between Nash and his brother. Not that Nash had allowed himself to spend any time thinking it over, either.

But now he had to consider it and the answer was an interesting one. Ever since he'd punched Ethan, a lot of the all-consuming anger had disappeared, leaving him with a weird hole in his chest and a bigger sense of confusion. It was strangely better than the hatred he'd lived with for so many years.

"I'm glad. Family is family," Florence said, echoing words she'd used often over the years.

"Me too." Kelly's heartfelt sentiment warmed him. He knew how much she wanted peace and reconciliation between the brothers and not just for Tess's sake but for his own.

Because she cared about him.

Before he could process that thought, his mother spoke up. "If you two don't mind, I need to turn in early. I volunteer at the old-age home and my shift starts at eight A.M."

"I'd like to stay and help you clean up," Kelly said.

His mother shook her head. "I have help coming in the morning and you already helped me rinse the dishes. Everything else can keep."

That was something he'd always admired about Florence. Everything got finished without her stressing over it. If she said it'd wait till the morning, it would.

"But —"

Kelly started to argue and Nash knew it would do no good. "She means it," Nash said, rising. He took Kelly's hand, indicating she should come along quietly.

"If you're sure . . ."

"I am."

"She is."

All three of them laughed.

They said their good-byes, Florence obviously happy he'd brought Kelly. Nash was still processing the fact that he'd done so, having never brought anyone except Annie to meet his family. Yet he'd been comfortable tonight and his mother's reaction told him the instinct to invite Kelly had been correct.

The trip back to Kelly's was a short one. Everything in Serendipity was a quick car ride from everything else, and soon Nash found himself parked behind Joe's.

He cut the engine and walked her to the door. With each day that passed, the air grew colder and he wrapped an arm around her waist. *For warmth,* he told himself, knowing it was a lie. He wanted her badly but he had no idea how this night would end.

Her apartment door was at the top of a long flight of stairs, but there was a bright light that at least made him feel she wasn't walking home alone in the dark at night.

He turned to face her, struck once again by how strongly he was drawn to her. "Thanks for coming tonight. I know it wasn't the most exciting way to spend an evening."

She blinked. "Why would you think that? I think I got more insight into you in one night than in all the time I've known you."

Her knowing smirk made him nervous. "What is it you think you discovered about me?"

"Oh, that's for me to know." She inserted her house key into the lock. "And for you to be left wondering about." With a laugh, she let them inside.

Instead of following her, he paused in the entryway. Though he'd been at a family birthday, he'd spent the night watching, waiting, wanting.

"Nash?" Kelly had taken off her coat and put her bag down on a chair. "What's going on?"

"You're home safe and sound. I should get going." Especially if she didn't plan on him staying.

Because after watching how smoothly she'd navigated what he thought of as his schizophrenic life — his wealthy adoptive mother and the man she thought he was versus the Barron brother he still considered himself to be — Nash was feeling things for Kelly he had no business feeling.

"Do you *want* to go?" she asked in a husky voice.

She'd worn a pink blouse, the color bringing out the natural flush of her skin. She reached for the top button and undid it, then followed with another one, and another. Beneath the blouse was a matching light pink bra, all lace and sexiness teasing him.

Her signals couldn't be clearer and he released the tension he'd been holding, meeting her in the center of the room. He stretched out a hand, intending to touch her, but she placed both hands on his shoulders, led him to the sofa, and pushed him down.

"You're playing with fire," he warned her.

"I can handle it." She shrugged and her soft blouse fell off one shoulder, revealing bare, creamy skin. "You wanted to know what I learned tonight, right?"

"Right."

"I learned you need someone that understands you. You're grateful to the Rossmans. You love Florence. But you hold yourself back because you feel guilty about Dare. Who, by the way, wouldn't want that for you."

"I can't have this conversation now."

Not while her fingers were hovering

around the hard ridge threatening to burst through his pants.

She met his gaze and grinned. "We're not going to do much talking," she promised, her eyes glittering with desire. "I just wanted you to know that I get you. And when you're with me, you can just feel what you're feeling and I won't judge. So tonight, you enjoyed a nice birthday dinner with a very sweet woman."

He nodded, his throat full, touched beyond reason that she'd thought so long and hard about him. What he wanted and needed. He wanted to express his gratitude, his feelings and once again he reached for her.

Once again she eased out of his grasp. "And now you're going to lean back and just enjoy. No thinking, Nash. Just feel," she said, and knelt down in front of him.

Her fingers no longer hovered. Instead, she opened the button on his khakis and attempted to push them down. She cleared her throat, obviously expecting him to lift up and he did, until she'd lowered his pants to his ankles. Nash retook his seat on the couch, and Kelly removed his shoes, then socks, after which she tossed his pants out of reach.

By the time she turned to him, still on her

knees, and wrapped her delicate fingers around his rock hard shaft, he thought he'd explode.

"Feeling anything yet?" she asked, her hand caressing him, from the base all the way up to the tip, pausing to spread the moisture around.

He sucked in a ragged breath, unable to formulate a coherent word.

"Nothing yet?" she asked, still the tease. "I have the cure for that." Then, while he watched, she shifted, moving closer until her knees hit the couch and she bent over, her hands on his thighs, her hair spilling over his skin.

"Kelly you don't have to —"

"I want to." She cut him off first with her words and then with her lips when she closed over him and took him inside her warm, wet mouth.

He let out a low groan, his entire body shaking in reaction as he fell back against the cushions, unable to withstand the sensations rocking through him and still remain sitting upright. But he wanted more than to just come — he wanted to feel connected — and he ran his hand over her hair, tangling his fingers in the strands, cupping her head as she began to move on him.

The suction of her lips, the slippery glide

of her tongue over and over his shaft, the complete rightness of the moment overwhelmed him. So did the way she gave, taking all of him, and sensation came at him from all sides, the wave building, slamming into him with driving speed.

He tugged on her hair, giving her warning, but her fingernails dug into his thigh and her other hand suddenly wrapped around the base of his shaft, pumping him with her fingers while she drew on the tip with her mouth. When he came, she was there until the end, milking every last bit of moisture and pleasure from his body.

Aftershocks still wracked him when she rose to her feet. Eyes gleaming, she stripped quickly, tossing her pants over his on the floor. And then she straddled him, arching her back, rocking her pelvis, making sure their bodies collided at just the right spot. He clasped her hips and held her in place, pumping his hips upward until she came, screaming his name.

Kelly woke up the next morning and Nash was gone, a note on her pillow in his place. *The night was as special as you are. See you later.* She laid her head down and smelled his masculine scent embedded in her sheets, a reminder of all they'd done last night.

Once on the couch, twice in bed. At least they'd slept in between, she thought wryly.

She dressed in nice sweats and sneakers. Though she told herself she was accommodating her work in the dusty back room, she was also accommodating her sore, tired body. Every time she moved, she remembered something else that made her smile. Nash's hard body entering hers, his masculine scent, his arms wrapped around her as she slept.

She felt closer to him than to anyone before, so close she was beginning to think Annie was right and she needed to level with him about her past and the problems looming in her future.

Annie. Before she headed to the coffee shop this morning, she put in a call to her friend, hoping she'd meet Kelly at Cuppa Café. Though Kelly had spoken to Richard directly only once since his surgery, she liked to check in periodically with his wife or daughter. He was progressing nicely.

But Kelly hadn't heard from Annie in a few days and she wanted to make sure her friend was holding up under the strain. She also wanted to find out how her date with Joe had gone.

Kelly dialed and the phone rang and rang and rang. She was just about to hang up when she heard Annie's voice.

"Hello?" Annie asked, sounding as if she'd just been woken from a deep sleep.

"Annie? It's Kelly. Did I wake you?"

"It's okay," she said, the standard answer when you don't want the person on the other end of the line to feel bad.

"Why don't you call me back?" Kelly suggested, though she was concerned that Annie was asleep so late in the morning.

"No, I can talk. I just haven't been feeling well, so I slept in."

"Is there anything I can do? Bring lunch? Dinner?" Kelly propped a hip against the kitchen counter, already thinking about where she'd go to pick up meals.

"No, thank you, but I have everything I need," Annie said.

Kelly narrowed her gaze, wondering if Annie would exaggerate just so she wouldn't be a burden. "How are you taking care of yourself?"

Kelly knew Annie's mother must be busy at the hospital with Richard, and from the sound of her voice Annie was too weak to do much for herself.

Annie remained silent for a second, but the answer had dawned on Kelly as soon as she'd voiced the question. "Joe's over, isn't he?" Kelly asked.

Annie sighed. "Not right now, he isn't."

"But he's the one coming by and helping you!"

"How did you know?" Annie asked, sounding brighter if still weak.

"Umm . . ." Kelly bit the inside of her cheek. "I was going to mention this to you at some point, just so you had a heads-up. Nash had a gut feeling something was wrong, so he drove by your house early yesterday."

"He didn't come in," Annie said, sounding tired and confused.

"Because he saw Joe leaving."

"Oh my God. Did he freak?" Annie asked.

Kelly gripped the phone tighter in her hand. "Depends on your definition of freak. Let's just say it was an eye-opener and he's okay with it. More than okay."

"Really? You're sure? As in you're not trying to make me feel better or not upset me when I'm sick?"

Despite herself, Kelly laughed. "No, none of the above." In fact, Kelly remembered everything about Nash's admission yesterday — from his surprise to the realization that he truly didn't care if Annie had a man in her life, to how he'd rushed right over and made love to Kelly on a table in the back room.

"Oh, that's great. I'm so relieved." Annie paused. "I'm sure you were too."

"You could say that." The details weren't something Kelly would share with anyone, especially Nash's ex. "So? You and Joe? What happened to the woman who didn't want to be taken care of?" Kelly teased.

"She's weak and she caved." Annie laughed. "He showed up for our date and I'd forgotten all about it! Then I practically passed out in his arms, and when I woke up the next morning, he was still there. Next to me. In bed."

Kelly squealed along with her, thrilled Annie had someone like Joe in her life.

"But I still don't want him to be with me out of pity. Or because he thinks I need someone to take care of me."

"No man comes back out of pity," she assured Annie. Besides, Kelly had seen the look in Joe's eyes when he watched her. The man had it bad.

"Well, to make certain he knows *me* or at least the me I want to be when I'm not laid up in bed, I want to plan a surprise for him. One that will make up for me forgetting the date and thank him for being there."

"What did you have in mind?"

"I haven't decided yet. Something he won't expect, though."

"Sounds like he's a lucky man," Kelly said, laughing. "When is this happening?"

Annie's groan echoed through the phone lines. "I wish I knew. I have to get better first."

They talked a few minutes more about her father's condition and Kelly hung up, promising to check on Annie later.

Right now she needed to work. She left home, stopped for coffee, and settled into the back room of the office. She took a long sip of her morning coffee and pulled out the first box to sort through. Her plan was to make sure that each file was labeled and placed in a new, sturdy box, marked by year.

Time passed quickly. When her legs began to ache, she glanced at her watch and realized she'd started at nine and now it was almost twelve thirty. She glanced at the open box and realized if she went through the last few files, she could finish this carton and at least start a new box later on.

She pulled out the remaining files, checked the name on the label, blinked, and checked it again.

Barron.

Kelly's breath caught in her throat. Like she'd done to all the files before this one, she flipped through the pages to make sure all the papers belonged to the same case.

But she couldn't stop herself from reading through things more slowly.

Richard had been the district attorney of Serendipity and had stepped down just after Ethan's arrest, going into private practice. He'd wanted to help the kids he'd been putting away. As he explained to Kelly, he'd seen something of himself in those teens, having been a hell-raiser in his youth. Most of the case files she'd looked at had been of downtown kids who'd gotten into trouble and needed help. Since Richard's real money came from his father's real estate business, he was able to concentrate a good deal of his legal practice on pro bono work, which Kelly admired.

Apparently the Barron brothers had been clients of a sort. Though Nash told her he'd had Richard to look out for him, she hadn't known details. Now they were in front of her. She hesitated, only to remind herself she hadn't thought twice about looking at files before.

Drawing a deep breath, she opened the file and began reading. By the time she was finished, Kelly was thrown by all she'd learned, most of which she didn't think even Nash was aware of. Information she knew would change how Nash viewed life from now on.

■ ■ ■ ■

Nash's first task this morning was to promote Bill Manfredi, from associate to junior partner. As Nash expected, an enthusiastic and grateful Bill accepted the offer, and Nash knew they'd both benefit by the change. With someone else in the office who had a stake in things, the solo stress Nash carried around with him was already easing.

An hour later, Kelly called and asked him to come over immediately. She wasn't prone to hysterics, but she did sound extremely wound up, so he dropped everything he was working on and drove over to Richard's office.

As soon as he stepped inside, he became hyperaware of Kelly; her scent, her essence, and of course the memories of what they'd done in that back room. He shook his head, reminding himself he wasn't here for sex, no matter how suddenly primed his body was.

"Kelly?" he called out.

"In the back."

He headed to the file room and found her waiting for him, her hand on a stack of legal files.

"What's wrong?" he asked.

She drummed her fingers on the stack of documents, then finally met his gaze. "Richard asked you to help out on anything I was doing in the office, right?"

"Right. Is there something you're having trouble with?" He took off his jacket and laid it over a stack of files.

She shook her head. "I've actually put current work on hold and I'm archiving old files."

He frowned. She couldn't possibly need his help on those.

"Some of these date back to the nineteen eighties."

"Okay," Nash said, still not sure where she was headed or why he was here.

She drew a deep breath, her nervousness contagious and his palms began to sweat.

"Let's say that I wasn't comfortable handing you a set of files to look at for no reason connected to any current case," Kelly said as if posing a hypothetical.

Lawyers were used to hearing those "what if" situations all the time, but that didn't ease his sudden anxiety.

"But," she continued, "if I were to need your help getting through all these case files, that would be different. And if, while helping me, you happened to read through this top file to make sure everything was in order, that would be in the regular course of doing business."

He glanced from her worried eyes to that file folder she hadn't taken her hand off of. There was something in there she wanted him to see but was obviously worried about violating confidentiality.

"Am I right?" she asked.

He nodded, recognizing that she was leading him to something important without actually handing him the information. "Whatever is in that file and how I came by it would never come back to bite you," he promised her, his heart beating faster, though he was still in the dark about the contents.

She blew out a deep breath. "Okay. So I'm going to step out and take a break. But I'll be in the other room if you need me." She eased closer and placed her hand against his cheek. "And I think you're going to need me," she whispered, before walking out.

More than a little uneasy and way beyond being merely curious, he picked up the folder she'd been touching and settled into a chair.

A quick glance informed him the main folder was labeled with his last name, and his stomach churned, agitated, as he opened to the first page. Ethan's arrest and court information stared back at him. The legal disposition of his brother's case followed. Subsequent letters and notes stapled together indicated Richard had reached out to Ethan after his release, offering to help get him settled with his brothers, find a job, and so on. But Ethan had left town and, as Nash knew too well, he and Dare became wards of the state. There was more paperwork about that too.

He flipped through some more useless information and then came the Rossman's application to be foster parents. Nash changed from scanning to reading more carefully. Each parent had to fill out an application, and Florence's came first in her familiar flowery script. She detailed why she wanted to be a foster parent, what she thought she could provide for a child, and then at the bottom, she requested specifically to be made a foster mother to *both Andrew (Dare) and Nash Barron.*

Nash blinked and read those words again, but they didn't change with any subsequent read. Florence had asked for both of them. His breathing now rapid and uneven, Nash flipped to Samuel's letter, his gaze immediately heading for the bottom part. Sure enough, he too asked to be made a foster parent to *both* Nash and Dare.

"I don't get it," he muttered.

He clearly remembered Richard coming to see him at a friend's house, where Nash had been staying in the initial days after his parents' deaths and Ethan's departure. Dare had gone to one of his friends' homes as well. Richard had sat Nash down and explained about the Rossmans and how they wanted to be his foster parents.

"What about Dare?" he'd asked, trying to be brave in front of Richard, who back then he'd viewed as a big bear of a man who seemed decent but who Nash didn't know at all.

"There's another special family who wants Dare," Richard had explained.

"But why can't the people taking me take him too?" Nash had persisted.

Richard's smile had been forced. Even a sixteen-year-old Nash had recognized that.

"Sometimes people only have enough room in their hearts for one child," Richard said.

Nash remembered those words because when he'd walked into the Rossmans' huge home, only a small suitcase in his hand, he'd immediately wondered why the two people welcoming him didn't have room in their hearts for his younger brother when they surely had rooms in their gigantic house.

Nauseous now, Nash kept flipping through the pages. There was information on the Garcias who'd taken Dare in and other papers that barely held Nash's interest.

All he could focus on now was the fact that Florence and Samuel had wanted both brothers, despite the fact that he'd been told otherwise for the last ten years.

Lies and omissions, Nash thought, disgusted and angry. *When will they end?*

Twelve

Kelly paced the small width of her office, wondering how Nash was taking the news, whether she should check on him or leave him alone to digest the information. The Rossmans had wanted to take Dare too? Even she couldn't process the fact, given what she knew of the Barron brothers' history.

When she heard what sounded like Nash's foot connecting with the metal trash can, she decided it was time to go back inside.

Steeling herself, she walked into the file room. "Nash?"

He turned toward her, his face a confused and angry mask. He didn't speak or move a muscle, maintaining a stony silence.

She rubbed her hands together, uncomfortable and uncertain of what to say. She settled for "I'm sorry, but I thought you should know."

She thought she saw a flash of gratitude

in his eyes. Just as quickly any emotion was gone. "You're the only one who thought I should know. Richard and the Rossmans lied to my face for ten years. They'd be happy to keep lying," he muttered, his voice raw, the depths of the betrayal he was experiencing painful to hear. "So the million-dollar question is, *why?*" he asked, meeting her gaze.

A rhetorical question, they both knew.

"Are you going to tell Dare?" she asked.

He shook his head. "Not until I know more. He's been through enough," he said, looking out for his younger brother as he always had.

Kelly smiled. She hoped Dare knew how lucky he was to be protected by this man. His loyalty and need to protect those he cared about ran so deep, he should have been the cop in the family. *A good, solid man,* she thought, not for the first time.

Yet Annie had given him up. In fact, his protective streak was the main reason she'd left. Kelly shook her head, accepting for the first time that *she* wouldn't be the one to walk away first. Her feelings for him were too strong and way more than she wanted to look into now.

"What?" His voice recaptured her attention.

"Nothing." If she wasn't ready to delve deeply within herself, she wasn't going to do it with him. Especially not now when his world had just shifted beneath him.

He narrowed his gaze. "You just shook your head like you thought of something."

She forgot how well he read her. "I was just thinking it's too bad you can't talk to Richard right now. He'd be the most logical, not to mention the least emotional person, you could question."

He straightened his shoulders. "And when he's up to a heated conversation, that'll be my first stop." Nash picked up his jacket from where he'd placed it earlier.

"Where are you going?"

"To talk to Florence."

At the mention of the woman who'd seemed so soft and caring, who so clearly loved Nash like any son she'd given birth to, Kelly felt a moment's panic. A muscle ticked in Nash's jaw and an accompanying vein throbbed in his left temple.

She ran her tongue over her dry lips. "Maybe you should calm down first." Because from his jerky movements and the way tension radiated off him in palpable waves, his anger was very much at the surface and she didn't think he should go alone.

"No. I've waited long enough for answers."

"Then I'll come with you."

"No."

The harsh word stopped her cold and nearly froze her heart. She instructed herself not to take it personally. She was the only target available to him at the moment.

She took a tentative step forward, but he ignored the overture and shrugged into his jacket, a determined look on his face.

"This is my problem. I lived their lie alone for years. I'll face it the same way." Each sentence came out clipped and biting.

"Fine," she said, not meaning it at all but knowing she couldn't stop him. "Go ahead. Talk to your mother. To Florence." She waved an arm, dismissing him.

As he spun around and stormed out, Kelly bit back the urge to tell him to go easy on Florence Rossman.

Without the facts, Kelly didn't know if the other woman deserved easy.

She stared out the doorway and her gaze fell to the file spread open on the table. What a mess. She still believed she'd done the right thing by leading Nash to the truth about his past. She only hoped she hadn't destroyed him.

He needed someone there for him, someone who understood. He clearly didn't want

her right now and Dare was still in the dark. Which left one person who just might be able to reach past Nash's anger and help him cope.

Hoping to God she was doing the right thing, Kelly picked up the phone.

"Why is it once you come home from vacation it feels like you were never away?" Ethan Barron asked his wife of a little more than a week.

Faith was in the walk-in closet of their bedroom and he wasn't sure if she even heard the question. That was okay. He only wanted a few minutes to think about anything and everything except the call he'd just received. A call that had dragged up the years he'd tried to put behind him and the truth, that he'd abandoned his brothers to a life of foster care, and the guilt that still ate away at him.

He'd much rather think about his wife. He still couldn't believe the girl he'd fantasized about when he was eighteen had actually married him. The bubbly cheerleader who'd lived in the mansion that to Ethan had represented everything he'd never have, believed in the man he'd become.

Ethan shook his head, knowing he'd just been handed the opportunity to step up and

be there for his siblings in a way he hadn't in the past.

"Who was on the phone?"

Faith stepped into the room and Ethan was immediately struck by her blond beauty and the intelligence behind those gorgeous eyes.

"C'mere."

He held out his arms and she stepped into his embrace, laying her head against his chest. "What's wrong?" she asked him.

He wasn't surprised she knew. Faith always knew what he needed, sometimes before he did.

"Kelly called. Nash just found out something that pretty much rocked the foundation of everything he was ever told about his past." Ethan went on to explain what Kelly told him about the documents in Richard Kane's office and how Nash had headed over to his adoptive mother for answers. "Kelly's worried about him. She said he wouldn't go to Dare with the news until he had more information, but she doesn't think he should be alone."

"She's right." Faith tipped her head back and met his gaze. "You know Nash and I didn't get along at first . . ."

"You're getting along now?" he asked sarcastically. They both knew Ethan had made a small inroad with Nash at the welcome-home party. Small was better than nothing and a hell of a lot more of an opening than he'd given Ethan before.

"Funny." Faith chuckled. "But I see how hard he tries with Tess, and even if I think his attitude stinks, I understand where he's coming from, and not just with you."

"He doesn't have the right to blame you for your father's crimes," Ethan said, his body going taut at the reminder of how Nash treated Faith.

"Well, his adoptive father had a heart attack and died not long after they lost a huge chunk of money in my dad's Ponzi scheme. And as a lawyer, he personally heard the stories of so many people who lost even more than the Rossmans. And he's been coming around."

"Sort of," Ethan muttered.

"Which is better than not at all." She rose up and kissed him on the lips.

Of course she thought just like him. "I'll go find him," Ethan said on a groan.

"You should. But while you're at it, don't beat yourself up for the past or things you can't change. You've come to terms with yourself. Don't let Nash bring you back to that dark place," Faith warned him.

He shook his head, amazed as always by

her wisdom and insight. "You know the irony of it all, right? Since I came back here, all I wanted was a chance to be there for my brothers, to make it up to them."

"And now you have that chance," she said, too brightly.

"Yeah." The opportunity to face down his demons, the mistakes he'd made and what his decisions had cost the brothers he loved.

What Ethan couldn't admit out loud was the ironic and scary truth. Now that he had the opportunity he'd craved, Ethan didn't know if he had it in him to be the brother they needed.

Nash spent twenty minutes driving around, attempting to calm down before confronting his adoptive mother. He needed to remember that the Rossmans had taken him into their home, given him clothes, food, an education that exceeded anything in his wildest dreams, and most important, love.

But the relationship had been built on lies.

He pulled up to the house, parking his car at the same time a black car parked on the street behind him. He climbed out and realized it was his brother's Jag.

"Ethan," Nash muttered, greeting his brother as he exited the vehicle. "What the hell are you doing here?"

"Saving you from yourself."

"Kelly called you," he said flatly.

"She's worried about you."

He would've expected anger that she'd sent Ethan after him. Ethan, of all people. "I know she is," he said instead. No anger at Kelly to be found. He figured it was all burning in his gut, directed at Florence and Richard. "You know everything?"

Ethan nodded.

"Fine. I'm going in to talk to her."

"I'm coming with you."

Nash cocked an eyebrow. "Playing backup in case I need you, big brother?"

"It's about time, don't you think?" Ethan shoved his hands into the pockets of his leather jacket, his steely gaze hidden behind his sunglasses.

Nash didn't reply, brushing past him and heading up the long drive. He had enough on his mind without adding his baggage related to Ethan to the mix. Odd thing was, having Ethan behind him didn't feel like baggage as much as . . . support.

Nash rang the doorbell and Florence answered. "Nash, what are you doing here?" she asked, sounding surprised but looking pleased.

"I need to talk to you."

"Of course. Come in." She glanced beyond him, seeing Ethan for the first time and her eyes widened in surprise.

As far as Nash knew, Ethan and Florence Rossman had never met. Their social circles wouldn't have crossed, he thought wryly.

"This is my brother Ethan," Nash said by way of introduction. "Ethan, this is my . . . This is Florence Rossman."

Ethan stepped closer to the open door. "Nice to meet you," he said, extending his hand.

Florence accepted the gesture. "To what do I owe the pleasure?" she asked, her confused gaze darting between them both.

"I need answers," Nash said, his voice rough with the anger he couldn't shake.

"I see," she said, but she was clearly confused.

"He does need answers. But first I'd like to thank you," Ethan said, surprising Nash. "For being there for my brother when I cou— when I wasn't."

In that brief instant, Nash saw the man his brother had become, and whatever walls remained crumbled to dust inside of him. Suddenly he wanted to know where Ethan had been all these years, what he'd lived through, and how he'd come out the other side.

But first . . . "Can we come in?" Nash asked.

Florence nodded. "Ethan, it was my pleasure, I assure you. Come," she said, and gestured for them to enter.

Nash found himself seated in the same family room he'd been in the other night with Kelly. This time his focus was different. His gaze fell to the row of pictures on the window sill behind him.

Ethan followed his line of vision, his lips turning upward in a grin. He strode over and picked up a photo. "Is this graduation?"

"High school, college, and law school," Florence said proudly, her fingers grazing lovingly over one picture at a time.

Nash could've done without the caps and gowns, but each represented a milestone in his life, one that wouldn't have been possible without the woman standing beside him.

"Why didn't you take Dare too?" Nash blurted out, unable to hold in the question any longer. And giving Florence one last chance to tell him the truth before he had to call her on the lie.

She stepped back unsteadily, her hand going to her throat. "Oh! I —"

"She didn't expect the question, Nash. Let's sit," Ethan suggested. He placed a guiding hand on the older woman's back and led her to the couch, where she eased herself down slowly.

His brother might want to give her a moment to compose herself but Nash burned with the need to understand. "Well?" he asked, his stare boring into hers.

"Some people . . . some couples . . . aren't equipped to have two children."

Some people only have enough room in their hearts for one child.

She was feeding him the same version of Richard's tale, Nash thought, both disappointed and disgusted. And he was no longer buying it.

"No more lies." His voice rose an uncomfortable notch. "I saw the original adoption request. You asked for us both."

Florence trembled, obviously stunned.

But Nash wasn't finished. He wouldn't be, not until he had the truth. "You wanted Dare too, so why the hell didn't you take him? Why did he end up in an overcrowded foster home on the other side of town?"

The years of sneaking food into his backpack for Dare, of making excuses for his missing clothes, came back to him, and Nash slammed his hand on the wood table in frustration.

Florence jumped, recoiling in horror.

Ethan shot Nash a warning glare.

"It's true," she said at last. "We wanted you both." She glanced down at her hands as she spoke, obviously searching for the right words to make him understand.

He wasn't convinced he ever would.

"Your father and I, we'd just lost Stuart." Her voice broke on her son's name. "He died when he was sixteen," she explained to Ethan. "Long story, but when we decided the house was empty and needed teenagers running around, we put in for both of you boys."

"Then why wasn't he here?"

Florence raised her bowed head to meet Nash's gaze. "You'll have to ask your brother that question."

Nash's gaze swung to Ethan before he realized Florence meant Dare. "Dare knows you wanted him?"

Of all the things she could have said, that possibility hadn't crossed his mind. The words, the news, blind-sided him.

Ethan remained coiled and silent behind Florence, listening and taking in every word.

Florence drew a deep breath and nodded. "We were told he refused to come. And though the state could have forced him, given the . . . circumstances . . . it was probably best that they didn't press the issue."

"Circumstances?" he asked sarcastically. "Is that the best you can do?"

"It's not my story to tell," Florence insisted. Eyes wide and moist, she spread her hands out in front of her, imploring him to understand. "But we wanted him too. Even after we found out why he didn't . . . wouldn't . . . come."

Nash could barely think or feel. His heart pounded so hard in his chest, unspeakable anger and frustration at still not knowing everything eating away at him.

The idea that Dare had the answers . . . Nash couldn't fathom it.

He couldn't.

"And how do you justify lying to me all these years?" Nash asked in a clipped tone.

"You have to remember where you were emotionally and what you were going through at the time. You'd just lost both parents in the blink of an eye. You'd been abandoned by your oldest brother." Her apologetic gaze shot to Ethan. "You were reeling and angry. You had one thing, one person you trusted, and that was Dare."

Florence rose. She walked to the small desk in the corner, pulled a tissue from a hidden box, and blotted her eyes.

Nash knew he ought to stop pushing and let her take her time, but he couldn't. He'd waited too long for answers.

Florence returned to her seat and met his gaze, crumpled tissue still in her hand. "Dare was young, but he had his reasons for not wanting to live with us. Here." She swept her hand around the room. "Richard and the social workers insisted he'd be better off if we didn't press the issue."

"And I still don't understand why you didn't just tell me the truth."

She shook her head. "Given how much you'd been through, if we'd told you that your brother wouldn't come live with you, we knew you'd be hurt. Furious enough to explode or turn your back on him in anger. *And we didn't want you to lose the only family member you had left.*"

Her words knocked some of his righteous anger down a peg. Barely.

A glance at Ethan told Nash he wasn't taking this story any better than Nash. Firsthand knowledge of the pain and destruction he'd left in his wake must be killing him, Nash thought, somehow able to see his brother's pain for the first time.

"I need to talk to Dare," Nash said.

Florence, the woman he'd called *Mom* when he was in this house, and referred to as *adoptive mother* when he was with Dare, held out a hand. He'd spent his entire life feeling torn in two, split by the life before his parents' deaths and the one after. Ridden with guilt that he'd been lucky enough to live here while Dare had been sent to the poverty-stricken Garcia family. Ripped apart by the gratitude he felt toward the Rossmans and his hatred for them for not taking his brother too.

And that's when he realized — they'd been willing to shoulder the lie, the burden, *his* anger, just so Nash could have a relationship with his only remaining sibling at the time.

Maybe they'd been misguided. They sure as hell should have told him and allowed him to make his own choices, but they'd acted in what they thought was his best interest.

They were his second set of parents and they loved him. It would take him a long time to forgive, but his anger wasn't clouding his emotions.

He reached out and placed his hand inside hers to tell her he understood what she'd done, at least a little. When he was finished with his adoptive mother, he headed out.

His next stop would be Dare. The last person he'd expected to have answers. The person Nash thought he'd have to break this news to. Because the brother he thought he knew best was now the brother he didn't know at all.

"If you keep pacing, I'm going to have to replace the carpet," Faith Harrington Barron said to Kelly, who'd shown up on her doorstep and hadn't stopped pacing since.

Kelly had hoped that Faith had heard from Ethan, but she hadn't. Knowing how many emotional land mines lay ahead of the Barron brothers, Faith didn't expect him to call soon. Or at all. He might just come home after he'd tried to help Nash, however long that might take.

"Sorry." Kelly stopped in the middle of the large family room, Faith's favorite room in the house, which she herself had decorated.

"Relax. I'm joking," Faith told the uptight other woman. "Ethan and Nash have a complicated family history. Now Nash has to deal with his adoptive mother and then tell Dare. It's not going to work itself out in five minutes."

With a prolonged sigh, Kelly flopped onto the sofa. "Something tells me it may not work itself out at all."

Faith narrowed her gaze. That was a negative attitude neither of them should entertain. "What makes you say that?"

"Other than Nash's intractable views on lying and betrayal?" Kelly jumped up and started pacing again.

She wore a matching set of sweatpants and jacket and she kept rubbing her hands over the velour on the arms. Soon she'd wear out that fabric too. Faith knew how important this revelation was to Nash. She also knew how hard it was for Ethan to track his brother down and insist on being there to support him — whether wanted or not. But she wasn't wearing a hole in the carpet or her clothing.

And she was married to one of the men involved. "Umm, Kelly?" Faith asked.

"Yes?"

"Why do I have a feeling there's more going on in your head than I know about?"

Kelly met her gaze. "Am I that obvious?" She groaned. "Who am I kidding? Of course I am."

"Let's start with this. You're in love with Nash, aren't you?"

A shocked look passed over Kelly's face. Then to Faith's horror, Kelly burst into tears.

Faith blinked, rose, and wrapped her arm around her, an unusual act, since Faith wasn't an overly demonstrative person with most other people. Except with Ethan. Then she couldn't keep her hands off.

"Tell me everything," Faith said.

Kelly obliged, revealing her entire past and future fears to Faith, who found herself grateful she was a happily married woman with all the uncertainty of the beginning of a relationship behind her.

She wished she could reassure Kelly that Nash would understand why she hadn't told him about her past, or that he'd get over whatever was being revealed this afternoon. But she couldn't. Faith barely understood Nash Barron. In her humble opinion, she'd landed the more simple of those two Barron brothers, and considering Ethan's own complexity, that was saying a lot.

Kelly finally pulled herself together. "Sorry. I've been holding in a lot of things. You didn't need me to fall apart on you."

Faith shook her head. "What do you think family is for?" Ironically, it was Ethan who had taught her the value of that.

Kelly looked up through damp lashes. "I have no idea."

"Considering the whole reason we met at all was because you did what was best for Tess, I beg to differ."

Kelly smiled. "Thanks for that. As far as Nash is concerned, I know him. No matter how good or bad today ends up, he won't get over it quickly. And I can't choose now to unburden myself. It would be selfish. He needs a clear head to focus on his brothers. That's more important than what I want or need."

It didn't escape Faith's notice that Kelly hadn't answered her question about being in love with Nash. Not overtly, anyway. But any woman who cared so much that she'd put what she thought was best for a man before her own concerns was definitely in love.

Even if she hadn't yet admitted it to herself.

Nash stormed out and headed for his car, Ethan following behind him. He expected his brother to climb into his expensive Jag and follow him to find Dare, but instead Ethan came up beside the passenger's side of Nash's car.

"What the hell do you think you're doing?"

"Coming with you."

Nash raised an eyebrow. Unwilling to waste time arguing, Nash shrugged. "Suit yourself."

Soon they were driving toward Nash's condo. "He'd better be home."

"She loves you," Ethan said into the silence.

Nash guessed it was too much to hope they'd make the trip in silence. "Yeah."

"You got lucky."

"And I've spent the last ten years feeling guilty that I did while Dare went to poverty row." Had his brother really made that choice? And if so *why?*

"Maybe he had his reasons," Ethan said of Dare. "Just like I had mine."

Nash gripped his fingers tighter around the steering wheel. "What were yours?" he found himself asking.

If today was a day of revelations, he might as well hear them all.

Ethan pushed the car seat back, stretching out as he spoke, his voice low and raw. "I hated myself and couldn't see beyond it. I'd been responsible for our parents being on the road that night, for them being killed by a drunk driver. I was eighteen and fucked up and I couldn't see past my own pain. I ran away like a coward."

Nash swallowed over the lump in his throat. He'd hated his older brother for as long as he could remember, but not once had he considered that Ethan had hated himself too. He remembered Ethan saying something similar during their first confrontation, after they'd found out about Tess, but Nash couldn't hear anything over the angry roar in his ears. The same buzz he'd heard every time he thought about Ethan over the years.

He listened now, though, clenching the wheel, torn between still-righteous anger at his sibling and understanding that at eighteen, Ethan hadn't been capable of making the right decisions.

"I should've manned up and stayed."

For the first time, Nash wanted to say more than his standard *You damn well should have.* "You can't change the past." It was all he could manage at the moment.

"No. But I wish I could. And whatever Dare's reasons, maybe he wishes the same thing."

Nash barely took in downtown Serendipity as he drove past, his thoughts on Dare and the betrayal that sat like lead in his stomach.

"Even if that's true, he's kept the truth from me for years. At least you weren't here facing me day in and day out. He knows how hard it was for me to accept all that the Rossmans offered" — including and most especially their love — "and all because I thought they deliberately withheld the same from him."

Ethan remained silent. Obviously even he couldn't come up with a response to that one.

"I ran away twice," Nash said, slowing the car down the closer they came to his condo. There were things he needed to say before he dealt with Dare.

Ethan obviously understood because he waited, his dark gaze on him.

"I couldn't accept so much when he had so little. I wanted to go with him to the Garcias'. To look out for him."

"Like I should've been looking out for both of you," Ethan said.

This time, Nash didn't know what to say to *that.* "When the cops brought me back to the Rossmans that last time, I knew I had to come up with a better alternative. I snuck him clothes and food. I thought I was so smart, getting away with it all."

"You think the Rossmans knew all along?" Ethan asked.

He hadn't, but now . . . "Yeah. They couldn't possibly believe I'd left my jeans in my gym locker or that I didn't know what happened. Not to mention the food that I took from the kitchen." Nash felt like an idiot,

"You did right by Dare," Ethan told him.

Nash laughed aloud. "So right I even

asked Richard Kane to keep an eye on Dare and on the Garcia house. He looked me in the eye and promised. I *trusted* him and he was lying to me too."

He'd finally reached the condo. Dare's car was parked in the extra spot outside.

"Ready?" Ethan asked.

Nash wished he could say yes, that he was prepared. But he wasn't. All he wanted was for his brother to tell him the paperwork was wrong, that Florence was making up stories, and Dare, the brother he'd devoted his life to protecting, hadn't lied and betrayed him.

Since that wasn't about to happen, he figured yeah, he was ready, because really how much worse could things get? Dare would confirm Florence's story, come up with an explanation Nash couldn't begin to fathom or understand, but the end result would still be the same.

Nash didn't know who his younger brother was. He never had. And that meant the world as he'd known it was gone forever.

Thirteen

Nash used his key and let himself inside his town house. Ethan, his shadow for the last hour, stuck close behind him. He stepped into his own home, on edge.

"Dare!" Nash shouted.

"In here."

Nash headed toward the sound of his brother's voice and strode into the den only to find Dare waiting for him, suitcase packed. He was still dressed in his uniform, obviously having just gotten off duty.

"Faith called," Dare said, before Nash could ask how he'd been prepared.

Nash glanced over his shoulder and glared at Ethan, who merely shrugged. Nash turned his attention back to his younger brother.

"So, you aren't going to tell me it's all one big mistake?" he asked, pointing to the packed bag, a sure-fire indicator Dare didn't think he'd be welcome here much longer.

Unlike his brother, Nash hadn't thought things through to its conclusion, and that Dare would move out over an argument turned Nash's stomach. For so long it had been Nash and Dare against the world, and he stared at his sibling now, willing him to make today's revelations go away.

Instead, Dare shook his head. "I wish I could." With his eyes so serious, Nash caught a glimpse of their mother. He hadn't thought of her in a while, rarely let himself revisit the years they'd been a family.

Fuck, Nash thought. Hating the jumble of emotions inside him, Nash got into Dare's face. *"Why?"*

Nobody in the room needed him to elaborate.

Dare jerked away and headed for the window, staring out, his back to Nash and Ethan. He was silent so long, Nash wondered if he'd ever answer.

"I couldn't live with them," Dare said at last. "I couldn't look the Rossmans in the eye day in and day out, knowing what I'd done." He shoved his hands into the back pockets of his pants and turned around. "Or should I say what I didn't do."

Nash set his jaw. He was finished with people talking in circles, not getting to the point. "Explain," he gritted out.

"The day the Rossmans' kid died at that party? I cut school. I was *there.*"

Nash did the math in his head. Stuart Rossman died about eight months before his own parents. The Rossmans were still grieving when they'd taken Nash in, having read about his situation in the paper and heard about him from Richard.

"You were all of what — fifteen?" Ethan asked, shock in his voice. "What the hell were you doing at an upperclassman party?"

"Following in the steps of my big brother," Dare shot back. He cocked his head to the side, meeting Ethan's stunned expression. "Cutting class, hanging out with older kids, and starting to drink. Because you did it. And because it was cool."

"I had no idea," Ethan muttered. Shoulders down, Ethan lowered himself into Nash's favorite leather club chair.

"Me neither," Nash agreed.

Dare shrugged. "It's not like you signed on to be my parents. And at that point Mom and Dad weren't paying all that much attention to me either." He clenched and unclenched his fists, his tension obvious.

"What happened?" Ethan asked, sounding calmer while Nash's stomach still cramped badly.

Dare propped a shoulder against the wall.

At this point, Nash figured he needed the support.

"The party was on the rich side of town. Everyone was out on the back porch of Brian McKnight's house. His parents were away on vacation. Somehow the party ended up an ugly mix of haves and have-nots. Public and private school. Add alcohol and you know the rest. There was a fight. McKnight threw the first punch at Stuart Rossman."

"Where was I that day?" Ethan asked.

"You went to school." Dare laughed, the irony in that one statement clear. "You had a test, then got out early, and took some girl over to the lake to make out. I remember because if you were going, no way would I have had the guts to show up."

Dare shook his head at the memory and Nash supposed there wasn't anything about that day his brother had forgotten. Silence descended on them, neither of the brothers speaking for a long while, each lost in their own thoughts.

"Might as well finish the story," Ethan said finally.

Dare cleared his throat. "Stuart was drunk enough that one hit took him down and his head cracked against the patio." Dare winced as if hearing the sound. "Blood was everywhere," he said, his eyes dark and unfocused.

Nausea filled Nash and he wondered how a fifteen-year-old had borne the burden of what he'd seen.

Back then, Nash had been a typical teenager, consumed with his own problems, not his younger brother's. He would've barely noticed if Dare's behavior changed. He hadn't been anyone's keeper. Not until his parents' deaths and Ethan's disappearance, when Nash stepped up, determined to be the man his older brother couldn't or wouldn't be.

"Everyone in the house panicked," Dare continued. "Either you were friends of McKnight's and stayed to clean up and get rid of the alcohol and evidence or you were from downtown and ran."

"Nobody called the cops," Ethan said. It was a statement, not a question.

Dare shook his head. "The newspaper said a bunch of his *friends* tossed him into their car and dumped him outside the hospital before speeding off."

"Some friends," Nash muttered.

"And nobody knew you were there? No one reported your name to the cops?" Ethan spoke again.

"It was one of those 'someone heard

there's a party, so let's crash' situations. Nobody knew anyone's name. The private school kids came from neighboring towns. We didn't know them and they didn't know us."

Ethan leaned back in his seat, eyeing his sibling. "You ran, came home, and never talked about it again?"

He continued to lead the conversation, being the adult, the leader of the family at last.

"Pretty much."

Dare glanced down, his shame so obvious, Nash wondered how he'd missed it for years.

"I buried it deep. I told myself I was going to be the happy kid nobody could ever tie to the tragedy."

The lighter brother, Nash had always thought. What a crock, he realized now. But Dare's reasons made sense. Dare's coping mechanism, pretending to be the happiest brother, had been a bizarre, opposite reaction to a dark, ugly situation.

And nobody had realized.

Nobody had noticed.

"And then our parents died and the Rossmans wanted to take us in." The sound of his own voice caught Nash by surprise.

Dare let out a long, harsh breath. "I

couldn't go. I couldn't live with them knowing that I hadn't done anything to help Stuart. But I thought that once they knew what had happened, they wouldn't want me anyway. So I told Richard Kane the truth and he told them." He blinked hard. "And damned if they didn't offer to take me anyway," he said, his amazement still obvious after all this time.

Nash already knew how generous Florence and Samuel were. He was now just understanding how big their hearts were.

But one question still remained. Haunted him. "Why the hell didn't you tell me?" Nash asked Dare.

Because of everything he'd learned today, that reality wounded him most. It was, he thought, the thing he might never get past. That his baby brother hadn't trusted him and had kept him in the dark for years.

Regret flashed across Dare's face along with something deeper and much darker. "That day changed me. I was only fifteen but I felt ages older."

Suddenly Nash remembered how sometimes he'd catch that same dark look on his brother's face and wonder . . . Only to look again, but all traces would be gone, replaced by Dare's normal, easygoing manner.

And now he understood what he'd been

seeing, if only for a split second.

"Look, I knew that telling you would screw up any chance you had with a decent family, a good life. As it was, you ran away from that house twice. If you knew what I'd been through, there's no way you would have stayed."

"So you decided to hide the truth. Just like Florence and Samuel decided to hide the truth." His voice rose. "Everyone thought they knew what was best for me, but nobody once thought to ask me what I thought. What I wanted."

Anger, the same anger fueling him all day, came raging back, full force, no longer dulled by the pain Dare had experienced but made sharper by his own sense of helplessness over having his choices taken away from him.

"Everyone did what they thought was right. I did what I thought was right," Dare insisted.

"You had no right." Nash poked his brother in the chest hard.

Ethan rose and placed himself between them. "We all did what we felt was best at the time."

"This is rich. News flash! You all did what was best for *yourselves.* Goddamn selfish bastards," he shouted at them. Blood rushed in his ears, his heartbeat pounded harder in his chest. "Get the hell out. Both of you." Nash pointed to the front door.

Ethan and Dare shared a glance.

Then they nodded and walked out.

Kelly headed home and waited, hoping to hear from Nash. Morning turned to early afternoon and then to evening without a word. From Ethan, Kelly already knew the highlights of the day and she understood Nash probably needed time alone to deal with all he'd learned.

By eight that night, she gave in and dialed his number, but her call went straight to voice mail. Unable to stand the waiting and worrying, she drove over to his house. His car was in the driveway.

She rang the bell and knocked, but he didn't answer, so she turned the doorknob.

Unlocked.

Drawing a deep breath, she let herself inside. And found Nash in the den. He was wearing unbuttoned jeans and a wrinkled shirt, and he lounged in a chair, a half-empty bottle of Jack Daniel's on the table beside him, a full glass in his hand.

"Is it too much to hope that bottle was half empty before you got started?" Kelly asked.

He turned, startled. His glassy eyes widened in surprise as he looked at her. "What are you doing here?"

"What do you think?" she asked, striding up to him and taking the bottle away.

He treated her to a grin. "Worried about me?" he asked.

"Should I be?"

"No." He rose from his seat and stood, steadier than she would have thought he'd be. "I can take care of myself."

She propped her hands on her hips. "I never said you couldn't."

"Nobody else thinks I can." He stared into the amber-colored liquid in his glass.

She understood the sentiment behind his words. She even got why he'd turned to alcohol. But his pity party was over. Kelly snatched the glass out of his hands before he could indulge further and walked out of the room.

"Hey! Where are you going with that?" he called out.

"To make you some coffee." At least she hoped he had coffee here because he obviously needed it. She placed the bottle and the glass into the sink.

Before she could turn, Nash surrounded her from behind. He bracketed his body against hers and wrapped his arms around her waist. He was big and overpowering and so male that heat enveloped her. Arousal rushed through her, thrumming in her veins. The erection pressing insistently against her back told her he wanted her too.

But the hint of alcohol on his breath reminded her that he was in pain. He needed more than sex to make him feel better, and she needed to tell him as much.

Before she could speak, he buried his face between her neck and shoulders, his warm mouth nibbling at her sensitive skin until she shivered.

"Nash," she said, trying to remain the rational one.

"Mmm." He nipped at her shoulder and her nipples peaked beneath her shirt.

"You need to talk about what happened."

He let out a low growl of disagreement. "What I need is not to think."

Without warning, he spun her around, her back to the counter, his hips aligned with hers, and his hard length pulsing against his jeans, pressing into her stomach. Delicious waves rushed over her and she swallowed hard.

She braced her hands on his shoulders, intending to push him away. Insist that they talk.

"You're not going to deny me the chance

to feel better, are you?" he asked gruffly, only partially teasing, she knew.

She looked into his wounded eyes and at that moment, she knew. Faith had been right. Kelly loved Nash.

She loved him.

Her throat filled and she fought back a tidal wave of emotion. "No, I'm not going to deny you," she whispered, wrapping her arms around his neck and sealing her lips against his.

With a groan, he thrust his fingers into her hair and kissed her like he was starving and couldn't get enough. Like he needed her for far more reasons than to just feel better. And because she loved him, really loved him, she gave him everything he needed. Of course what he needed was exactly what she wanted too.

Next thing she knew, he broke the kiss. "Wrap your legs around me," he ordered.

She jumped up and he lifted her so she could lock her legs around his waist. Then he headed for the dark bedroom. He deposited her on the mattress and stared down at her, his gaze consuming her.

"The clothes have to go," he said.

Kelly agreed. She lifted her shirt up and over her head, conscious that she'd changed into sweats and a T-shirt earlier. No bra.

His eyes darkened to a stormy haze and every nerve in her body tightened with need.

Next she hooked her thumbs in the waistband of her sweats and pulled them down, making sure to take her panties along with them.

Finally she lay naked, legs dangling off the bed, her arms over her head. "Happy now?" she asked.

A muscle worked in his jaw. "Getting there," he said, as he stripped off his shirt followed by the rest of his clothes. "Are *you* happy now?" he asked.

Unable to take her eyes off him, naked and erect, all she could manage was a nod.

"You told me earlier I was going to need you." Nash placed his hands on her legs. "You were right."

Palms hot, he branded her with his touch and liquid heat trickled between her thighs. It was all she could do not to twist and moan and beg him to stop talking, to fill her and never stop. But his needs came first tonight and she bit down on the inside of her cheek, determined to lie silently and let him take as long as he wanted. Even if her body was coiled tight with need.

He spread her legs and leaned over her until the head of his hard penis teased her moist center. Stars flickered in front of her eyes and she arched her hips, trying to pull him inside her.

His gaze intense and never wavering, he thrust deeply, filling her completely. She felt him everywhere, not just in her body but in her heart and also her soul. She'd admitted her feelings to herself and now she was ravaged by them, emotions clogging her throat. And when he started to move, oh God, she was undone.

"Nash, harder please." She needed to feel him everywhere.

He complied. Every shift of his hips brought him deeper and she was drowning, lost in sensation and in watching his expression, wanting so badly to believe the emotions and feelings were shared.

Nash gazed down at Kelly, her beautiful body spread out before him. His position gave him leverage and power and he used it, manipulating her pleasure. From how fast he pumped into her to how much of him filled her, he was in control — and that was something he needed badly. But he'd underestimated her effect on him and soon, his control snapped, no match for being cushioned in her moist heat, her inner walls squeezing him tight.

A quick shift and he separated them long enough to ease her farther back so he could join her on the bed. Straddling her with his body, he placed his hands on either side of her head and came down on top of her. Skin to skin, hot flesh touching hot flesh. *Now* he had the closeness he craved. That he could find it at all caused a sense of relief to wash over him, even as he demanded more. Back and forth, round and round, he shifted his hips against her, until finally he found her, pushing his slick member in with one hard, smooth thrust.

Kelly cried out and every hot inch of her contracted around him. Her nails dug into his shoulders and she bent her knees, taking him deeper.

He raised his head, looked into her eyes. What he saw in those brown depths went beyond just sex. He knew it. Felt it. Didn't know what to do with it.

"Just love me," Kelly said.

He hoped it was that simple. And when he began to move inside her, it was. He owned her with deep, hard thrusts that left no space between them, no barriers. No question that he was demanding everything she had to give and not holding back either.

She met his rhythm, accepted his need for hard and fast, grinding her body into him each time he plunged deep. Everything came down to the connection between their bodies until her small moans came faster and faster.

"That's it, sweetheart. Keep coming." He clenched his teeth and tried to hold himself off, wanting her to milk him, ride hers out as long as possible.

"God, Nash, please." Her voice echoed in his ear.

Her muscles pulled at him, urging him to join her, and he pumped his hips faster and faster until his world exploded.

A few minutes later, they'd shifted until they were beneath the covers and he pulled her into his arms, her back snuggled into him.

"Thanks for coming by," he said, feeling like she was the only safe haven he had in a world that had suddenly shifted beneath him.

"You'd have done the same for me," she said over a yawn.

"You sound sure."

She shrugged. "I am."

He pushed her hair out of the way and settled himself more comfortably against her. She had faith in him. "I had that kind of faith in Dare."

"You still can. He was just looking out for you."

Nash stiffened. "At the age of fifteen, I

understand. As we got older? What's his excuse for not telling me then?"

Kelly let out an almost painful sigh. "Sometimes the longer we wait, the harder it is to admit the truth. The right time never comes."

Nash gritted his teeth, so tired of everyone else thinking they knew what was best for him.

She rolled over, facing him, her eyes solemn and serious. "I'm so sorry for all you went through today." She brushed his cheek with her hand.

"It wiped me out," he admitted.

"Then we should stop talking and let you sleep."

He grabbed her hand and pressed a kiss against her wrist, pausing to run his tongue over her skin.

She shivered and her eyes darkened. "I thought you were tired."

"Mentally drained. I didn't say anything about being physically tired." He grinned and rolled her on top of him.

They didn't talk or sleep again for a good long while.

For the first few days after the revelation, Nash ignored everyone except for his office staff and new partner. Burying himself in work seemed the safest way to cut off his emotions and so he ignored everyone. Including Kelly.

In the beginning, his brothers had been persistent, but obviously they caught on and he hadn't heard from Ethan or Dare in a few days. Even Ethan's wife, the woman with whom he'd had a confrontational relationship from the moment she returned to town, had tried to get through to him. She'd had no family unit for so long that now that she was married to Ethan and understood the value of family, she wanted him to do the same. He wasn't ready.

The one person who could have gotten through to him was the only person who gave him space from day one. After spending the entire night losing himself in her, feeling as if she'd opened her veins and bled for him, giving him everything she had, he'd heard nothing since. Kelly, of everyone, understood. He'd needed that night and then he thought he'd needed solitude.

That he was wrong didn't negate the fact that she'd been in tune to exactly what he thought he wanted. But he'd realized he needed her. Desperately. And so from the third day on, he'd taken to showing up on her doorstep after work each day and not leaving until dawn, when he'd head home to shower and dress for work. She welcomed him with open arms, didn't force him to talk about anything in particular, just gave of herself when he needed it and provided company when he wanted to sit in silence. When the days got tough and he couldn't turn off his thoughts, he knew he'd have her to turn to at night. Her small apartment became a safe haven, a place where nobody tried to call or push him to come to terms with things before he was ready.

She just gave.

He'd have been happy to continue this routine forever, but real life intruded. Richard had been home from the hospital for a week. Two weeks in total had passed since his surgery. But since his return home, Nash hadn't been by to visit. Since there was no way he'd have been able to see Richard and hold back on questioning him, he'd waited until he thought Richard could handle it.

Today was the day.

Nash had been so busy thinking of himself and his problems, he hadn't thought about running into Annie at her parents', but sure enough, when he rang the bell, his ex-wife answered the door.

"Nash!" Annie seemed surprised to see him. She met his gaze for a brief second before looking away, an unusual blush staining her cheeks.

"Can I come in?" he asked. "Mary said Richard was up for a visit."

She nodded. "Of course you can."

He joined her in the foyer. She stood in front of him, twisting her hands together, obviously uncomfortable. He wasn't feeling much better himself.

He hadn't seen her since he'd caught Joe leaving her place, but she couldn't know that. Unless . . . "Kelly told you I saw Joe leaving your house last week, didn't she?"

Annie blinked, her pretty eyes showing her shock at his blunt question. "Well, yes. I didn't expect you to blurt it out like that."

"There's something to be said for honesty," he said. Heaven knew he'd had that lesson reinforced lately.

She nodded. "I would have told you if I'd seen you . . ."

He forced his tone and his expression to soften. He wasn't angry at her. "You don't owe me an explanation, Annie. Your social life is none of my business. But since we're getting everything out in the open, I'm with Kelly now," he admitted, unable to believe he and his ex-wife were discussing their love lives, even in a roundabout way.

Annie nodded. "I'm happy for you. Really happy. You deserve someone to love you the way I couldn't."

"I don't think . . ."

Love?

The word, the very thought, startled him. Nash hardly thought Kelly loved him. But a flash of her warm eyes and her open expression as she took him inside her body broadsided him, clogging his throat with emotion.

Annie grinned, watching him intently. "You'll figure it out," she said, patting his cheek.

"Do you love Joe?" he asked.

"It's all so fast. I was sick and he stayed to take care of me. And we're going out tonight."

He cocked his head to the side. "Everything you didn't want from me." He was surprised to find the truth didn't hurt the way it once had.

She spread her hands in front of her. "I don't know what to say. It's . . . different with Joe."

Just like it was different with Kelly, Nash thought. "I wish you nothing but the best. I just want you to be happy," he said to his ex, meaning every word.

"I want the same for you.

Her smile put him at ease, freed him from any remaining obligation he might have felt toward her. And he hoped he'd given her the same gift.

Now to deal with her father.

Fourteen

"Nash, my boy! Come on in." Richard beckoned him with his deep voice.

"Are you sure you're up to company?"

In bed, Richard held a large pillow in front of his chest. "I'm sure. I'm so bored I'm going out of my mind. Don't mind this pillow. In case I have to cough or sneeze, they tell me to hold it against my chest." He winced at the thought.

Nash stepped into the room and sat down in a chair Mary had put by the bed for visitors. He glanced around the room, decorated with sunny yellow walls and old wooden furniture before resettling his gaze on Richard.

"Good to be home?" Nash asked.

The older man let out a groan. "Better than you know. If only my wife would stop hovering," he said in a hushed tone, obviously not wanting to get caught.

"She's worried. You gave everyone a

scare." Nash included, and despite the gnawing ache and ever-present anger, he couldn't stop his love for the man from pushing through.

"I'll outlive you all," Richard promised. "Though I have to say when you face your mortality, it forces you to think about a lot of things." His voice along with his expression grew pensive.

Nash leaned forward, until his arms were almost touching the bed. "Things like lies told years ago?" he asked pointedly.

What little color Richard had drained from his face. "What exactly are you referring to?"

Nash dipped his head, wishing the older man wouldn't make him restate the facts. "That the Rossmans wanted Dare too. That he refused to live there and you all deliberately lied to me about it." Pain shot through his skull at the reminder.

Richard suddenly sucked in a shallow breath and began coughing, holding the pillow to his chest as he winced and groaned through the post-op pain.

Nash shook his head. "I should've waited to do this." He rose from his seat.

Annie had left after their talk, but Mary came running into the room. "What's wrong?"

Nash glanced at Richard's wife, knowing his guilt was probably obvious in his face. "I should have waited to come by. I'll just go now."

"No!" Richard said.

Mary wrinkled her forehead, confused. "I don't know what's going on, but I have a feeling Nash is right. Now's not the time."

"There's never been a good time, damn it!" Richard yelled. "I'm not putting this off any longer." He coughed again, probably due to the exertion of yelling.

Mary closed her eyes in frustration and shook her head. "I'll tell you what. If you can manage to talk softly, Nash can stay. Otherwise he goes and you do this in . . . oh, about four to six weeks."

Nash recognized the obstinate look on his ex-mother-in-law's face. He'd seen it often enough in her daughter's. Nash had just chosen to disregard her feelings instead of realizing that by ignoring her needs, he'd doomed their marriage. Of course it didn't help that though they'd been adults, they lacked the strong chemistry they'd now found with other people, he realized now.

"Richard?" Mary's voice brought Nash back to the present. "Do you promise to speak softly and not get upset?"

Richard forced a nod.

Nash understood. What else could the man do when faced with such a strong woman? God, he'd been so young and stupid when he'd been married.

"Nash?" Mary turned to him, her hands on her hips.

"I promise. I won't agitate him again." Though Nash wondered how either one of them would keep their word.

Mary shot them warning looks. "I'll be right in the other room," she said.

Nash waited until Mary had walked out before sitting back down. "I shouldn't have brought this up now."

"No, I shouldn't have waited so many years. I should have told you myself instead of letting you find out on your own." He paused to gather himself. "How?" he finally asked.

"The files Kelly's archiving have the original foster care application Florence and Samuel filled out." Nash glanced down at his hands, then up at Richard. "Now I have a question. Why *didn't* you tell me?"

Richard pointed to a glass on the counter.

Nash reached for the water and handed it to Richard, waiting while he took a sip and slowly swallowed. Richard gave him back the tall glass and he replaced it on the coaster on the nightstand.

"Dare begged me not to. He said you were so angry at Ethan he couldn't handle it if you turned on him too. And you were the only family each of you had left. Florence, Samuel, and I agreed that preserving your bond with your brother was the best thing we could do. For both of you."

Nash bowed his head, gathering his thoughts, waiting for his temper to cool. "I understand you making the decision when Dare was fifteen and I was sixteen," he said, hating it but understanding. "But ten years have passed. Ten long years. We've been like father and son. How . . ." He shook his head, determined not to berate the older man.

Richard was weak and tired and he needed his strength to recuperate.

"You're not saying anything I haven't thought over the years. But the more time passed, the harder it was to bring it up again, let alone tell you. And we all agreed it was Dare's story to tell. Not ours."

It all came back to Dare, who hadn't trusted Nash enough to confide in him. The whole crazy story blew Nash's mind. "Everyone in my life made this decision about what I needed to know. Nobody once thought about the life I was living." Nash forced himself to remain in his chair, to speak in low, steady tones, when everything in him wanted to pace and yell.

"Nash, we tried to look at things from your perspective."

"And did that perspective include the fact that I was torn in two? Gratitude, on the one hand, that the Rossmans gave me everything. They put a roof over my head, food on the table, and a private school and college education. While at the same time I *hated* them for not taking Dare. I hated myself. Why me, I asked over and over. Why me and not Dare?" Nash braced his hands on his temples, as if he could steady the thoughts rioting through his brain. The thoughts that had tormented him for as long as he could remember.

"I don't have answers that will satisfy you," Richard said at last. "I'm not even sure I can satisfy myself."

A glance at Richard told him the man had aged another decade in the last five minutes, and damned if despite being the wronged party, Nash still felt guilty for upsetting him now.

He rose from his seat. "Get some rest, okay? There's plenty of time to go over this when you're better."

Richard nodded in agreement. "I'm sorry," he said.

"I know." Nash inclined his head. That Richard never meant to hurt him was a given. So was the fact that he had. "I've got to get going." There wasn't anything more to say anyway. "Get some rest and I'll check in with you again tomorrow," he said, because the only way Richard would heal and to return to his normal self was with rest.

And no stress.

Nash reached the bedroom door.

"Do you forgive me?" the older man asked.

He turned and gripped the doorframe. There were many lies he could offer in reply, the most glaring being "There's nothing to forgive." Richard was too smart to believe a platitude designed to make him feel better and too weak to hear the truth.

So Nash settled for an old standby. The truth. "In time," he said. And then, "I'll talk to you tomorrow." Walking out, he shut the door with a soft click.

Joe stepped out of the shower, one eye on the clock as he dressed for his date with Annie. He was supposed to pick her up at seven, and because he was shorthanded at the bar, he was running late. They'd agreed to a casual night, so he pulled on a pair of jeans and a long-sleeved light blue shirt his sister had bought him for his birthday last year. He tried not to get overly excited about tonight. After all, he'd spent plenty of time with Annie over the last two weeks, first while she was recuperating and then whenever he could find time to stop by and say hello.

When she started insisting she didn't need him bringing her meals, he'd known she was feeling better and switched tactics. He asked her to take on the bar's accounting, but she'd seen the request for what it was — a blatant excuse to spend more time with her. Eyes blazing, cheeks pink with anger, she'd called him on it.

Her honesty never failed to both amuse and arouse him, and he wasn't about to take no for an answer. By the time he was finished praising her accounting skills, she was impressed with his due diligence in asking her current business clients about her work, and she'd agreed to take him on.

Score another point for me, he thought, pleased with himself. But it was also a smart business move. His old accountant had been his father's crony, half drunk and mostly incompetent. The change was long overdue.

He was about to grab his keys and head out when his doorbell rang. He was in no mood for a delay and he swung the door open, ready to rip his visitor's head off. Until he saw who stood on his doorstep.

"Annie!"

A vision in form-fitting denim and a gold turtleneck that set off the color of her hair, she greeted him with a smile. "Hi! Are you ready?"

He narrowed his gaze. "I thought I was picking you up."

"Surprise!" She dangled her keys in front of him. "So? Are you ready?"

He grinned, liking this impulsive side of her. "I sure am. Want me to drive?" he couldn't help but offer.

"Nope. You're going to need all your skills and energy for later." She wriggled her eyebrows seductively.

"I'd like to think you mean *later* later," he said in a gruff voice. Because all he could think about was her bed or his and them together in it. "But for some reason I think you have something else in mind."

She laughed. "Maybe I have both things planned." Her voice dropped a sexy octave.

Unable to resist, he slid his hand around the back of her neck and pulled her against him, sliding his lips over hers.

"Mmm," she moaned, softening her

mouth and opening for him without coaxing.

He tasted her, toyed with her, touched his tongue to the corners of her lips before nipping lightly in the center.

"If we keep this up, we'll never get out of here," he warned her, never breaking contact with her mouth.

"Darn it." She stepped back and he realized she'd gripped his shirt with both hands, curling the fabric into her fists. "I have too much planned to give in. Much as I want to." She smiled and reached for his hand instead.

He shifted, trying to get comfortable when his jeans felt ten sizes too small. But he knew she'd planned something special. For him. The notion pleased him. And he wouldn't deprive either one of them of whatever it was. Then he'd pick up where they'd left off.

"Where are we going?" he asked.

"Ever raced a car?" Her grin was miles wide and sexy as hell.

"No, you?"

"Nope. Ever hear of Grand Prix?"

He raised an eyebrow. "The racing place. Guys in the bar have talked about it." He'd just never had a chance to experience it for himself. Go-karts and genuine tracks. Real racing suits and helmets. "You're up for that?"

"Ever since I was diagnosed with MS I told myself that I wanted to experience new things, not let my life or disease hold me back. I left my husband, but other than that I haven't done one thing to act on my desires."

The word rippled through the air around them, sending currents of awareness shooting through his veins.

"Then you pushed through my defenses. You asked me out, you didn't get angry when I forgot. Instead, you took care of me and for some reason it didn't feel the same as it did when Nash tried to do the same thing." She ran her tongue over her lips. "I saw him earlier. He knows about us and he actually wished me well. He's over me."

Losing Annie. Joe shook his head, actually feeling sorry for the man. "You sure about that?"

"He can't see past Kelly. And I? I can't see past you."

Her lashes fluttered over her blue eyes and he lost a part of himself to her.

"The way you talk to me," she continued, unaware of his emotions, but expressing so much of what he actually felt, it was like she was inside him.

"It's like you understand who I am and you treat the MS like it's a side order, not the main course."

He grinned. "That's because *you're* the main course, baby."

She smiled right back. "You have this whole laid-back attitude, but I know you too. You took care of your mom and your sister, and I know the bar is a huge responsibility. So I thought we could release some excess energy together. At the racetrack." She drew a deep breath. "And then we could get rid of the rest of it . . . in bed."

The flush in her cheeks told him how hard all this was for her to explain and admit. That she'd chosen him made him feel like the luckiest guy in the world.

He brushed his hand down her cheek, loving how she trembled at his touch. "I would love to release *all* my energy. With you." He swiped his tongue over her lips. "In you."

Her entire body vibrated with need. Need he'd take full advantage of later. "We have a racetrack to get to," he reminded her.

This would be waiting for them when they returned.

On Saturday, Nash was surprised by a phone call from Faith inviting him to stop by the house. She hadn't said what she wanted to discuss and she'd evaded the question when he'd asked. When he pulled up the long driveway, he saw Kelly's car parked in one of the extra spots and a kick of pleasure spiked through him. Considering he'd been in her bed last night and woke up with her snuggled against him this morning, the pleasure shouldn't be so acute.

Yet it was.

He couldn't get enough of her.

He rang the doorbell and Faith answered. She wore jeans and a navy pullover sweater, and her blond hair fell around her face in a casual way. She wasn't his type, but he appreciated a beautiful woman. And Faith was beautiful, something he hadn't let himself think about or notice before, when all he felt for Ethan and anyone connected to him was painful betrayal. It hadn't helped that her father had bilked people out of their money, Nash's adoptive parents included, without a thought to the damage he'd cause. For Nash, Faith had been an easy target.

But the anger he had lived with for so long had begun to recede and left almost completely when Ethan had shown up when Nash needed him. Despite rightfully thinking Nash hated him, Ethan had had his back while his life crashed around him.

"Nash, thanks for coming!" Faith greeted him with a warm smile.

"I was surprised you invited me," he said honestly. Their relationship had been beyond rocky.

She nodded. "Well, I thought it was time we talked. Come on in."

He followed her inside.

"Let's go to the sunroom. It's bright and a nice place to talk."

"What's Ethan up to?" he asked as they passed the closed door to his brother's office.

"He's tied up in his office on a conference call. Business." Faith led the way through the marble entryway and through the den, giving Nash the chance to admire the huge home with an unbiased eye for the first time.

He knew Ethan had parlayed his love of computer games and his army education and training into a lucrative software business that sold military software to the government for a small fortune. Nash hadn't let himself be impressed by his brother before. He did now.

They ended up in a room he'd never seen before, wall-to wall-windows with an incredible view of the property. The foliage and trees were burnt orange, yellow, and brown, thanks to the end of fall, and the sky above seemed to go on and on.

"Beautiful," he said.

"Thank you. I love this room and its view." She swept an arm around. "Have a seat." Faith settled into a large club chair, propping her feet on an ottoman.

Nash chose to sit across from her on a small sofa. Like the rest of the house, this room was decorated in muted neutrals and masculine browns, yet there was enough warmth in the decor and accessories to assure a homey, family feel.

"So." He wrapped his arm over the back of the couch and met her gaze.

"You're wondering why I asked you over?"

He nodded. "I am."

Faith had never been one to mince words. He'd had it out with her before, over Tess, her relationship with Ethan, and her father's actions. He doubted she'd hedge now.

"The other day when Ethan followed you to Florence Rossman's . . . I wanted to thank you for letting him in." She tapped on her chest, directly over her heart, leaving Nash no doubt what she meant.

"I didn't let him in." His denial was an automatic, ingrained response.

"You most certainly did." Faith dropped her feet to the floor and leaned forward in her seat. "By not telling him to get lost, by letting him come with you to face Dare, you most certainly did let him in."

"I sure as hell did tell him to get lost," Nash felt compelled to tell her.

Faith grinned. "You couldn't have tried too hard."

Nash opened his mouth, then closed it again, forcing himself to think.

Hadn't he just admitted to himself that he'd all but forgiven his older brother? Why was he denying Faith's words? For the sake of continuing an old argument that wouldn't serve any purpose except to maintain distance?

"It wasn't easy," Nash said at last. "A part of me is still angry with him." The abandoned little boy, Nash knew. The adult had forgiven.

"You're hurt. There's a difference." Faith's eyes flashed determined sparks. "But the more you get to know Ethan now, the more you'll see he isn't the same kid who ran away and left you behind."

Silence filled the room. Nash wasn't sure how to respond. Spilling his guts didn't come easily but Faith seemed happy to let him think over her words.

"My brother's lucky to have you in his corner," he finally said to his sister-in-law.

There was a time when Nash had been

envious of what Ethan and Faith shared. The open honesty, the commitment. But he was finding those things for himself now.

In Kelly.

And though he didn't know where things were headed, he sure as hell liked where they currently were.

"I'm the one who's lucky," Faith said. "Which brings me to the main reason I asked you over. I thought that since you're dealing with Ethan in a more rational manner, maybe you and I could make our peace too." She drew a deep breath. "I understand why you hate my father, but I'm not *him*. I'm more a part of your family than mine, and I know it would mean so much to Ethan if we could get along."

She surprised him. But Nash sensed her sincerity and as he looked into her open, honest eyes, he wondered how he hadn't really seen her before. She wasn't like her father. She was just a daughter who'd been as blindsided by her parent's actions as everyone else in town. A woman who'd had to make a fresh start alone. With her father in jail and her mother a town pariah, Faith had returned, recently divorced and betrayed. She should have been fragile, but she'd been strong.

Instead of seeing her strength and integrity, Nash had been blind. He'd already blamed his adoptive father's fatal heart attack on Martin Harrington's Ponzi scheme and he was already angry at Ethan, so Nash had lashed out at Faith too, calling himself justified.

He shook his head and forced himself to meet her gaze. "I'm not sure why you want to make peace with me." He clasped his hands together in front of him. "It's not like I've given you a reason."

She shrugged easily. "Like I said from the beginning, Tess needs her family. You, me, and Ethan coming together would give her a huge foundation from which to build."

Nash noted she hadn't mentioned Dare. "You're right about that," he agreed. "Tess judges everyone by how they treat Ethan." At one time that would have had him gnashing his teeth. Now it just was.

Faith grinned. "He can have that effect on women."

Nash rolled his eyes, not wanting to discuss that aspect of his older brother's character.

"I haven't been fair to you, but I'm willing to start over too. And I appreciate you giving me a chance."

Faith exhaled a long breath and laughed. "Well, that was easier than I anticipated."

He shook his head, embarrassed by his past actions. "I've been pretty tough on you."

"Nothing I couldn't handle."

"But you shouldn't have had to." Which led him to another question. "I'm glad you reached out to me, but I have to know why. Why now?"

Faith met his gaze. "Because it took guts for Kelly to come over here and ask Ethan to go after you. Considering how you felt about Ethan, Kelly had no way of knowing whether he'd laugh in her face or throw her out."

Nash did his best not to wince at the too-true description.

Of course now he'd transferred that anger to his younger sibling. As much as Nash wished he could blink and make it all go away, he couldn't. Dare had betrayed him in an elemental way, an adult way, and he didn't know how to come to terms with that.

"Anyway," Faith said, her voice bringing him back to the present, "if Kelly thought you were worth the risk, I decided you must be. So I called and asked you to come by."

He cocked his head to one side, surprised. So he had Kelly to thank for this, did he? He'd have to find a way to show his gratitude. A way that involved that claw-footed bathtub in her apartment.

He shifted uncomfortably and forced himself to focus on his sister-in-law's peace offering. "I'd like to start fresh." He rose to shake her hand.

Faith startled him by pulling him into a warm embrace.

Ethan cleared his throat. "Am I interrupting?" he asked as he stepped into the room.

To her credit, Faith didn't flinch at being caught hugging him. She just turned, keeping one arm around Nash's waist. "I was making peace with your brother," she said with a big grin.

"Is that so?" Ethan eyed Nash warily.

Not because there was a chance in hell Nash would make a move on his brother's wife, and Ethan knew that. They all knew that. But because Nash had been such an ass to Faith for so long.

"Apparently your wife believes in second chances," Nash said to Ethan. He wanted to step aside, but Faith held on to his waist, keeping him beside her.

He understood her. She wanted to make the point that they were a family. Nothing more to hide.

"As long as you aren't harassing my wife, I'm all for peace," Ethan said, but his tone remained wary.

It seemed his big brother had no problem extending his own olive branch, but he was a hell of a lot more protective when it came to someone he loved.

Nash admired that particular quality. "No harassment. No insults," he assured him.

"Good." Ethan's expression relaxed, his frown turning into more of a smile. He held out a hand and Faith eased from Nash's side right into her husband's. "How are you holding up?" Ethan asked Nash.

"I'm fine." Working and trying hard not to think about things he couldn't change. Every time he tried to understand Dare's lies, he only lost sleep and valuable time he could be spending doing other things.

Which reminded him. "I saw Kelly's car outside?"

Ethan caught his gaze, letting Nash know he wasn't buying his "I'm fine" lie.

Faith merely grinned. "Kelly and Tess are in the kitchen baking cookies."

"I'll go say hello on my way out," Nash said, ignoring them both.

"Actually, we're going to take Tess over to the youth center. My friend Kate Andrews wants to start up an art program there. Tess asked one of her teachers if she had time to volunteer. We're going to talk about how to proceed," Faith said.

"And Faith figured Tess would get something out of helping others," his brother added.

"Which means . . . you might have to help Kelly finish the cookies," Faith told Nash in a teasing voice.

Kelly sat with Tess in Faith and Ethan's gorgeous kitchen baking cookies for an upcoming fund-raiser at Tess's school. The money raised would pay for a trip to the Museum of Modern Art in Manhattan, something she knew Tess would love. Since Kelly's kitchen was tiny, Tess asked her to come and bake at her house. They'd started with all the ingredients to make cookies from scratch laid out on the counter and had progressed to almost getting the entire mixture ready. As for cleaning, Rosalita had the day off and Kelly was on her own, something she was used to anyway.

She glanced down at the large bowl of batter in front of her. "Betty Crocker I am not," she muttered, as she added eggs to the cookie mixture. "Tell me again why we couldn't use slice-and-bake cookie mix for your fund-raiser at school?"

" 'Cause it's a cookie recipe swap, so we also have to have copies of the recipe available. Now keep mixing. It has lumps," Tess ordered, sticking the spoon in for a taste.

"Hey!" Kelly playfully swatted her sister's hand. "Quit eating all the profits and get back to greasing the cookie sheets."

"Slave driver. Did you remember to preheat the oven?" Tess asked.

Kelly nodded. She finally mixed the batter until it was smooth. Together they placed the dough on the sheets, spacing each cookie far enough apart that they wouldn't spread into each other when heated. Finally, they placed the full set of baking sheets in the oven and Kelly set the timer.

"Why do you like Nash so much?" Tess asked, taking her off guard.

Kelly bit the inside of her cheek, wondering how to answer. "Your brother's a good man."

"That's not what I mean." Tess hopped onto a stool by the counter, propped her dough-filled hands under her chin, and stared at Kelly wide-eyed. "Forget Nash is my brother. Why do you *like* him like him?" The teenager pushed in the way that meant Kelly wasn't getting away without answering.

"Yes, Kelly. Tell Tess why you *like* me like me."

Kelly jerked her gaze to the door, where Nash stood watching them. Eyes glittering with amusement and heat.

"What are you doing here?" she asked.

"Well?" Tess pushed. "Answer me!"

Kelly couldn't help it. She leaned against the counter for support. "There's no explaining chemistry," she murmured, more to herself than to Tess.

Nash couldn't tear his gaze from hers.

"God, grown-ups!" Tess shook her head in frustration.

"Tess, you about ready to go to the youth center?" Faith's voice called to her from the other room.

"Coming!"

"Go wash your hands," Kelly told her.

"Yeah, yeah. Thanks for making cookies. But don't think we're done with this conversation!"

Kelly bit the inside of her cheek to keep from laughing as Tess ran from the room. "What are you doing here?" she asked Nash.

He walked over and sat on a stool next to her. His warm cologne assaulted her senses, reminding her of falling asleep beside him and waking up in his arms the last few mornings. "And I thought the cookies smelled good," she said.

"What was that?"

"I said you smell good." She leaned in, nibbled on his ear, and was rewarded with a low growl. She grinned. “So what are you doing here?” she asked again.

“Faith invited me. We made a sort of peace.” He shook his head, obviously still surprised.

She wasn’t.

“I’m glad.” First Ethan, then Faith. Slowly but surely, the walls he’d built around himself were crumbling.

If there was anything good that had come out of this mess with Dare, it was that Nash had begun to warm toward his older brother. In turn, Tess continued to warm toward Nash, asking questions about them as a couple instead of being angry. Now they just needed him to do the same for Dare and this family might just become whole.

It was too soon to mention it now. Just like it was still too soon to tell him she loved him.

Not when she was still reeling from the knowledge herself.

Nash was in a better place, but he wasn’t there yet. And she was still learning to accept and understand what loving Nash meant.

Suddenly she had an idea. “Are you busy this weekend?” she asked, before she could chicken out.

He leaned in close, his body heat sending her senses into overload. "What did you have in mind?"

"I thought we could go away? A bed-and-breakfast or something for the weekend?"

His eyes lit up at the suggestion. "That sounds perfect," he said, his voice rich and warm.

"I'll research and find someplace. We can leave early Saturday morning after Tess's art show Friday night?"

"You bet." A low groan rumbled from deep in his chest as he pulled her to him and kissed her long and hard.

As usual, she lost herself in his arms, his tongue sweeping over her lips and demanding entrance. She let him inside for a brief, delicious moment, before breaking the kiss.

"You taste like cookie dough." He dampened his mouth with his tongue and grinned.

"Go. I have to clean up here and then go find us a bed-and-breakfast." She swatted his shoulder. If he didn't leave, she'd end up embarrassed in Ethan's kitchen.

With a sexy wink and a grin, he stole one more kiss and headed out.

Kelly sighed happily. When was the last time she had this much peace in her life? She couldn't wait to get Nash alone. Someplace away from family and problems.

A place where they could focus solely on each other.

Fifteen

Kelly found a small bed-and-breakfast in Rockport, Massachusetts, an almost four-hour drive from Serendipity. The inn boasted a view of the Atlantic Ocean; the rooms provided decks, jet tubs, and a private entrance. It sounded perfect, and though she hoped they wouldn't spend all that much time clothed, she still wanted to buy something special to wear.

On her lunch break, Kelly took the opportunity to shop. She walked the short distance to the center of town and headed into Consign and Design, the store next to Faith's business.

The chimes rang as she opened the door, announcing her presence. A woman with a cherry-colored haircut in a funky style Kelly thought Tess would love came rushing out of the back to greet her.

"Welcome!" she said.

"Thank you. This is a beautiful place you

have here."

Kelly glanced around the beautiful shop, taking in the mint green walls. "I love the clothes, but these walls and this shelving are so cool!" She brushed her hand over the unique carved-wood free-floating shelves.

"Thanks! My brother Nick just put those in. I'm April Mancini, by the way."

"I'm Kelly Moss. And Faith Barron has told me all about you. I was hoping you could help me pick out some clothes for a trip I'm taking this weekend?"

"I'd love to." April hooked her arm through Kelly's as if they were old friends. "Business or pleasure?"

Despite herself, Kelly blushed. "Pleasure."

"Aah. Anyone I know?" the other woman asked.

Kelly, having spent so many years in Manhattan, was still getting used to people — strangers — asking her personal questions and expecting answers.

But April was warm and friendly and Kelly didn't mind. "Nash Barron," she admitted.

April grinned. "Oh those Barron boys were always so bad. Nash was always the hardest to read."

Kelly nodded. "You have to get close before he lets you in."

"Well, I'm glad to see he's found someone. I know his divorce hit him hard. Come on. I take it Faith told you that most of my items have been taken in on consignment, but I recently started expanding, using my own designs."

"Faith said she sold you some truly expensive designer items and you turned them into unique pieces."

"I was going to sell them on eBay because I honestly didn't think the wealthy would shop in a consignment shop, but it turns out that word of mouth is a wonderful thing. I couldn't imagine how Faith's pieces would boost my business." April glowed with the pleasure of success. "I also decided to carry select items so people can shop here even if they're not looking for gently used clothing or high-end new designs."

"An eclectic bit of everything?" Kelly asked with a laugh.

April let out a long sigh. "That's the problem with me. I can't stick to one thing. I like something, I take it in and hope to sell it."

Kelly smiled. "Sounds to me like you need a business plan."

"Are you offering?" April asked hopefully.

"Sorry, not my forte. But I'll keep an ear

out in case I hear of someone who can help you."

"Thank you. Now, let's get out started. First up? I took in a line of sexy lingerie for the discerning consumer. Something tells me you'll love them." April led her to the back of the store, to a separate section of clothes and dressing room.

Half an hour later, Kelly had purchased a set of lingerie the likes of which she'd never thought to own, a sexy lounge wear set for hanging around the room, and a dynamite April original for dinner on Saturday night. All bought with Nash in mind.

Kelly knew she was more in love with him than any man she'd ever been with. His mix of strength and vulnerability drew her, as did the fact that with her he didn't hide himself. He trusted her and she had every reason to trust him.

Sometime during this weekend, Kelly would tell him everything about her past with Ryan, the mistakes she'd made, and the deposition she would probably have to face in the future. If she came clean, he'd understand. He'd had too many people lying to him for too long. Kelly didn't want to be one of them.

The night of Tess's art show, the school

parking lot was crowded with expensive cars. Kelly pulled in and parked a few spots away from Ethan's Jaguar. Surrounded by other high-end vehicles, Kelly's subcompact looked like a cheap toy. This place always made her feel less than, in a way not even Ethan's mansion managed to do.

Tess bounced out of Ethan's car, and her wide smile made Kelly forget about feeling out of place.

"Now, remember, don't forget to check out Sara Murphy's projects. She thinks she's the most talented artist in school and that her shit don't stink!"

"Mouth!" Kelly, Ethan, and Faith said at the same time.

Kelly had arrived at school at the same time as the other three and they walked in together.

Tess popped a huge bubble with her gum.

Kelly frowned and held out her hand. "Give it," she said, cringing as she made the demand.

"Wait, I have a spare tissue," Faith said, not bothering to hold in a laugh.

"You know there's no gum allowed in school," Ethan said. "Can you at least behave for the next hour or so that we're here?"

Kelly watched Tess's face as she came to a

decision. "Okay. As long as all my brothers get along," she said with a sly grin that indicated she was looking for trouble.

Kelly wasn't sure how much Tess knew about the problems between the three brothers, but her little sister was perceptive, especially when it came to any change in the dynamics between them all. And she clearly knew there was trouble brewing now.

"Your brothers always get along." Kelly prodded Tess to walk faster. "And since tonight's about you, I don't think you have anything to worry about. Your brothers will be fine."

"I'm not worried about them." Tess gnawed her bottom lip, taking off the lip gloss Kelly had helped her apply seconds before.

"Well, don't worry about your showing either. I've seen how good you are," Ethan assured her.

He was about to ruffle her hair when Faith grabbed his hand and threaded her fingers through his. Meeting Kelly's gaze, the other woman grinned.

And Kelly blew out a sigh of relief. Only another female would realize that Tess had probably stood in the bathroom with the straightener for an hour to get her hair so perfect. One touch by Ethan would mess up the whole thing.

Kelly liked these little changes in Tess. Her asking for lip gloss, the time spent on her hair, caring about school. In the few weeks since Ethan had been back, Tess hadn't asked about transferring. She still spent a lot of time with Michelle, and though the girls might have met because others ostracized Tess, there was no denying the teenager had been a good influence on Kelly's harder-edged sister. Combined with the art Tess loved so much, maybe this private school would work out after all.

They strode into the building surrounded by other parents and eager kids. Tess said hello to both girls and boys Kelly didn't recognize as she led her family to her station. The kids had been set up alphabetically, so Nash and Dare would have no trouble finding them.

Tess's artwork, like the other kids', had been proudly displayed on an easel. She was supposed to stand by her designs, and when parents passed by she'd been instructed to explain her creations and the mood and reason behind them.

Kelly took her time going through Tess's portfolio, amazed anew at her sister's talent. She'd only been in school for two short months and Kelly felt certain she was looking more at Tess's innate abilities than anything her instructor had taught her. But there was a definite refinement in her drawings Kelly had never seen before, a more deliberate choice of color. Yes, this school would give Tess opportunities Kelly would never have been able to give her on her own.

A lump in her throat, Kelly met Ethan's proud gaze and mouthed a silent thank-you. She'd never be able to repay him for taking Tess in when she'd been at her wit's end and for turning the teenager around in such a short time. Whatever he'd been or had done in his past, Ethan was an extraordinary man now.

And when Kelly felt a warm hand on her back, she knew the more extraordinary Barron brother — at least in her estimation — had arrived.

Tonight couldn't be easy for him, knowing he had to see and be civil to Dare, but he was here. For Tess. To Kelly, that said everything she needed to know about the man.

"Hi there," she said softly.

Nash took in her happy-to-see-him expression and grinned. "Hi." He pressed a kiss against her cheek, remaining close to her side.

"Well," she said, a wealth of questions in

that one word.

"Not hiding us," he explained.

He'd spent most nights in her bed, finding so much more than solace and comfort. She wasn't his nighttime-only secret. He was ready to take this relationship to the next level. They were an official couple and he didn't care who knew.

Her eyes lit up with pleasure and a distinct sense of rightness overwhelmed him. It wasn't something they'd discussed, but everything in him had felt lighter since he and Annie had in effect released each other from any remaining obligation.

"Hey! No BlackBerry or I'm calling security to throw you out!" Tess interrupted them. As usual. She folded her arms over her chest, telling them she meant business.

Nash rolled his eyes at her dramatics. "Show me your artwork, twerp."

Tess led him to the easel, biting on her fingernails as he looked through her portfolio. She used to be hesitant about sharing her work, and there were times Nash had resented how she'd turned so readily to Ethan, trusting him first. Now she resorted to a nervous habit, as if his opinion mattered to her.

He studied each piece. Tess liked to focus on dragons and fantasy figures in bold colors. Her recent drawings pulled up her favorite colors, black and purple, with accents of orange. He couldn't help but notice that the art teacher had let her choose her own style, teaching her how to grow within what she liked, keeping her attention that way.

"Great job! Who would've thought you had it in you?" he teased.

She punched him in the arm but, from the grin on her face, his approval meant something to her. Just as their growing closeness meant the world to him. He liked her a lot and wanted her to feel the same. Hell, the kid had stolen his heart already.

Apparently there was a lot of that going on, he thought with a glance over his shoulder at Kelly, who watched them, appreciation in her soft gaze. *He* appreciated the way her black jeans and white sweater hugged her body.

"Hey." Dare suddenly joined them, pulling Tess into a brotherly hug.

"Dare!" Tess said, excited her last brother had arrived.

Too bad Nash didn't feel the same way. His entire body stiffened and the sweet family scene he'd been enjoying disappeared.

He'd done his thing with Tess and stepped back to let Dare have his time. Nash headed back to Kelly before Tess noticed anything was wrong.

"Want to walk and see the other kids' stuff?" In truth, he wasn't interested in anyone's art except his sister's. But as an escape, a tour of the room would do. He needed a breather.

Kelly tipped her head to one side, sizing up the situation accurately, Nash was certain.

"Sure," she said.

He threaded his fingers through hers and they started up and down the aisles of the large gymnasium.

"Look. Our favorite teacher." Kelly tilted her head toward the far end of the room where Ms. Julie Bernard stood with another teacher, the perpetual frown on her face.

"Ethan put a call in to Dr. Spellman, the headmaster. Apparently he gave the woman a good talking to. Hopefully that translated into how she's treating Tess," Nash said.

Kelly nodded. "Whatever works. And Tess does seem happier, don't you think?"

"It's only been a few weeks, but you're right. She's more relaxed. She does better when Ethan's home."

A low hum escaped Kelly's throat. "There was a time when that might've hurt, but now I'm just glad someone can relate to her," she admitted.

"Agreed." They had that in common too, Nash thought.

"Even if that someone is Ethan?" Kelly met his gaze with her perceptive stare.

"If that's your way of asking if I've come to terms with him . . . more and more." More and more. Which still surprised him. His anger at Ethan had been such a part of him, the thaw took getting used to.

"And Dare?" she asked.

He replied by tugging on her hand, stopping them from rounding a corner into the next aisle. Instead, he pulled her through a doorway that took them into a dimly lit stairwell.

"What are you doing?" she asked, somewhat breathless.

It seemed obvious to him. "Getting you alone." He backed her against the wall, savoring her body heat.

She licked her lips and he followed the movement, every muscle in his body tensing in reaction.

"Why?" she asked.

Again, he thought the answer was obvious. "Because ever since I left your bed this morning, I've missed you." He paused and decided to admit the rest. "And to get you to stop asking me questions about my family."

A grin lifted the corners of her mouth. "And just how do you plan to get me to stop asking questions?" she asked, deliberately pushing him.

Teasing him.

All but asking him to kiss her.

"Like this." With a groan, he leaned in and sealed his lips over hers.

Every time he touched her was a revelation, and now that his feelings were so close to the surface, there was so much more to learn. He let the kiss go on and on, his tongue in her mouth, demanding, taking, and giving as she accepted his desire and gave of her own. He swirled circles around the inside of her mouth, drinking in her sweetness and wanting more.

His erection pulsed against the zipper in his pants, begging for release and reminding him of where they were. And why they couldn't do this now.

With regret, he forced himself to lift his head and break the kiss. "Tess will miss us," he murmured.

"I know."

He heard the disappointment in her voice and chuckled. "I'll make it up to you tonight."

"Promise?" she asked, wriggling her hips against his.

He bit back a groan. "You're going to make it damned difficult for me to walk back out there, you know."

She batted her lashes at him, too innocently.

"Just for that I may not let you out of bed this entire weekend."

Her eyes opened wide. "Promise?" she asked again, shifting her body against him.

His threat and her reaction did nothing to alleviate the ache in his groin, only making it worse.

Finally, she stepped aside and out of his way. "Why don't I go out first and give you a chance to get yourself under control?" she offered, her sultry stare on the bulge in his pants.

"Good idea." He kissed her hard once more. "Go. I'll meet you at Tess's booth soon."

She waved at him, a grin on her well-kissed lips, her eyes flashing with pleasure.

Then she was gone, leaving him to think about anything that would dim his arousal — like the people in his life who thought they knew what was best for him, kept secrets, and lied.

In a flash, he was ready to head back into

the room. Instead, he decided to take his time. Why deal with Dare before he had to?

Ethan shoved his hands into his pockets and plastered a smile on his face, unwilling to let Tess see he was worried about his whole family. Nash barely tolerated Dare right now and nobody held a grudge like his middle brother. Until Nash and Dare made their peace, Ethan wasn't just worried about them but about Tess too. So far she was too wrapped up in her art to notice that the brothers who normally got along were ignoring each other, but she was smart.

She'd catch on soon.

Meanwhile, Nash and Kelly had taken a walk, Dare had gone out for air, and Faith was off talking to the headmaster, making sure the situation with Ms. Bernard was under control.

Ethan had stepped away from the easel to let Tess explain her presentation to other parents who stopped by. Ethan turned back to see who Tess was talking to and immediately realized something was wrong. His sister's body language screamed tension. She rocked on her heels, much the way she used to rock in her black lace-up army boots in the dead of summer, all attitude and anger.

Narrowing his gaze, Ethan strode up to the man who stood by her side. Before Ethan could only see a sport jacket and bald spot. Now, he realized, the guy clearly didn't look like one of the parents. His jacket was too old and out-of-date.

Ethan stepped into the other man's personal space. "Ethan Barron, Tess's brother," he said, holding out his hand for an introductory shake. "And whose parent are you?"

The stranger's gaze ran over Ethan and he stepped back. "Roger Grayson." He slipped his sweaty palm into Ethan's for a flimsy shake.

Ethan narrowed his gaze. "I didn't hear you say whose parent you were?" He pushed the other man harder.

Tess nudged Ethan in his side. "That's 'cause he didn't. He was asking me about Kelly, like how long did she live with me in your mansion and did she leave me alone at night and stuff like that."

Now Ethan wasn't wary — he was pissed. "Who the hell do you think you are, cornering a teenage girl?" Ethan placed a hand on his sister's shoulder, then turned and caught sight of his wife coming toward them, equal concern in her expression.

"What's going on?" Faith tucked a strand of blond hair behind her ear and looked to all three of them for answers.

"Do me a favor, princess? Take Tess for a walk. Let her go see her other friends' artwork. I have some business to take care of here."

"But who is he?" Tess asked. "He was asking me questions. I have a right to know who he is and what he wants!"

"When I know, I'll tell you." He nudged her toward Faith.

"Come on. Let's go," she said, turning Tess around and practically pushing her down the aisle.

God, he loved that woman.

Ethan focused his attention on Roger Grayson, if that was really his name. "Now spill."

The other man reached into his pocket and handed Ethan a card, which he gave a cursory glance. "Okay, so you really are Roger Grayson. You're also a PI. So what the hell do you want with Tess? And why are you so interested in Kelly?"

"I was hired by a woman who —"

"Ethan?" Kelly walked over, pointed concern on her face. "Where's Tess?" she asked, her gaze darting around for her sister.

"I sent her for a walk with Faith. This man" — Ethan jerked his thumb at Grayson — "was asking Tess questions about the two of you."

The color drained from Kelly's face. "Who hired you?" she asked.

"Leah Muldoon."

"Who?" Ethan and Kelly asked at once.

The beefy man turned to Kelly. "I was hired by your mother."

Kelly narrowed her gaze. "My mother's name is Leah . . . Moss."

"Her married name is Muldoon."

Kelly blinked up at the man. "Married," she said on a groan. "Why am I not surprised? So why did she send you instead of just looking me and Tess up herself?"

The man rubbed a hand over his balding head. "You'll have to ask her that."

"I've been trying to track her down," Ethan said, deciding he'd have to fire his investigator.

"I'll let her know you want to talk." The PI slowly stepped backward and Ethan realized his hands were balled into fists at his side, scaring the PI.

He wasn't about to start a fight at Tess's school but let this guy think whatever he wanted. While Grayson slunk out of the building, Ethan made a mental note to discuss better security with the school board, which he was now on.

Then he turned to Kelly, whose color had

slowly started to return. "You okay?"

"I am. But are you thinking what I'm thinking about my mother?" Her voice was tinged with a combination of anger and concern.

Ethan understood both. "Yeah. If Leah bothered to hire a PI to slink around, that can only mean she wants Tess back."

"Because she knows that without ammunition, she doesn't stand a chance in court." Kelly exhaled a hard breath and met Ethan's gaze.

He studied the woman who'd been a stranger a few short months before. She'd shown up on his doorstep and put blind faith in him when nobody else in his family would give him the time of day. She'd given him a moody, sullen teenager who'd turned out to be his greatest gift.

Kelly, with her brown eyes, her expressions so like his sister's, and a trusting warmth and generosity, had become part of his inner circle, the people closest to him. And Ethan didn't have many.

He cleared his throat. "Kelly, I have to know. Are we on the same side in this?"

"Oh my God, yes." Her eyes filled and she wrapped her arms around his neck, pulling him into a sisterly hug.

"Good. Good."

She stepped back and shot him a determined smile and Ethan knew. They weren't giving Tess up without a fight.

Kelly's hands shook and she rubbed them together, trying to calm down. When she'd heard the PI had been asking about her at the coffee shop, she'd assumed he'd been hired by Ryan's wife. Never in her wildest dreams had she imagined her own mother was looking for dirt on her daughter.

Kelly shook her head in disgust and dismay. Of course she was on Ethan's side. Leah had walked out on her teenage child without looking back. She'd cast Kelly into the role of Tess's mother, over and over, without thought to what it would cost her or Tess. And then she'd gone and gotten married.

"What else is wrong?" Ethan asked.

She propped her hand on her hip and glared. "Why are you Barron brothers so damned perceptive?"

"Your hands are trembling and you can barely stand. You've survived your mother leaving and we're a team when it comes to keeping Tess. I figure something else has to have you so shaken." Ethan placed a firm hand on her shoulder, offering his support. "What is it?"

She met Ethan's gaze, surprised he had to ask. "Didn't Faith tell you about my ex-boyfriend, Ryan Hayward?"

Ethan shook his head, waiting patiently for her to explain. Apparently Faith had kept her secret. Kelly hadn't specifically asked her to remain silent, but Faith had respected her privacy. The woman was an even better friend than Kelly had given her credit for being.

"I left behind a problem in New York," Kelly admitted to Ethan. If she trusted him with her sister, she sure as hell could trust him with her secrets.

She quickly explained the situation to Ethan, knowing Tess or Nash could return any second. "So this private investigator could just as easily have been hired by Ryan's wife to dig up dirt on me before I'm subpoenaed to testify at their divorce hearing."

She pressed her hands to her flushed cheeks. "And if this hits the newspapers, I'll be labeled a prostitute and Tess will know how I met Ryan. She'll be in for horrible embarrassment at school and she'll think I'm the worst kind of hypocrite, preaching good behavior to her while I . . ." She trailed off, shaking her head.

Ethan placed a comforting hand on her

shoulder. "Tess loves you. She'll stand by you no matter what. So will I."

He couldn't know how much his support meant. "Thank you," she said, tears filling her eyes. "I didn't know you when I gave Tess to you, but I trusted Richard. And you turned out to be the miracle she needed."

He dipped his head in embarrassment. "I just happened to get her because we're alike. As for your problem with your ex —"

"I have a bigger problem than Ryan and his wife." Kelly drew a deep breath. "I've been hiding this secret, afraid of what you all would think of me."

"Nash doesn't know, does he?" Ethan said on a groan.

She shook her head. Her insides cramped and nausea swamped her as she realized how badly she'd screwed up keeping her past a secret. "At first I was hoping it would just go away. And when I heard this guy was asking questions about me at Cuppa Café, I called Ryan and he swore he had things with his wife under control. By the time I decided to tell Nash the truth, his life imploded and it was too late. I couldn't add to his burdens with mine. I was going to tell him this weekend when we were away from everything."

But they couldn't leave town with her

mother's investigator hovering, so she'd have to find another time and place.

"He's had a lot of shocks. Maybe Nash will take it better than you think," Ethan said, trying to offer comfort.

"Maybe I'll take what better?" Nash strode up behind her.

They'd been so caught up in conversation that neither she nor Ethan had seen him approaching.

Kelly closed her eyes and shook her head. *When will life get simpler?* she wondered, and glanced at Ethan once more.

Nash looked from his brother to Kelly. He'd clearly interrupted something. And he'd walked up in time to hear Ethan say his name. "What's going on?"

Kelly wrapped her arms around herself. "My prodigal mother's returned and there's every chance she wants Tess."

Ethan explained what Nash had missed.

Listening, thinking about how easily the bastard strode into the school and singled out his sister thanks to the alphabetical order of the setup, Nash's gut tightened in anger.

"He had no right to talk to her at all. How the hell did he get in here?"

"Walked right in among all the other parents," Ethan muttered.

Nash glanced around him. "Where's Tess now?"

"Faith took her for a walk," Kelly said.

Ethan nodded. "Look, before Tess gets back, I need to make something clear. You and I have problems," he said, gesturing between himself and Nash. "And now you have issues with Dare. I don't care how legitimate these things are, until we find out what Tess's mother wants and how far she'll go to get it, we're a unit. *All* of us stick together and nobody gives her ammunition to use against us in court. Understood?" He stared at Nash, daring him to disagree.

At one time Nash would have hauled off and hit his brother or told him where to shove his orders. But somehow enough time had passed for Nash to see how Ethan had changed. How committed his brother was to raising Tess and doing it right.

Yeah, part of him hated to admit it. Another part respected him for it. As for Dare, that was Nash's personal issue and he'd keep it out of the family dynamic. He had to for Tess's sake.

So Nash met his older brother's gaze and held out his hand. With a distinct look of relief on his face, Ethan shook it.

"I'm not handing Tess over to your mother," Ethan promised. "Married, not married, she's going to have a fight on her hands."

Nash didn't doubt it.

But for all Ethan was worried about Tess, Nash had another concern and that was Kelly. Because she'd be siding against her own mother. And no matter how much she believed Tess belonged with them, she had to be hurting inside.

And he wanted to be the one to make her pain go away.

"There are Faith and Tess. I'll go talk to her," Ethan said.

"What will you tell her?" Kelly asked.

"That we're not sure who the man was or what he wants, but I'm looking into it and she shouldn't worry." He spread his hands out in front of him. "A white lie, sort of."

"Works for me," Nash muttered. No need to upset Tess. Not until they knew for sure if her mother wanted custody or just to say hi. *We should be so lucky,* he thought to himself.

Ethan headed to his wife and Nash turned to Kelly.

He took her hands in his. "You're cold." He rubbed her hands between his.

"Cold hands, warm heart," she tried to joke.

He frowned. "I think that's feet and quit

trying to make light of this. When we get back to your place, we'll talk about your mom," he promised her.

She shook her head. "I can't even think about her without wanting to do bodily harm. Tess isn't a toy to be passed back and forth."

He lifted her hands to his lips and pressed a kiss against her knuckles. "Ethan's taking care of Tess. What about you?"

She wrinkled her nose. "What about me?"

"What about what your mom did to *you?*"

Kelly blinked up at him in surprise. "What do you mean? It's Tess she wants."

"But it's you she's targeting. Your life she's digging into. You're the one she left in charge without asking whether it was a job you wanted or could even handle." He released one hand and slid his finger down her cheek. "How about for one second you think about yourself?"

She looked into his understanding eyes, obviously stunned. "You're the first person who asked about me."

"Get used to it," Nash said in a deep voice he barely recognized. He wrapped his arm around her and pulled her close.

"Don't make promises you can't keep," she whispered.

"Kelly —"

"Let's go!" Tess shouted at them. "We're leaving."

"Coming," Kelly said, abruptly turning away.

Nash groaned. Fine, they'd continue this discussion later.

They all walked out to the car, Dare maintaining a safe distance from Nash. He knew he'd have to deal with his brother eventually, but Dare didn't seem inclined to talk and Nash was still too pissed to think rationally.

They'd lingered in the gymnasium so long the parking lot was fairly empty. No sooner had they walked toward their cars when a woman stepped out of the shadows.

"Tess, come say hi to your momma!"

Sixteen

Ethan grabbed Tess's hand and Nash supported Kelly with an arm around her waist.

The overhead lighting was dim, but Nash was able to make out Leah Moss's bleach blond hair. She had similar features to Kelly, but her nose and jaw were more angular and harsh. Kelly was softness and warmth. Tess, it seemed, resembled Nash's side more than her mother.

"Aren't you going to give me a hug?" Leah held her arms out to Tess, gold bracelets jangling in the silence.

Nash glanced at his sister, who'd shrunk into Ethan's broad body. Looking at her pale, frightened face, his heart nearly broke in two. She stared at her mother as if she were looking at a ghost. Tess didn't respond or run over for an I-missed-you hug.

"What are you doing here?" Kelly asked, her voice colder than Nash had ever heard.

Leah gripped her small silver purse tighter

in her fingers. "I want to see my girls. Is that a crime?"

Ethan knelt down until he was at Tess's eye level. "Do you want to see your mother now?"

The teenager shook her head back and forth almost violently.

Ethan rose and placed his hand on Tess's shoulder. "Dare, Faith, take Tess home," Ethan instructed.

"Tess, baby, it's me, Mommy!" Leah called to her.

"Not now," Kelly bit out.

In tense silence, Faith and Dare each held out a hand. Tess eagerly grabbed for them and let them lead her away.

Kelly waited until Tess was out of earshot before turning to her mother. "It's not bad enough that you left without saying good-bye, but you have to show up the same way? You upset her." She folded her arms across her chest.

"That's not fair, Kelly."

Nash thought it was pretty damned accurate.

The wind blew around them, as cold and unfeeling as this woman apparently was.

Leah cleared her throat. "Roger Grayson told me you were looking for me."

"And you didn't have to travel far to get

to us. Were you waiting in the parking lot?" Kelly asked in disgust. "Instead, you sent a strange man in to scare Tess. A private investigator you hired to dig up dirt on your own daughter."

"You packed up and left Manhattan. I had to know what I was dealing with before I saw you again." Leah whined her explanation.

Kelly let out a laugh that Nash knew held a world of hurt. "You mean keeping in touch with me never occurred to you before now? Checking on Tess never crossed your mind?" She raised an eyebrow, her expression as cool as her eyes when she looked at her mother.

To Leah's credit, and Nash gave her very little, the woman glanced down, appearing ashamed. "I had to get myself together before I could come back."

"You mean you had to find a man to take care of you?" Kelly asked. "I heard you were married. Forgive me if I don't congratulate you."

"I can't believe you aren't happy for me," Leah said, pouting, like a little girl.

"Mom, go home, okay?" Kelly said, sounding exhausted.

Over Kelly's head, Ethan met Nash's gaze. They'd just been given a glimpse into how

Kelly had had to parent her own mother.

Nash studied Leah, trying hard to see what had drawn his father and allowed him to betray his family. Whereas Nash's mother had had a natural beauty, Leah, in her form-fitting red dress with shirring, clearly meant to call attention to attributes Nash doubted were God given. Instead of making her look younger, Leah looked old and used. Alcohol had probably contributed. Hell, maybe her artificial looks had been attractive when she was younger, but Nash couldn't see any beauty now. And given how she'd treated her children, there wasn't much inside to like either.

"I can't go home," Leah insisted. "We need to talk first."

Kelly would have laughed at her mother if this whole situation weren't so pathetic. If she wasn't doing everything she could to stay on her feet. The last thing she'd expected was her mother to show up now. But as soon as the PI had said who hired him, Kelly realized she should have.

Impulsive, selfish, that was Leah. No thought to what was good for anyone but herself. "What do you want?" Kelly asked her mother again, eager to get rid of her.

Kelly didn't want to be around her any more than she wanted Nash and Ethan subjected to their father's onetime lover.

"I don't think we should have this conversation in front of them." Leah pointed at the men without meeting their eyes.

"Why not?" Kelly asked. "We're not going to talk about me. You want to talk about Tess. And she's *their* sister too. Unless you've forgotten that you slept with their father?"

"Kelly!" Leah said, horrified, her perfectly red lips opening in an *O.*

Kelly rolled her eyes. "It's a little late to be embarrassed, don't you think?"

Leah dragged her gaze upward, looking from Nash to Ethan for the first time.

Uncomfortable silence followed.

"You both have your father's good looks," she said at last.

Nash remained quiet.

Ethan glared.

"Kelly, please. We need to talk alone."

Kelly shook her head, confused. She knew her mother wanted custody of Tess. She just didn't know why. Why had her mother discovered her parenting genes all of a sudden? And what did her new marriage have to do with bringing her daughter home? Kelly was dying to know but until Leah mentioned the word *custody,* Kelly would be damned if she'd give her the opening.

"Nash and Ethan stay," Kelly said.

Nash shrugged. "We stay," he told Leah.

Ethan didn't have to utter a word. His dark, dominating visage said it all.

"Your father loved you boys," Leah said unexpectedly.

Kelly sucked in a startled breath and looked at Nash.

He winced but kept quiet.

"If their father loved them so much, he shouldn't have cheated on their mother," Kelly muttered.

Leah kicked a foot petulantly against the blacktop. "It always comes down to that, doesn't it?"

Kelly braced herself for the oncoming tantrum. Heaven knew she'd lived through enough of them. "To what?" she asked.

"To me having an affair. You've always looked down on me because of my relationship with Mark Barron."

"Because he was married! You knowingly slept with a man who had a wife and three young children!" And Kelly couldn't stand the thought or the sight of her mother since she'd found out.

Dimly she was aware of Nash and Ethan surrounding her on both sides, the conversation as awkward and awful for them as it was for her.

Her mother strode up to her, invading her space, wagging a finger in Kelly's face. "My God, you're a judgmental hypocrite. But you were no better than me when you slept with Ryan Hayward!" her mother spat back.

The words hit Kelly like a slap and she struggled for air. "Ryan was legally separated," she said through gritted teeth. "I made damned sure I saw papers before I got involved with him because I had no desire to be like you." She trembled with hurt and rage.

Her mother had been around during the time she'd been involved with Ryan. She just happened to take off while Kelly had been trying to cope with the end of the affair, the pain and the betrayal. Not that Leah had cared about her older daughter's emotional well-being. Nobody's feelings mattered but her own.

The lump in Kelly's throat grew larger and tears threatened, making her unable to speak or fight back.

Leah had no such trouble. "It's so easy for you to judge," she went on. "Why is that? Where does that moral righteousness come from? You met Ryan while you were working as an escort! Where do you get off judging me?" Leah asked, sounding hysterical now.

Kelly whipped around, her gaze darting from her mother and the vile words she spewed to Nash and the stunned expression of disbelief on his face.

"How the hell would you know that?" Kelly asked, horrified.

"Escort?" Beside her, Nash stiffened and Kelly's entire world crashed around her.

"It's not as bad as it sounds," Kelly said, the words sounding pathetic and lame, even to her.

"It's in the reports my investigator gave me," Leah mumbled, sounding at least a touch ashamed of the route she'd taken.

Not that it mattered. Nothing did.

"That's it," Ethan said suddenly. He stepped forward, placing his hand beneath Leah's elbow and leading her away from Kelly, giving her much-needed breathing room.

"You have no right to speak to your daughter that way. Her situation was nothing like yours. She was the victim. And a decent mother wouldn't use her painful past against her. You've had your say, and now it's time for you to leave."

"What the hell is going on?" Nash asked. "What does Ethan know that I don't?"

Nausea swept through her and Kelly's knees threatened to buckle.

"I'm going." Leah shook free of Ethan's grasp. "I didn't want it to be this way, Kelly. I thought when I came back you'd be happy to give your sister back to me and get on with your life. Then I discovered you didn't even keep her. You pawned her off on half brothers she didn't even know."

"That's not what happened!" Kelly yelled at her, tears streaming down her face.

She'd done her best for Tess. Her very best until she was afraid of losing her sister altogether. Giving her to Ethan had been a last, desperate resort to save Tess, not dump her.

"Shh," Nash said, softly, wrapping his arms around her and holding her tight, but Kelly sensed his confusion and knew once he understood everything in her past and, worse, that his brother already knew, his feelings of betrayal would end anything good they'd shared.

"I didn't mean to hurt you, Kelly. I'm your mother and I love you. But you judge me so harshly and I just wanted to point out that in reality, you're no better than me."

Kelly shook her head, wanting to deny those words with everything in her. But her mother was right. And that was what Kelly had been running from for so long.

Unaware of her thoughts, her pain, Leah

continued on. "I'm Tess's mother. And I want her back." Leah straightened her shoulders, trying to pull herself together. "The next time you hear from me it'll be through my lawyer."

"Why?" The word ripped from Kelly's chest. "You hated being a mother. You weren't a parent when you were home. Why in the world would you want her back now?"

Leah glanced away. "My husband has money, so don't think I won't fight you." She turned and headed across the lot to her own car.

"You won't get Tess," Kelly called to her mother's retreating back. "I'll fight you in court. Ethan, Nash, Dare, and I will fight you. You aren't worthy of being her mother!"

Kelly's legs shook so badly as Ethan unlocked the car door that Nash had to lower her into the passenger's seat of his truck.

"Calm down," he said gruffly. "Take deep breaths."

She slowly drew in air and let it out, over and over until the anger and dizziness receded. "I'm okay," she said.

"Are you sure?" Ethan asked, concern etching his features.

Nash kept a comforting hand on her shoulder.

"Yes. I'm sorry you had to deal with her."

Ethan shook his head. "It'll be okay. I'm sure she has enough skeletons for us to dig up and use. Tess isn't going anywhere."

"He's right," Nash said. "I have a great guy on my payroll. I'll call him first thing in the morning."

"Good, since my guy couldn't manage to locate Leah before she found us," Ethan said in disgust.

"We need to find out why she wants Tess." Kelly's gut told her the answer to that question was the key to beating Leah in court.

"We will," Nash promised.

Kelly glanced up at Ethan. "You need to get home to Tess. She's going to be upset and confused." Just like Kelly was. "Do you want me to come over?" she offered.

"Ethan can handle Tess," Nash said. "We need to talk." His fingers suddenly tightened on her shoulder.

Her stomach cramped and she forced herself to meet his gaze. One look and she saw how quickly things between them had changed. Gone was the desire in his eyes from the stairwell earlier. Instead, there was wariness and distrust, two things she never wanted him to feel toward her.

She swallowed hard. "I know we do. Can you handle Tess?" she asked Ethan.

"Of course." He shot her an apologetic glance. "I'll have Tess call you later," he promised.

"Thanks." She rose to her feet and shut the door to his car.

Ethan raised his hand in good-bye. He climbed into his Jag, started the engine, and drove away, leaving Kelly to face the man she loved.

Nash's wary stare merely cemented the reason Kelly had told him not to make promises he couldn't keep. When someone Nash cared about disappointed him, he shut them out. And she knew her news would do that and more. It had been seductive to think she could rely on him, but as her mother taught her, then Ryan, people rarely stayed around.

So though she loved Nash and had foolishly allowed herself to believe they might have a future, she'd been deluding herself. She was now facing both him and the end.

Nash's gut cramped as he studied Kelly. Shaken and upset, he knew now wasn't the time to push her for answers, but he had no choice.

More revelations. More secrets. More lies. He wondered if they'd ever end.

"What haven't you told me that my

brother already knows?" he asked, keeping his distance as he spoke.

"I want to do this but I need to sit."

He glanced around and caught sight of a swing set on the nearby grass. "Come on."

She followed him to the large iron swing, lowering herself into one.

He leaned against the metal support bar, arms folded across his chest. He hated this feeling of being in the dark and he was dealing with it way too often lately.

"What did your mother mean about you being an escort? And why did Ethan seem to already know everything?" he asked, sounding cold and unable to help it.

Kelly concentrated on kicking the dirt beneath her feet. Though she sat on the swing looking lost and alone, he found himself unable to offer her warmth and comfort, not until he'd heard it all. And maybe not after.

She curled her fingers tighter around the swing's chains. "You already know I didn't want to get involved with another man who had ties to his ex. That's because I was in a serious relationship with a man in Manhattan. His name is Ryan Hayward and he works for a large investment firm there."

Nash's stomach roiled at the thought of her with anyone else. Ridiculous considering he'd been married and divorced, but his feelings for her ran so deep and so close to the surface, he had a hard time being rational.

Somehow he remained silent.

"Ryan and I met under . . . unique circumstances. My friend worked for an escort service. We both owed so much money in student loans and she found this way to make extra cash. I never wanted anything to do with it, but one night she was sick and she had this appointment. If she canceled at the last second, she knew she'd lose the job permanently, so she begged me to take her place. She promised there was no sex involved, so . . . I said okay." She wrapped her hands around her waist, rocking in the swing.

She drew a deep breath and continued. "It sounds so much worse than it was. I didn't sleep with him that night. We just really connected. He wanted to see me again, but I already knew his marriage situation, so I made him prove to me that they were separated and he did. I thought it was okay, but my mother was right. It wasn't. He had a family and a child and I should have stayed far away." Her voice cracked and she kicked harder at the dirt under her feet.

Nash remained silent, letting her gather her thoughts before going on.

"Long story short, after about eight months, Ryan went to discuss something with his ex. One thing led to another and he slept with her. She got pregnant and he went back to her. To try to keep his family together."

Her voice cracked and Nash winced, knowing the pain that had to have caused her. No wonder she'd resisted so hard when she thought Nash was still in love with Annie.

"In the end, Ryan and his wife couldn't make things work and their new divorce proceedings are ugly. She's accusing him of sleeping with an escort, and anything more she can dig up before I have to testify at the divorce proceedings, she'll use. So when I found out the guy talking to Tess was a PI, I panicked. Ethan noticed and asked what was wrong. I just told him tonight. He hasn't known long," she said, looking up at him with big, imploring eyes. "Are you disgusted?" she asked in a small voice.

"God, no." He shook his head. She could never disgust him. "Do you really think I'd judge you for choices you made?"

Even as he asked, the truth dawned on him. Of course she thought that. Why else wouldn't she have confided in him?

She exhaled long and hard. "Thank you for that. I know I should have told you."

And that was the crux of things. He dug his fingers into his jacket. "Why didn't you?"

"In the beginning, I didn't know what you would think. You were so angry all the time. At Ethan, at Faith. Later, Annie begged me to tell you but —"

"Annie knew?" he asked, stunned. "My ex-wife, my older brother . . . Who else knew your past before me?" He felt himself choking on the depth of the betrayal, which was just now setting in.

"Faith," Kelly admitted.

Every muscle in his body tensed up and he stared up at the dark, starless sky, waiting for the pain to come, to explode in his head, but he felt . . . nothing.

Before this revelation, he'd already been raw, hurting, betrayed by everyone he knew at one time or another. This was just one more thing added onto the heap.

"I'm sorry." Her voice broke into his thoughts.

Looking at her tearstained face, he realized she wasn't the one who should apologize. "You know what? There's no need. You don't owe me an explanation. We've been together what? A few weeks? A month?"

But it felt like so much more.

She stood up and grabbed his face, turning his head toward her with chilled hands, forcing him to meet her gaze. "They were intimate weeks. Long enough for me to know *I love you.*"

He jerked back, startled. Not that he should be. He'd been damned close to falling himself. When he looked at her, cheeks red from the cold, eyes damp, she was so damned sexy she took his breath away. But inside him everything had shut down.

He couldn't take any more caring, feeling, or most of all, hurt.

He gripped her wrists and pulled her hands away from his face. "You don't love me, Kelly. We've had great sex. Lots of fun. You were there for me when my world fell apart and I'm grateful." His voice sounded like sandpaper and she winced as it grated over her skin.

Her lower lip trembled. "Are you telling me you don't care about me?" she asked point-blank.

"Of course I care. But we haven't been together long enough for it to be love. Besides, people who love each other trust each other." He thrust his hands into his jacket pockets to avoid touching her, pulling her close, and using her as an escape from his pain. She'd been there for him, but she hadn't trusted him enough to confide in him. That truth gnawed away at him like acid.

He thought he'd stepped up, been the brother Dare needed, the husband Annie wanted, the man Kelly could love. But nothing he'd done had convinced any of them he was trustworthy. Obviously he didn't know the first thing about the people in his life.

And he didn't know the first thing about himself.

With energy to spare and frustration to work out, Nash woke up early the next day and headed to the Y where he normally worked out. He stepped inside and was greeted by the receptionist.

"Hi, Nash."

"Erin, how are you?"

"Pretty good."

He held out his membership card for her to scan. "You're all set."

"Thanks."

She treated him to a wide smile. One that held an invitation . . . if he wanted to take her up on it. He didn't. He nodded and walked past the desk, his mind on one woman only.

He and Kelly were supposed to be on their way to a bed-and-breakfast for the weekend, not broken up with no hope for the future. Neither had discussed the trip. It seemed obvious to Nash that with a custody threat looming over Tess, this was not the time to get away. Combined with the argument and his declaration that it was too soon for her to be in love with him, he assumed she figured out all on her own that the trip wasn't happening.

Nash gestured for a friend of his to spot him, and he lifted weights for a good thirty minutes, promising to return the favor when the other guy was ready.

He wiped his face with a towel, debating whether to hit the treadmill or the elliptical when he felt someone beside him.

"Hey."

Nash glanced at his older brother. "Don't you have a fancy home gym?" he asked.

"Waiting on a few machines to be delivered. Besides I like getting out of the house once in a while." Ethan flicked his towel at Nash like he used to do when they were kids. "You okay?"

Nash let out a groan. "No."

"Want to talk about it?"

Nash looked at Ethan. He'd have thought he'd slit a wrist before he turned to him for anything. "Yeah," Nash said, surprising himself. "I do."

Ethan lowered himself onto an empty bench.

Nash copped a seat beside him. He stared down at his hands, not knowing what he wanted to say. "When you left, I stepped up. I had no choice. I felt responsible for Dare. And we were always close, or I thought we were. He tagged along with me and my friends, and I let him." Nash shrugged, remembering their younger days. "He never once let on there was anything more to his going to the Garcias'."

"Maybe he had to work through things on his own."

Nash turned his head. "At fifteen? More like he didn't think he could come to me." He wondered if Dare would've gone to Ethan if he'd still been around.

"You can't know what he was thinking."

"How about Annie? We were inseparable since we were sixteen. The first time I heard about her being unhappy in our marriage was when she asked me for a divorce. She couldn't come to me either."

"I imagine it's not easy to tell someone you love that you're unhappy," Ethan said.

"Tess didn't exactly warm to me right away."

"She bonded with me first. She was just being protective."

Nash cocked an eyebrow. "What about Kelly? What excuse are you going to come up with for the fact that the woman I was sleeping with didn't think she could tell me about her past and her problems?"

Ethan rested his elbows on his knees and blew out a harsh breath. "My leaving did a number on you. I'm not going to make excuses or say I'm sorry again. I'm just stating the facts. You're loyal. You're someone everyone in the family knows they can depend on."

"But?" Nash asked, needing to hear the truth. Even from Ethan.

Hell, especially from Ethan. He'd been gone for ten years and was completely objective. He might be the only unbiased one left to tell it to him straight.

"But you're a hard man. The first thing people think when they see you is, he's rigid. Inflexible. And as they first get to know you, they think, he sees things in black and white. No shades of gray."

Nash set his jaw. "Explain."

"Ethan left. He's a bastard. His reasons don't matter. Kelly dumped Tess on my doorstep. You thought she had no heart. Until you finally learned differently. Annie's sick, and therefore she's needy. It didn't matter how many times she told you to back off and let her be independent. It was your way or no way." With a shake of his head, Ethan blew out a breath. "Shit, I hate this."

"I asked for it," Nash muttered. And because he had, he listened and tried to process what his older brother was saying.

"And Kelly?" He balled his hands into tight fists.

Ethan leaned his back against the wall. "She told me she hoped it would all just disappear, and by the time she wanted to tell you, your life had imploded. She didn't want to burden you. But Faith said that after Kelly told her everything, even Faith wasn't sure how you'd react."

Nash groaned. He'd asked for the truth and Ethan hadn't held back. He supposed he owed him for that. He'd never realized how damned intractable he'd become and had a lot to think about later.

"She said she loved me." Nash surprised himself with the admission. His entire body warmed at the memory of her unexpected declaration. Part of him had wanted to forget everything else going on and tell her he loved her right back. But the pain of betrayal had already swamped him and he'd immediately lumped her in with everyone else in his life who hadn't trusted him with the truth.

Like Ethan just said, Nash saw things in black and white.

"Do I want to know what you said back?" his brother asked.

Nash winced. "That it was too soon for love. That we had a good time and great sex."

His brother shook his head and rose from his seat. "Good going," he muttered, slapping Nash on the back. "Know what I think?"

Nash didn't answer.

"I think you should go home and figure out how you feel about this woman. Because if it's what I think, then your window to fix things is damned small so you'd better get moving."

Wise words. Too bad Nash hadn't a clue how to make things better with himself, let alone with Kelly.

Seventeen

Kelly's head hurt like she had a hangover. She slept in, unable to pull herself out of bed to deal with the most basic things like showering and eating breakfast. The one thing she did do was call Tess and force cheer into her voice as she spoke to her sister and promised they'd find a way to let her stay with Ethan.

In the interest of fairness, she told Tess she should keep an open mind about seeing her mother and having a relationship with her if that's what Tess wanted.

Her sister launched into a foul-mouthed tirade the likes of which Kelly hadn't heard since the day she'd dragged her to Ethan's this past summer. Her ears still ringing, Kelly made Tess promise to talk to her therapist about Leah. No matter her own feelings, she didn't want Tess to wake up one day, an adult with regrets over impulsive teenage decisions. Which didn't mean she wanted Leah in Tess's life, not unless her mother had done a real one eighty and was now Mother Teresa, which Kelly doubted.

By noon, she rolled out of bed and made herself a cup of vegetable soup. She was drinking it when she heard a knock at her door.

Her stomach flipped for a quick minute before she remembered Nash didn't want anything to do with her. She padded to the door and opened it wide, only to find a process server waiting for her on the other side.

She glanced at the blue papers in her hand. A quick read told her this was what she'd been expecting. A mandatory summons to appear on Friday, 11:00 A.M., in Manhattan at a deposition in the divorce proceedings of Mr. and Mrs. Ryan Hayward.

Kelly was both nauseous and oddly relieved. At least this part of her life would be over soon. And even if the scandal hit the Manhattan papers, Tess had more to worry about than her sister's issues. And the rest of the Barron family already knew her deep, dark secrets.

The irony was, now that she'd received the summons, things didn't look as bad as she might have thought. In fact, it felt like she'd panicked for no good reason, at least as far as the family was concerned.

Considering she'd lost Nash over withholding the truth, Kelly couldn't say she felt any better.

After a long weekend, Kelly returned to work on Monday. She'd barely begun to tackle her work for the day when she heard the sound of footsteps and then a familiar voice.

"Hello? Kelly?"

"In my office, Annie," Kelly called out.

Annie stepped into the doorway. "Where were you this morning? I picked up my coffee and waited, but you never showed. And you never miss your morning coffee run."

Kelly shook her head and managed a laugh. "No wonder I feel so fuzzy. I forgot," she admitted.

Narrowing her gaze, Annie stepped toward Kelly and placed her hand against her forehead. "Are you sick? Fever?"

Kelly shook her head.

"Well, you look like shit," Annie said bluntly.

"Why, thank you." Kelly would have liked to throw back a snappy retort along the lines of *So do you,* but she'd be lying. Annie, in her brown sweater, with her big eyes and bright complexion, was glowing. She looked gorgeous.

And happy.

Kelly's stomach twisted hard. "Things with Joe are good?" she asked, as pleased for her friend as she was unhappy herself.

"Amazing." Annie pulled a chair closer to Kelly. "What is wrong? You can tell me. I'm your friend. Just because I'm Nash's ex-wife doesn't mean he has my loyalty. You do," Annie assured her. "We are living our own lives, going our separate ways."

Kelly nodded. "I know. I do. And I value our friendship more than you can imagine." She hadn't had many close friends, and Annie, who'd accepted her so quickly, confided in her about her MS and about Joe, held a special place in Kelly's heart.

"Then talk to me. Please."

Kelly swallowed hard. "My mother wants custody of Tess." She poured out the story of the PI. "And then she showed up at school and held her arms out to Tess, like she hadn't been gone for more than a year." Kelly's heart beat faster at the memory. "We argued. In front of Ethan and Nash. She said I always judged her for her affair with Mark Barron because he was married, but I was a hypocrite. By getting involved with Ryan, I was no better than she was." Kelly stared at the stack of documents on her desk without really seeing them. "The worst part is, she's right." She started trembling, like she had that night.

Annie jumped up and grabbed her hands. "Your mother is a selfish bitch. You are nothing like her. Do you hear me?"

"Ethan said the same thing," Kelly said with a small smile.

"And Nash?" Annie asked softly. "What did he say?"

Kelly blinked back tears. "When he realized Ethan already knew everything? When I let it slip that you'd begged me to tell him, so you knew too?"

"Oh God. I'm so sorry."

"I told him I loved him and he said we weren't together long enough for it to be love. That we had great sex and a lot of fun. He was grateful for how I helped him through a tough time. But love required trust and we didn't have that." Kelly shrugged, looking up at Annie. "And he was right about that too." Kelly swiped at a tear dripping down her face.

"I'm going to kill him," Annie muttered. She rose and began pacing the small room.

"For letting the sum of his past experience dictate his response? Come on, Annie. You know he has every right to feel betrayed. Add up the people in his life who didn't come to him with one thing or another."

"Then he needs to grow up and take responsibility for that. There's a reason nobody comes to him. You told other people because you knew they'd understand. He's so damn rigid and set in how he thinks. By the time you get up the nerve to talk to him, there's too much water under the bridge, you know?"

Kelly shook her head. "Nice analogy, but I knew him. I knew his weaknesses. I should have trusted him. If he'd heard it from me first, the right way, maybe he'd have come around eventually. Or maybe he'd have surprised me and just understood and not judged. I'll never know and that's *my* fault." She shrugged. "Who knows. Maybe there's enough blame to go around, but any way you cut it, it's over for us."

"I disagree."

Kelly ignored her. That discussion was closed. "In the meantime, guess what I got? A summons to appear at a deposition Friday in Ryan's divorce."

"When it rains, it pours."

"You said it."

"Want me to come with you? For moral support?" Annie asked.

An easy smile lifted Kelly's lips and her spirits. "You're such a good friend. But I'm okay. And I need to do this myself and put it behind me once and for all."

"You're one of the strongest people I know. I admire you." Annie hugged her, made her promise to call if she needed to talk about anything, and took off.

Kelly didn't want to spend another minute thinking about her complicated life, so she dove back to work. She and Richard had a scheduled conference call later in the afternoon during which she hoped he'd sound stronger than the last time they'd spoken. His plan was to return to work for a few hours midweek, see how his stamina held up, and go from there.

In the background, Kelly heard his wife arguing that he'd be there for one hour on his first day, no more.

Kelly grinned. If Mary was fighting with her husband, Richard was definitely on the mend.

She spent the rest of the afternoon working on questions in Richard's next scheduled deposition, which had been postponed until next month. The word *deposition* only served to remind her that perhaps she should bring a lawyer of her own to Ryan's deposition. Even President Clinton had gotten himself in trouble and slapped with a perjury charge after going it alone. Kelly didn't intend to lie, but as a paralegal, she knew better than to take a deposition lightly.

She didn't want to upset Richard, and the only other local lawyer she knew was Nash — the last person she would turn to for help. Instead, she called Ethan, who referred her to his attorney, who promised to have someone call her tonight.

Before heading home for the day, she checked in with Ethan, who assured her that Nash had his own PI digging into her mother's life and he was certain they'd find enough ammunition to fight her and keep Tess.

Then she headed home to her small apartment to spend another night alone. She never knew how quickly you could get used to having another person in your life, or how big a hole they left when they were gone.

The first night Nash spent in his apartment after the art show, the emptiness ate at him. He hadn't spent time there since Dare left, except to pick up clothes or take an occasional shower. The fridge was empty and the place needed a good dusting.

He bit the bullet and called the cleaning service he occasionally used and arranged for them to come first thing Monday; then he went food shopping on Sunday. Of course he was too distracted to make a list, so he forgot a half dozen things, including milk.

After work on Monday, he stopped by the grocery store on his way home. Better to kill time out than to head home to his lonely apartment. Funny, in all the time he'd spent at Kelly's, he'd never cared how small her place was. They'd shared one sink in the bathroom, his toothbrush sat next to hers, his razor kept falling into the sink because there was so little space on the counter, and he just hadn't cared.

Because he'd been with Kelly.

Now he was alone and his big empty condo annoyed the hell out of him.

He pushed the cart down the aisle, slowly picking up the items he needed, using the time alone to think. To come to terms with the things Ethan had told him. He'd had to replay his past in his mind, his attitude toward friends and family and his reactions to people and situations.

Self-reflection sucked.

So did the conclusions he'd come to, because looking inward, Nash didn't like the uptight man he'd become.

Hadn't he thought Dare the more easy-going brother and himself the darker, more uptight one? And he hadn't even known the pain Dare harbored for most of his life. Yet faced with the knowledge, Nash's thoughts had been all about himself and how he'd been betrayed, not about what his little brother had gone through.

As for Kelly, he'd been worse. Instead of being there for her in the aftermath of her mother's scene, harsh words, and threats, he'd walked out on her. Then he'd thrown her love, the one thing he wanted more than life itself, back in her face.

He had so much to fix, so much to make right.

A simple *I'm sorry* wouldn't cut it. Even if Kelly were willing to take him back on an apology alone, it wasn't good enough for Nash. He needed to prove to her that he would change, become someone both she and his family could come to in the future. Only then would he be able to apologize and ask her to forgive him.

As his father used to say, actions speak louder than words. Too bad Mark Barron hadn't lived by his own mantra. But Nash would.

As soon as he figured out how to accomplish his goal.

"Nash!"

He turned at the sound of Annie's voice.

He swore to himself, realizing she'd left a

message on his cell. He'd seen that she'd called, but he hadn't bothered to play back the message yet.

"Hi," he said, pausing to wait for her to catch up to him.

"Hi." She greeted him with a smile, then kissed him on the cheek.

He hugged her and stepped back.

"Fancy meeting you here," she said.

He shrugged. "A man has to eat."

"Didn't you get my message?" she asked, sounding curious, not mad.

He nodded. "I saw you called. I didn't have a chance to listen yet."

"That's progress," she said, sounding pleased. "You didn't rush to call me back, which means you have more important things on your mind." She studied him with inquisitive eyes that saw too much because she knew him too well.

"Anything important?" he asked.

"Depends on whether you think me calling you a dumb-ass is important." She folded her arms across her chest and glared at him.

"What did I do now?" he asked, though he had a hunch he knew. Annie had been talking to Kelly.

She grabbed his jacket, pulling him away

from a few other people who were shopping.

And staring, since she'd yelled at him.

"Are you so stupid that you're going to let Kelly go just because she found you too intimidating to confide in? That's your hang-up, not hers!" Annie jabbed him in the chest as she spoke. "I suggest you learn from past mistakes or you're going to end up alone."

Face flushed, eyes blazing, she looked healthy in a way he hadn't seen in a long time.

"Trust me, I have no intention of growing old by my lonesome," he assured her. "But it's nice to know you care."

"I care about Kelly. You're too stubborn and dumb for me to worry about any longer," she said, but a knowing smirk curled at the corners of her mouth.

She cared. She just didn't want him to know it.

"Seriously, Nash. You can't let her go."

"Do you really think I intend to?" He cocked an eyebrow her way.

Annie lifted her shoulders. "I don't know. Based on what Kelly told me, why should I think anything else?"

"Just because I'm stubborn doesn't mean I can't learn. Relax. I've got it under control." At least he hoped he did.

"Before or after Kelly goes to give her deposition against her ex-boyfriend?"

He stiffened. "When did that come up?"

"She was served over the weekend."

"On top of everything else she's had to deal with?" He ran a frustrated hand through his hair.

"That actually sounds like you care."

He jerked toward her only to find her blue eyes sparkling with mischief.

"Sorry. I couldn't resist." She shook her head and laughed. "Nash, what are you doing to yourself?" she asked, sounding concerned.

"Finding out who the hell I am. If I'd been at all aware, maybe we'd still be married."

"Or maybe we wouldn't have gotten married at all?" she asked softly. "I've done a lot of soul searching too. You were my best friend. The person I trusted most in the world. But we were so young, we didn't even know ourselves."

He agreed. In part. "How could you say you trusted me? You never once let on you were unhappy."

"Because I didn't know myself!" She toyed with the button on her jacket as she spoke. "It wasn't until I was diagnosed that

I looked at life from a whole new perspective. After that I *was* unhappy. I wanted more but didn't know what that more was, so how could I tell you?"

He nodded in understanding. "Thank you for that."

A part of him was sad they hadn't had this talk until now. Another part was grateful for the insight into a difficult time in his past that until now he'd tried hard not to dwell on.

A sad smile crossed her face. "The hard truth is that ever since my diagnosis, you smothered me and I didn't want that. I didn't tell you because I'd always let you make the decisions in our relationship. That was my failing, not yours."

He reached for the shopping cart, grasping it in his hand, letting the cool metal soothe him. "It's not like I listened when you talked either."

At least now he knew why. After Ethan left, Nash had felt a compulsive need to take charge and control. He'd done that with Annie, and as she said, she'd allowed it. But even after their divorce, he hadn't listened when she'd asked him to back off. And regardless of what she said about her own failings, he knew he made it difficult for people to come to him.

Dare was another story entirely. His brother had kept a secret from the time he was fifteen. Nash might be tough, but he couldn't shoulder all the blame for his brother's choice either. Not that it mattered, he realized now. He'd either have to accept what Dare had done or not.

It was over. Nash couldn't change the past and he sure as hell didn't want to lose his brother any more than he wanted to lose Kelly.

"I can't believe we're having this conversation in the cereal aisle," Annie said, giving him a welcome break from his thoughts.

Nash grinned. "Better than the ice-cold frozen-food one."

"Are you going to be okay?" she asked.

He nodded. And for the first time in a long while, he actually believed he'd be just fine.

Nash called a family meeting at his condo. He included everyone, from Kelly to Dare to Ethan and Faith. He told Ethan to keep Tess home with Rosalita.

Nash hadn't seen Dare since Tess's art show. Though they hadn't talked since their argument, Nash knew Dare had spent a couple of nights in a motel before Ethan talked him into moving into a spare room at his house. The place Dare was building wasn't ready and, besides, he had a buyer and he'd soon be finished with the place, making himself a nice profit. So it came as no surprise that Ethan, Faith, and Dare arrived together. Kelly pulled up a short time later.

They gathered in the family room. Everyone knew they were there to discuss Tess, so civility reigned.

Cold civility.

Dare nodded at him when he walked in, but they didn't have any one-on-one conversation, and since Kelly showed up after the rest of the family, there was no time or opportunity.

Still, Nash couldn't tear his gaze away. She wore a pair of navy sweats that rode low on her hips and rolled at the ankles along with a white tank top beneath a hooded zip sweatshirt. All he could think about was the body beneath the heavy clothes. He wanted to pull the zipper down slowly, expose her skin, and lick every part of her he could see before getting to work on the parts she had hidden.

She'd pulled her hair into a ponytail and hadn't bothered with makeup, clearly not caring if she impressed him or not.

She did.

The dark circles under her eyes told him she wasn't sleeping any better without him than he was without her. That was all he needed to know.

"Thanks for coming on such short notice," he said. "The private investigator I hired had some interesting information and I thought you should all hear it together."

Ethan leaned forward, eager for information, while Faith wrapped an arm around his shoulder, there for him in whatever way he needed.

Nash envied them the easiness between them. The love that existed and could be counted on. He had a lot of work to do before he'd get Kelly to believe he wanted those same things with her.

But they all had to deal with Leah Moss first. "Okay. Apparently when Leah left Tess and Kelly, she headed to Atlantic City with her then boyfriend. He proceeded to lose a ton of money at one of the casinos, couldn't cover his marker, and ended up in jail. Instead of sticking by her man, Leah moved on in search of the next target. Of course she had no money, so she took a job as a waitress in one of the larger casino restaurants."

He glanced at Kelly, who listened with little reaction to give away her feelings. His heart clenched, wishing he could hold her while he told them the rest, but they weren't at that place anymore. He could only hope they'd get back there — soon.

"While working, Leah met Sean Muldoon, a wealthy man who wanted a more mature wife, since the second Mrs. Muldoon, a twenty-something-year-old, had divorced him and hooked up with someone closer to her own age. The first Mrs. Muldoon had given him two now adult children and was long gone."

"This sounds like a soap opera," Faith said. Her gaze shot to Kelly. "Sorry. My family's actually worse."

Kelly replied with a weak smile.

"Go on," Ethan said.

Nash nodded. "Whirlwind courtship and marriage. His adult children aren't happy, of course. They see their future inheritance dwindling. Muldoon lives near Livingston, New Jersey."

Dare whistled. "Nice area."

"With families who send their kids to private school, who attend their sports games . . . and art shows," he said pointedly. "In other words, to get in with the 'in' crowd, Leah needs to play the role of doting mother. Prove Muldoon's kids are wrong and she's not a gold digger, just a loving mother who fell in love with their father."

Dare cleared his throat and looked at Ethan. "Nash's PI found this damn fast. How the hell did your guy miss this?"

"He wasn't looking. The man got lazy and greedy. Last case he worked for me concerned a business issue with my ex-partner. I had no problems there, so when he told me he kept hitting a dead end on this, I believed him. He was taking his retainer and enjoying his life," Ethan muttered.

"I take it you fired him?" Nash asked.

"And reported him to the licensing agency." Ethan drummed his fingers against the table. "What business is Muldoon in?" he asked, changing the subject.

"Manufacturing. Old family business that his brother runs while he pulls in a predetermined share."

"So far we have a nice claim, but how can we use this to keep Tess? If they tell a judge they can give her a good life, a child's mother has a much better chance than a sister or brother." Kelly hugged her arms tight to her chest, her fear for Tess obvious.

"Because there's more," Nash said, looking into her eyes, searching for a glimpse of the feelings she'd said she had for him.

Right now he saw bleak desperation, but

he hoped to change that. Soon, he promised himself. Once they got through this mess with her mother.

"Muldoon is a functioning alcoholic. According to the report I have, he has a fully stocked bar, visits his country club daily where he passes the afternoons watching the stock market on the TV screen, and he always has a drink in his hand."

Kelly's eyes lit up with hope. "And my mother? Is she still drinking?" She flexed and unflexed her fingers, over and over. "I hate it that I'm hoping my own mother is still a lush just so we can keep Tess." She looked down, shamed and embarrassed.

"You aren't a bad person, Kel. You're human." Dare eased closer and wrapped an arm around her shoulder.

Brotherly, Nash knew, but it had him grinding his teeth anyway.

"Nash? What did you find out about my mother?" Kelly asked, the first time she'd spoken directly to him.

"Let's just say from the people my guy talked to, Leah and her husband enable each other's drinking. Day and night. We can paint an ugly picture for the court."

She nodded and kept up the rhythmic clenching of her fists.

Nash waited for his family to process the

information for a few minutes before picking up the file that had been expressed to him earlier in the day.

"Here," he said to Ethan, handing everything over to him. "I'm sure you have a good family-law attorney, but if you need names, let me know." Nash handled more business and real estate law, though he did the occasional favor for a friend that involved something more personal, and he'd even tackled family court.

But Nash wouldn't let his ego stand in the way of hiring the best person to protect Tess.

Ethan slapped the thick folder against his thigh. "I'm hoping to avoid court altogether. My hunch is that the Muldoons' reputation in the community means more to them than getting custody of a kid they don't really want. The last thing they need is to have their dirty laundry aired in the community, and if they take us to court, that's exactly what will happen. I'll make sure of it," he swore, his tone so dark even Faith trembled.

"And you'll make sure my mother knows it before this goes so far," Kelly said, awareness of his intentions dawning. "I'll go with you."

"No." Ethan shook his head, speaking before Nash could say the same.

Good thing or Kelly would probably accuse him of being as controlling as Annie had. He'd just wanted to protect her, but as he'd learned with his ex, Kelly didn't need his protecting. She needed him to stand by her, support her, but let her know he believed in her abilities and strength.

It wasn't easy. Hell, it went against every guy instinct he had. But this change in him was worth the reward.

"She's my mother."

"And she'll play dirty, using your emotions to rile you up and set you off." Ethan didn't have to remind her of her reaction to Leah's threats the other night.

Nash saw the memory flash in her eyes.

"Let me deal with her," Ethan said. "I can play this as cold as I have to. Without you there for her to try and manipulate, I'll have the upper hand."

"I'm prepared now. There's no way I'd let her get to me like that again."

Kelly straightened her shoulders and Nash was proud of her resolve. "I know you wouldn't," Nash said, unable to hold back.

A quick flash of gratitude flickered across her face before she masked all feelings toward him once more.

"I know that too," Ethan assured her.

Kelly blew out a long breath. "But I see

your point. Our position is stronger without me there."

Now Nash admired the strength of character it took to admit she'd be better off backing down.

"We'll have custody papers drawn up for her to sign," Ethan said. "Hopefully when I show Leah the consequences of pursuing this, she'll do a full retreat."

Kelly nodded. "I can't believe I'm asking this, but . . . what about visitation? She is Tess's mother. Granted, she hasn't been much of one, but shouldn't Tess have the choice as she gets older if she wants to see Leah?"

Ethan paused in thought.

"I'd insist that she get help, get sober first," Kelly added. "I'm not looking to put Tess in any emotional or physical danger, but growing up without a mother or knowing your mother didn't care can leave emotional scars."

Nash closed his eyes against the pain in those words.

"We'll deal with that in the agreement," Ethan promised. "Sober and Tess's choice."

"Thank you," Kelly whispered.

Family meeting over, everyone rose, said their good-byes, and filed out the door.

"Kelly, can you stay for a little while?"

Nash asked before she walked out.

She turned, her eyes wide with surprise. He saw the war going on behind the mask of her expression that hid her emotions from him. Or tried to.

She shook her head. "I can't."

He reached for her but she stepped back. " 'Won't,' you mean?"

"Can't." She set her jaw. "I have plans."

He inclined his head, studying her for a brief minute before nodding. "Okay, then. Have a nice night."

"Thank you."

Too soon, she was gone and Nash was alone. A place he'd created for himself. Now it was up to him to rectify his mistake.

Kelly walked out of Nash's condo, head held high. The minute she heard the door close behind her, she backed herself against the wall and drew in a long breath.

She had plans, all right. Plans to go over her testimony with the lawyer Ethan found for her. God, it was hard to be in the same room with Nash and not be with him. It was worse than breaking up with a friend who ran with the same crowd because she couldn't avoid family events. Well, she'd just have to learn to cope.

Being alone with him wouldn't help her

deal any easier, so it couldn't be part of the plan.

EIGHTEEN

Nash knew Dare took lunch at the Family Restaurant. He considered meeting up with him at Ethan's, but he didn't want Tess subjected to tension between her brothers, so he opted for a public meeting.

A surprise meeting.

Nash waylaid his brother's partner, Mac, handed him a twenty, and asked him to get fast food and come back to pick up Dare later.

Heavy-handed and controlling? Yeah.

But necessary if he wanted peace.

Nash waved to Macy, indicating she didn't have to seat him by pointing to Dare in the back booth. She nodded and refocused on the couple who walked in behind him.

"Mind if I join you?" Nash asked his brother.

Dare's blue eyes grew wary. "Mac's coming in a second."

"He's giving us a few minutes." Nash

might have commandeered this meeting, but he wasn't going to force his brother to talk to him.

Dare waved at the empty booth. "Sit."

Nash lowered himself into the bench across from his brother. "How've you been?"

"Fine."

"Work good?"

"Also fine."

Nash gripped his hands beneath the table. "This how it's going to be? Like pulling teeth?"

Dare shrugged. "I'm not sure what you want me to say."

Nash ran a frustrated hand through his hair. "Jesus. I don't want to dictate what comes out of your mouth. Just talk to me."

Dare leaned back in the booth and glanced up at the ceiling before looking at Nash once more. "If I had to make that same choice again, whether or not to live with the Rossmans, I'd do the exact same thing."

"Fair enough. I can't fathom what you went through back then."

"Who are you and what have you done to my middle brother?" Dare asked. "Did you really just accept that?" Shock rippled through Dare's voice.

"Yeah. I did." Nash's lips twisted in a wry

smile. "Look, none of us can change what happened back then. If we could, our parents would still be alive. I want to go forward as best we can."

"I lied to you for years," Dare said, pushing him.

Nash figured he wanted to be sure they put everything behind them. "Yeah, you did. And I still want to kick your ass for doing it."

"Try it." Dare grinned. "I have academy training."

Nash shook his head and groaned. "I can't tell you I understand why you kept silent all these years. But we've all made so many mistakes, me included, I think it's better to let it all go."

"I wish it were always that simple," Dare muttered, his eyes darkening to a deep, stormy blue.

There it is, Nash thought. The glimpse of darkness and inner torment he occasionally sensed in his brother.

"But if you're game for forgive-and-forget, I'm grateful. I want my brother back." Dare held out a hand.

Across the table, Nash shook it.

Another heavy weight lifted from his chest. Breathing came easier again. He'd never not had Dare in his life, and the last weeks had been a hell he didn't care to revisit.

"You want to move back in?" Nash asked.

"Are you hiring yourself a Rosalita?"

Nash shook his head and laughed. "Getting spoiled?"

"It's temporary. I'll be out before you know it. Besides, I figure it's only a matter of time before you get Kelly to forgive you for being an ass."

"Burgers for the Barron boys," Gina, their waitress said, placing their plates down in front of them.

Nash raised an eyebrow. "I didn't order yet."

Gina patted him on the shoulder. "You never vary. I figured why wait. Yell if you need anything else," she said, and headed for another table.

The delicious aroma of hamburger and thick French fries assaulted him and his stomach grumbled, reminding him he was starving.

"Well?" Dare asked as Nash took a large bite of his food.

"You get Kelly to forgive you for being an ass yet?" Dare began eating too.

Nash wiped his mouth with the napkin before answering. "What makes you think I was an ass?"

"You trying to tell me the breakup was her fault?" Dare poured ketchup onto his plate, then passed the bottle to Nash.

He rolled his eyes. "I'll fix things."

"Waiting for anything in particular?" Dare asked. "Like another guy to step in?"

Nash curled his hands into tight fists. "Do you know anything?" he asked, recalling her saying she had plans the other day.

Dare let out a loud laugh. "No, but it was worth the show to see your reaction. Seriously, what are you waiting for?"

"She wouldn't stick around to talk to me the other day, but don't worry," he said, as much to assure his brother as himself. "I have a plan."

On Thursday, Kelly picked Tess up after school to take her for ice cream. Tomorrow she would go to the city for the deposition and then hopefully that part of her life would be over for good.

She just wished she knew what the future held.

She placed her order, coffee ice cream and hot fudge, while Tess ordered Monster Mash ice cream and marshmallow fluff, which Kelly thought looked like green goop. Neither of them cared that the weather was cooler now — ice cream was a treat they always enjoyed.

Kelly nabbed a window seat at a table in the corner of the shop, where she and Tess could talk in private. She gave her sister a few minutes to enjoy her ice cream before broaching a subject she wished they could avoid.

"We need to talk about Mom."

"Hell no," Tess said and began to shovel spoonfuls of green goop into her mouth to emphasize her point.

Kelly sighed. "Fine. I'll talk. You'll listen."

Tess shoved her spoon into her cup so hard the plastic handle cracked in her hand. "She left me," Tess said in a small voice.

"That's why we're making sure she can't just come back and insist you live with her now." Kelly was having a hard time talking to Tess while her sister's entire mouth was covered with green ice cream and white fluff.

Kelly handed her a napkin and pointed to her mouth. Tess grabbed it and wiped her face clean, then leaned back in her seat.

"You trust me, don't you?" Kelly asked her sister.

For the first time, Kelly wondered. She'd left Tess with Ethan, just as her mother had left her with Kelly. The realization about the similarity was too long in coming, and

Kelly wanted to kick herself for not coming to that conclusion sooner.

"Yeah, I trust you," Tess said.

The teen sounded sincere but Kelly needed to know for sure. "Even though I left you with Ethan this summer?"

Tess bobbed her head up and down. "Yeah. I was a pain in the ass. You had no choice." She stared down at her dessert, suddenly not so interested in the treat.

"Hey." Kelly waited till Tess looked back up. "Yes, you were a pain, but you were going through a hard time. We both were, and I turned to Ethan for help. I realize now that in your eyes, that could make me no better than Mom, but I swear to God, Tess, I love you and I will be there for you no matter how big a pain in the ass you are."

She softened the last part with her tone, knowing she could always joke with Tess, even over something as serious as this. Neither of them could deny Tess had been difficult.

To Kelly's surprise, Tess blinked hard and tears fell from her eyes, showing her big, tough Tess wasn't so tough after all.

Kelly's heart broke at the sight. "What is it?"

"We're a team," Tess said, repeating something Kelly had often told her in the middle of the night when Tess would get scared and crawl into bed with her.

"Yeah, we are." Kelly smiled, the pain in her chest easing, somewhat.

"But so are Ethan and Faith."

Kelly narrowed her gaze, confused by Tess's comment. "I don't get it."

Tess began to rock in her seat. "They just got married. They don't need a kid hanging around them all the time. Isn't it just easier for them to let Mom take me?" she asked, wide-eyed and truly afraid.

Kelly folded her hands on the table and leaned in close. "You listen to me. If I thought for one second that Ethan didn't want you, I'd move you in with me and fight Mom all by myself," she said, meaning every word.

"Then why don't you?" Tess didn't meet her gaze. Instead, she stirred her spoon around the now melting ice cream in front of her.

"Because in my heart and soul, with everything I believe inside me, I know Ethan loves you, wants you, and will do everything in his power to keep you with him. Faith too. And let's face it. Aren't you happier in a house that's a real home than you would be in my one-bedroom apartment?"

Kelly waited for an answer, swearing to

herself that if Tess said otherwise, she'd pack her sister up tonight and move the teenager in with her.

"You won't be insulted if I tell you the truth?" Tess asked.

"Considering this is the first time you'd be *asking* to express your opinion? Of course not. Go for it." Kelly encouraged her sister to open up.

"Then, yeah. I love living with Ethan and Faith, and having my own room. I can have friends over and there's always someone home after school. And I don't miss you too much because I see you all the time."

"Of course you do. I make sure of that." Kelly tipped her head to the side. "So you believe me? About Ethan and Faith wanting you?"

Tess nodded. "It's just . . ."

"That people close to you have disappointed you and let you down, so you're afraid to trust."

Tess perked up in her seat. "How do you know exactly what I'm thinking?" she asked.

Kelly laughed. "Because I'm older and wiser, that's how."

Tess rolled her eyes and grinned, and Kelly knew they were finished with the hard part of the afternoon.

"So how come you and Nash aren't together no more?"

Kelly nearly choked. So much for the hard part being over.

"*Any*more." She managed to correct her sister's grammar, buying time with which to come up with an answer. "Because sometimes two people can care about each other, but because they've had bad experiences in the past, it affects how they react to each other in the present." Kelly nodded, pleased with her explanation. "Do you understand?"

Tess shook her head. "Nope."

Kelly sighed.

"Good afternoon, ladies."

Kelly stiffened at the sound of Nash's familiar, too-sexy voice.

"Hey, Nash! We were just talking about you," Tess said, obviously back to her happily nosy, troublemaking self.

"Oh, yeah?" Nash grabbed one of the white iron chairs, turned it around backward, and sat down beside Kelly. "Do tell."

"Do not speak," Kelly warned Tess. Instead, she fished through her wallet and pulled out a ten-dollar bill. "Here. Go buy yourself a new ice cream. Our talk ruined yours before you had a chance to eat it." She waved the bill in front of her sister.

Tess glanced between the two adults, then grabbed the money, hopefully realizing her life was on the line.

"Please buy me a bottle of water while you're up there," Kelly said.

Tess glanced over to the counter. "There's a long line," she complained.

"Go!"

Tess stomped toward the counter.

"Not so smooth," Nash said with a smile.

"Hey, she's gone for a few minutes. Mission accomplished."

He laughed and Kelly almost forgot they'd broken up. Almost but not quite.

He looked handsome in his work suit, a navy pinstripe with a pastel multicolored tie. The mental reminder of their distance came as a swift kick to her heart.

"So what's the special occasion?" He pointed to Tess's melted ice cream.

"I picked her up from school. I wanted to talk to her about Leah. See how she really felt about everything."

Nash nodded in understanding. "Is she okay?"

Kelly appreciated that he was being civil despite their breakup. She knew it was for Tess's sake, since they'd have years of family get-togethers ahead of them. But she couldn't say it didn't hurt.

"She will be once we take care of things legally. As long as she feels like she's in limbo, she's going to question everyone's feelings for her."

Anger flashed in his eyes for a moment before he banked the emotion. "It's not fair for her to go through so much emotional turmoil so young."

"Nobody's immune from pain or disappointment." He ought to know that first-hand, Kelly thought.

"You're right. And sometimes that pain causes us to say or do stupid things to the wrong people. People who don't deserve it." Nash met her gaze and held on.

There was so much he wanted to say, to explain.

He'd missed her like crazy but he knew from Annie that Kelly had her deposition tomorrow and he'd just dropped off legal documents at Ethan's, for him to use to confront Kelly's mother. It didn't seem fair to ask her to discuss *them* right now.

Which meant he was holding back. For good reason. Suddenly Ethan's words about Kelly came back to him. *By the time she wanted to tell you, your life had imploded. She didn't want to burden you.* Just like he didn't want to burden her now, by forcing her to deal with their relationship when the rest of her world was crumbling around her.

God, he'd been so arrogant and selfish,

yelling at her and casting her out of his life.

"That almost sounds like an apology." Kelly's voice interrupted his thoughts and gave him a much-needed opening.

He took her hand, enjoying the soft feel of her skin. He'd missed this, missed her. "Maybe because it is one."

She looked down at their joined hands, then pulled away. "Thank you."

He smiled. "I mean it, Kelly. I've made mistakes. More than I can go into now. More than you need to deal with at the moment." He paused, then said, "I heard your deposition's tomorrow."

She nodded and looked around, probably checking to make sure Tess wasn't coming back yet.

"I'm not looking forward to it," she admitted.

"I can only imagine. Is there anything I can do to help? Legal advice? Moral support?"

With every word he spoke, he confirmed his reasons for not pulling her into his arms and kissing her senseless in front of Tess and every other ice-cream-eating customer. He couldn't put more pressure on her now.

"Thanks, but I need to do this on my own," she said.

He nodded slowly, reminding himself he'd

expected that answer. From the minute he'd seen Kelly and Tess through the window, he'd planned to walk in here and offer his support. He'd also figured she wouldn't accept. "And I respect that. If you change your mind . . ."

"I won't."

He inclined his head in acceptance. It wasn't easy when every instinct screamed at him to argue and force her to let him go with her.

But just because he was backing off now didn't mean he'd let her just walk out of his life. Tomorrow, he assured himself. Tomorrow would be soon enough.

Time to move on to the next subject. "I spoke to Ethan a little while ago. He plans on driving to Jersey tomorrow to talk to Leah and her new husband."

Kelly let out a groan. "What a nightmare my mother is."

Nash agreed. He couldn't imagine her torment, knowing her mother was willing to dig out her own daughter's skeletons to get what she wanted.

"Don't worry. Ethan's more than up to the challenge. Hopefully Leah and her husband will care more about appearances in their social circle than they do about Tess. If we're gambling correctly, Ethan will come back with signed custody papers tomorrow."

"I hope you're right." Kelly's smile was tight. "Thanks for letting me know. I heard my phone go off earlier, but I was at the school parking lot and let it go to voice mail. Maybe he called to fill me in."

The small talk was killing him. But the dark circles under her eyes spoke to how much strain she'd been under. It didn't help that she'd been single-handedly running Richard's office. She'd sent a few new cases Nash's way, but the bulk of the burden had been on her shoulders.

But tomorrow, the deposition and custody threat with Tess would hopefully be over. Then Kelly's mind would be clear to could focus on what she wanted out of life.

He hoped like hell that something was still him. Because he wanted a life with her in it.

Sunny skies marked the day of the deposition. Kelly drove to Manhattan, planning to arrive an hour before she was scheduled to appear so she could talk to her attorney. She was determined to get through today and the only way she could face both Ryan and his wife was to put all the other problems and issues she was having out of her mind.

She couldn't think about Ethan squaring

off with her mother and her new husband over Tess. She couldn't think about how scared Tess actually was. And she definitely couldn't think about Nash.

As if she could think about anything else? He'd been so kind yesterday, so caring. Not only had he apologized but there was none of the residual anger she'd always sensed deep inside him. She'd been too overwhelmed with everything else in her life to let the conversation get any deeper, not with Tess just a few feet away.

Her cell phone rang and she answered on speaker. It was Annie calling to wish her luck and thankfully keep her mind busy as she drove.

The ride passed quickly, as it always did when you were heading toward something you were dreading. She'd planned to meet her lawyer at a Starbucks down the street from the law office where the deposition was being held.

She recognized him from Googling his name on the Internet. Mitchell Yale was a young-looking yet experienced family lawyer with dark brown eyes and a slightly receding hairline that did nothing to detract from his good looks. The right client would find him sexy with shoulders broad enough to cry on.

Not Kelly, who was still hung up on Nash Barron.

Her lawyer, who insisted she call him Mitch, reminded her to tell the truth, to answer questions succinctly and not embellish. Yes or no replies were best, and she should elaborate only if pushed. He further warned her not to engage in on-the-record conversations with Ryan or his soon-to-be ex-wife.

It sounded simple. Kelly knew from her years as a paralegal and the rapid pounding of her heart that the experience would be anything but.

She walked into the conference room, acutely aware of all the eyes on her. She'd chosen a simple black skirt, pale pink blouse, and pearls. Yes, she looked like the picture of innocence. No, she didn't care what anyone thought of her. She just wanted this day over. That she had any impact on another couple's divorce case made her feel both sick and ashamed. Two emotions she could not let show.

The seating arrangements at the large conference table were strategic. Doreen Hayward sat beside her attorney. Across from them was Ryan and his lawyer, and adding to the solemnity of the occasion, the court reporter was positioned at the far end of the table. Her time there passed in a blur. Kelly was dimly aware of Doreen's resentful glare. She thought Ryan tried to get her attention, but as her attorney suggested, she focused on the lawyer asking her questions and nobody else.

It was as ugly as Kelly had imagined. Doreen Hayward's attorney had dug into Kelly's family situation, bringing up in his questioning the fact that her father died when she was young. He asked if she'd raised her sister and then basically insinuated that Kelly had been looking for a father figure when she'd worked as an escort and again when she'd gotten together with Ryan. Kelly pointed out that a onetime occasion didn't make her an escort, but her attorney tapped her arm, reminding her not to engage.

In turn, Ryan's attorney phrased his questions to imply that Kelly, a younger, broke woman had preyed on Ryan, a wealthy married man, who couldn't resist her charms. More than once Kelly caught sight of Ryan arguing with his attorney over his tactics, but she refused to acknowledge what was going on.

All she needed to do was testify and leave. She'd managed to separate Kelly the paralegal from Kelly the witness. She didn't know nor did she care about fault, no-fault, cause of action, or anything else. From a personal standpoint, this whole ordeal seemed to be about humiliating her, but she refused to succumb. The end result of today's deposition had nothing to do with her and everything to do with how they divided up Ryan's money. So she answered the questions and tried not to engage anyone in an argument. By the time it was over, Kelly was emotionally and physically drained, numb to any and all emotion, as she took the elevator downstairs and said good-bye to her attorney.

In the lobby, she turned to head for the parking lot where she'd left her car, when she heard her name being called and recognized Ryan's voice.

Her stomach cramped, and though she wanted to keep walking, she'd never been a coward. She came today because she'd been subpoenaed, but she acknowledged that the day also provided closure. So she swung around to face Ryan in person for the first time in more than a year.

Nineteen

Kelly stared at the man she'd once loved, or thought she had, looking at him in an objective way. He was a handsome man. Women turned to stare at him on the street and she couldn't deny his charisma. The gray around his temples was new but only added to his good looks. She'd been intimate with him once, but now she felt like she was looking at a stranger.

"I am so sorry you had to go through that," Ryan said, stepping toward her.

Wary, she held herself back, hoping he'd take the hint and give her personal space. "Thank you. I'm just glad it's over."

"How have you been?" he asked.

"I'm fine." She deliberately glanced at her watch. "I don't mean to be rude, but I really need to get going."

"Please wait. I'd like to talk."

Kelly frowned. "I can't imagine what's left to say."

"Then let me tell you." He smiled, one of his patented charming grins. "I'm sure you understood why I had to try and make the marriage work once Doreen told me she was pregnant, but it's really over this time."

She didn't know whether to say she was sorry or to congratulate him, so she remained silent.

"You and I had something special," he continued, in what she used to think of as his bedroom voice. "Kelly, you have to know I never stopped caring about you. And now that Doreen is out of the picture for good . . ." He trailed off, obviously assuming his meaning was clear.

Kelly shook her head in denial. "You went back to your wife," she reminded him. "It's been more than a year since you've seen me and we've only spoken once since you ended things!"

He reached out and touched her shoulder. "A long, painful year." With his soulful, dark brown eyes, he pleaded with her to believe him.

There was a time when she'd have fallen into the trap, but she wasn't the same girl she'd been when they'd first met, and he no longer drew her the way he once had. But even if she had still been attracted to him, she hoped she'd have learned her hard lessons and been strong enough to walk away.

The way she planned on walking now.

Kelly lifted his hand off her shoulder. "You made your choice and it wasn't me. I'm sorry it didn't work out for you, but I've moved on."

And she had, she realized. She'd moved to a new town, she'd become part of a new family, and most important, she'd found a new man. A man she loved with all her heart, no qualifications and nobody else in the picture. A man she'd lost when she'd let fear of who she'd been take over. Even when Nash asked her to stay and talk after the family meeting, she'd run away.

But she wasn't afraid anymore.

She wanted Nash — not Ryan — and she intended to get her man back or at least know she hadn't let him go without a fight.

Ryan shook his head, denial in his posture and his determined expression. "You only think you've moved on because I gave you no choice. But things are different now. I'm free. *We're* free to be together."

Kelly stared at him. He wasn't listening. He wasn't hearing her. "I'm not free, Ryan."

"There's someone else?" He raised his voice, shock rippling through him, as if he'd never considered the possibility.

"There is." Kelly hoped that ended this

discussion.

"You heard the lady, she's taken." Nash's deep voice startled her. She was sure she had to be dreaming.

But when he stepped forward and slipped an arm around her waist, she knew she was fully awake.

She looked up at his handsome face. "You're here. In New York." She shook her head. "I don't understand."

Nash never broke eye contact, letting her look straight into his heart. He wanted her to see him. To know him. To believe in him.

"You said you didn't need anything during the deposition, that you could handle it alone." He paused. "But you didn't say anything about not wanting me to be here for you afterward."

"You came," she murmured, the pleasure in her tone warming him. "How did you know where I'd be?"

"I had to drag the information out of Ethan," he admitted. And his brother had only parted with the address when he fully understood Nash's intentions.

"Excuse me for interrupting," the other man said, sarcasm making his annoyance clear. "But who are you?"

"Ryan Hayward, meet Nash Barron. Ryan, this is Nash."

"Her *someone else,*" Nash said pointedly.

Ryan narrowed his gaze and glared at Nash. "Kelly's not the kind of woman you can stake a claim on. She's independent and smart." He squared his shoulders, ready to take Nash on, so certain he knew Kelly best.

Nash bristled at the assumption. "I agree. Kelly is smart. Too smart to wait around for you to decide things didn't work with your wife, so now she's good enough to take back."

Kelly stiffened against him. "Kelly can speak for herself," she said, obviously feeling the need to at least defend herself.

Ryan scowled. "This man doesn't know the first thing about us or what we had." His words were bluster. His shoulders dropped and he'd lost his defensive stance.

Nash almost felt sorry for the man.

"Actually, Nash knows everything about me."

Those words thrilled him beyond reason. "What I know is that you had her, you lost her, and she's mine now. Is that good enough to convince you?" He wanted this man gone so he could kiss the woman he loved.

And he did love her. Her independence, her ability to stand up for herself and her sister, to take on whatever life threw her way and succeed.

Ryan finally lowered his head. "It's enough that she's not denying a word you say." He raised his gaze and looked at Kelly. "I wish you well," he said at last.

"I wish you well, too."

Ryan extended his hand to Nash. "Do a better job taking care of her than I did."

Nash hesitated but knew he could afford to be magnanimous and clasped the other man's hand.

Seconds later he was gone.

Kelly pulled out of Nash's hold and turned to face him, hands on her hips, her pink-glazed lips turned downward.

Uh-oh. "Should I apologize for acting all caveman?" he asked.

"Ryan was right, you know. I'm not the kind of woman you can stake a claim on," she informed him.

Nash's heart skipped a beat. He felt sure he stopped breathing.

He'd had been waiting downstairs in the lobby for more than an hour. When the man he'd assumed was Ryan Hayward called Kelly's name, Nash wanted to intercede. He wanted to get to Kelly first, make his case. Then he remembered his resolution. He wouldn't judge and he wouldn't take control.

If Kelly wanted that prick, Nash would have had to let her go. But her body language had informed him she wanted nothing to do with Hayward, freeing him to join in the conversation. He was just glad Kelly had given him such a good opening.

But now she wasn't happy. "Are you telling me that was all an act to get rid of him?"

Fear rippled through Nash, worse than anything he'd felt in the past and that was saying something.

"I'm telling you no man can claim me unless I want him to." She smiled and wound her arms around his neck, pressing her body intimately close to his. "And Nash? I want you to claim me."

Pure sweet relief rushed through him as he lifted her off her feet and spun her around before setting her back down and dipping his head for a kiss.

"Let's go." He tugged on her hand.

"Where? My car's in the parking garage around the corner."

"And I booked us a hotel room at the London NYC."

Her eyes opened wide in surprise.

"Before you say no, I wanted to make it up to you for missing the trip to the bed-and-breakfast. Not to mention I thought you'd need to relax, not drive home today.

But if you don't want to go —"

"Stop! Yes! Of course I want to go. I'm still getting over the fact that you came all the way here. For me."

He cupped her face in his hand. "Honey, I'm always going to be where you are. Now can we please go to the hotel? We can talk about anything you want as long as we're alone." He'd had enough of this sterile lobby to last him a lifetime.

And a lifetime was exactly how long he wanted to be with Kelly.

Nash had thought of everything. Kelly stepped into a hotel suite on a high floor with a view that overlooked the bustling city below. Chilled champagne sat on the counter beside the large king-sized bed.

Her head still reeling with the events of the day, she lay down on the bed and stretched out, letting her body melt into the deliciously comfortable mattress. "This is heaven," she murmured.

"I hope it's going to get even better." Nash sat down beside her, his eyes warm and filled with emotion. "I really wasn't sure how you'd react to seeing me today."

"I'm glad you took the risk." She pushed herself back into the pillows. "Talk to me," she said, needing to understand what changed for him, what brought him here.

He lay down beside her, sharing the large bed. It felt so good to be here with him, so right. And though she didn't know what he was thinking regarding the future, she loved him enough to take it as slowly as he needed to.

"It's hard to look at yourself and discover everything you believed was a lie," he finally said.

She narrowed her gaze and waited for him to continue.

"I thought I was an amazing brother to Dare and a great husband to Annie. Ethan was the jerk and I was the good guy. When I realized everyone else knew your secrets before me, it was easier to get angry at you than to look at the reasons why the people I loved couldn't come to me." His expression darkened, disappointment and pain radiating from him in waves.

"Nobody's perfect. Not even you."

He managed a laugh, and her heart filled with love as she realized how difficult the last few weeks had been for him too.

"Kelly, did you hear what I just said?" He levered beside her, propping himself up.

She had. He'd been talking about why the people he *loved* couldn't come to him. He'd put her in that category, but she'd let her mind skip over it, too afraid to believe he could really mean it.

"Say it again," she said, looking into his eyes.

"I love you. And I will never again be a pompous jerk who judges you first and asks questions later."

The lump in her throat was so big she could barely speak. "Even after I saw you in the lobby, even after we walked into this room, I couldn't let myself believe," she whispered.

"You can," he assured her, his voice gruff. "Because I *love* you."

She smiled wide. "I like the sound of that. And I love you too. So much it hurts." She threaded her fingers through his hair and touched her forehead to his.

The intimate gesture filled Nash with a contentment and happiness he'd never known before. He sealed his lips over hers and kissed her like he hadn't seen her in a century, relearning the deep recesses of her mouth, licking her lips, tasting her over and over again.

She moaned and he rolled her on top of him, never breaking the connection between them. She straddled him, her hips aligning with his, and something hard pressed into his thigh.

"Wait," he said, unable to believe he'd forgotten something so important.

"Haven't we waited long enough?" She wriggled her hips against his, obviously frustrated by their clothing.

"One thing first." He rolled her over so he could slip his hand into his front pants pocket. "I wish I'd come back to you sooner, but I wanted to give you space to deal with everything that was going on in your life. Your mother, this deposition . . . And during that time, I realized I was holding back how I felt. The same way you withheld the past from me. Because I was going through too much for you to burden me with."

Kelly nodded, her eyes glazed and happy.

He loved seeing her happy. "The time apart also gave me a chance to prove to you that not only did I want to change but that I actually could. I want you to be able to come to me with anything and know I'm not going anywhere, no matter what you have to say."

"You never had to prove anything to me."

He shook his head. "Maybe I needed to prove it to myself then. Anyway . . ." He opened his hand and revealed a ring he'd bought this morning as soon as he'd reached Manhattan. "Think you can bring yourself to marry me and spend the rest of your life with an arrogant jerk who occasionally sees the world in all black and white?"

"Yes. Yes. Yes!" She rained kisses over his lips and face, her reaction everything he could have hoped for and more.

He slipped the Tiffany setting, a traditional white gold band with a solitary diamond, on the third finger of her right hand. Only then did he pull her back on top of him where she belonged.

And later, when they were both undressed and he slid back inside her, he knew he'd found the one thing he'd been looking for his whole life.

In Kelly, Nash found home.

The Barron family gathered in Ethan's family room for a celebration. A joint party in honor of Nash and Kelly's engagement and Ethan's success in dealing with Leah Moss and her new husband.

Dare Barron enjoyed the celebration, but he'd needed some breathing room and sat down on the sofa to think and reflect. Their family was amazing, he thought. Especially in light of their shared history, some recent, some old. Watching them laugh and share jokes, nobody would know that the men in the Barron family had recently been estranged. Or that before three months ago, no one had even known Tess existed. Or even that Faith and Kelly were recent additions.

As a unit, the people in this room were closer than any families Dare had encountered. They impressed him, these people in his life, the things they'd lived through and overcome. There were times he was damned sure he didn't deserve them. Especially not Nash, who'd done more for Dare than any parent, yet who'd blamed himself for Dare's mistakes.

Dare shook his head to dispel those damned ghosts from the past. Most days he could keep them in the shadows where they belonged. Sometimes they came back to haunt him when he least expected it. Since having it all recently resurrected, Dare had begun having nightmares about the night Stuart Rossman died.

He shivered, though he wasn't cold. He thought those dreams had been put to rest years before. Unwilling to go down that dark road, Dare focused on the present.

On Tess, who brought light, laughter, and a smart mouth into all their lives. Thank God they'd judged Tess and Kelly's mother correctly. As they'd all hoped, just the threat of a scandal had panicked the couple.

Ethan had sworn to reveal their dirty

laundry in a custody scandal he assured them would be covered by their local news. And Ethan had enough contacts in enough places to guarantee placement. It was one thing for Muldoon to drink and be a functioning alcoholic, quite another to let the world know the truth. And if their country club friends found out Leah had abandoned her daughter and not enrolled her in an exclusive boarding school as she'd claimed, the lives they enjoyed would be over. Leah and her husband only wanted Tess as a trophy to parade around so Leah could claim she was as good a mother as the other women at her club. In twenty minutes, Ethan had destroyed their plan and had signed papers giving him and Kelly custody of Tess.

For such a big threat, it had been handled quickly, efficiently, and easily, but the emotional damage would take longer to recover from.

Still, it was over.

"Hey." Tess bounced over and sat next to him on the couch. She curled her legs beneath her and looked into his eyes. "Why are you sitting by yourself?"

"I'm just resting. I worked a long shift last night."

"Do you like being a cop?" she asked,

wrinkling her nose at the mention of his profession.

"Brat," he said, laughing. "You say that like it's a disease."

"You said it," she muttered.

He rolled his eyes. But he knew her question was a serious one. "I like it a lot," he told her. It was the one way he felt he could atone for past sins. Not that he'd admit that to his fourteen-year-old sister. "I like knowing I'm doing good things, like protecting people," he said instead.

She nodded. "That's cool, I guess."

"If you say so." Dare studied her.

She wore a pair of skinny jeans, a tank top with a sweater over it, and a headband that pulled her dark brown hair back from her face. She looked like a fresh-faced teen, so unlike the juvenile delinquent who'd arrived on Ethan's doorstep a few months ago.

"Hey, kid?" He liked the nicknames he used for her.

"Yeah?"

He braced his arm on the back of the sofa and turned to face her. "Did I tell you I'm really glad you're one of us?"

Her eyes opened wide. "No." She stared at him with serious mistrust.

Given how her mother had treated her, Tess had good reason to be wary. She'd come far in a short time, but Dare knew any serious talk or show of affection between them had been rare. In the beginning, he'd tried to reach her on the casual level he thought she'd relate to and she'd responded.

But now? He felt protective of her and damned if he didn't adore the little brat. "I mean it, Tess. I love you." He heard the gruff tone in his voice and wondered how she'd react to the admission.

To his surprise, she jumped forward and hugged him tight. Her skinny arms wrapped around his neck and he felt like a goddamn hero.

Then she was gone, running across the room to Kelly, who stood in the circle of Nash's arms. Come to think of it, Faith was wrapped in Ethan's embrace too.

Dare groaned. The room was thick with romance and love. As happy as he was for his siblings, Dare was just fine with his single status and his bachelor life. At twenty-five, he was in no rush to commit like his brothers had done.

His cell phone rang and he grabbed it, grateful for the distraction.

A quick glance told him it was work and he answered immediately. One of his long-time friends on the force knew there was one person Dare kept track of and he let

Dare know if the guy was picked up, whether or not Dare was on call.

Brian McKnight, a screwed-up rich boy, who'd thrown the party that changed Dare's life forever. McKnight had been trouble at sixteen and hadn't improved himself since. Apparently he'd been arrested outside Joe's tonight on a drunk and disorderly.

For Dare, this party was over.

He made it his mission to make sure McKnight's screw-ups didn't go unpunished. At least he tried to. Unfortunately, his sister usually managed to show up with a high-priced attorney and a bunch of bullshit excuses on her brother's behalf.

Liza McKnight had been getting under Dare's skin since he was a horny teenager. He might have told his brothers he'd gone to that party to hang out with the older guys, but the truth was he'd gone to see her. An older, rich girl way out of his league.

If Dare had listened to his brain and not his cock, he'd never have been a witness on that fateful day. Never have run away with his friends without calling the cops. Maybe Stuart Rossman would still be alive. And who knew how different Dare's life might have been? After all, Liza hadn't been home and the party had been a bust for Dare in more ways than one.

These days, their differences were just as pronounced. As a cop, Dare was still out of her class and out of her league. He rarely saw her now, except when she showed up to bail out her bother. Out of jail, of trouble, sometimes both.

Dare rose and headed for his family, saying his good-byes and excusing himself to go to work. It wasn't just that he wanted to make sure Brian got what was coming to him.

He still liked to see Liza when he could. He still thought with the wrong head. As much as he hated to admit it, if there was a chance Liza might appear, Dare hated to miss the show.

The employees of Thorndike Press hope you have enjoyed this Large Print book. All our Thorndike, Wheeler, and Kennebec Large Print titles are designed for easy reading, and all our books are made to last. Other Thorndike Press Large Print books are available at your library, through selected bookstores, or directly from us.

For information about titles, please call:
(800) 223-1244

or visit our Web site at:
http://gale.cengage.com/thorndike

To share your comments, please write:

Publisher
Thorndike Press
10 Water St., Suite 310
Waterville, ME 04901